"Dead Rage:

A Zombie Apocalypse"

Nicholas Ryan

Copyright © 2014 Nicholas Ryan

Acknowledgements:

A fair amount of research went into writing this book.

I would like to thank Mike, Charlie and Al. These three men all have personal knowledge of the military, and have been with me, advising and guiding, since I wrote my first zombie novel, *'Ground Zero: A Zombie Apocalypse'*. They're great guys and have been very generous with their time.

I'd also like to give a special mention to Samuel C. Garcia. Sam was a Black Hawk pilot in the US army, and his help with the intense combat sequences in this novel was invaluable.

So too was the help of Dale Simpson. Dale is retired Special Forces. His expert knowledge helped shape the combat and military facets involved in the story, giving them a wonderful sense of authenticity.

Finally I'd like to thank the skippers and crews of the long-line boats I boarded here in Australia as I was preparing the manuscript.

Also available by Nicholas Ryan:
'Ground Zero: A Zombie Apocalypse'
'Die Trying: A Zombie Apocalypse'

Part One.
Chapter 1.

Low rain clouds had turned the ocean grey as steel, so the sky and sea merged together at the horizon into a dull blur without definition.

Steve Bannon leaned against the spoked wooden wheel and peered hard through the wheelhouse windows.

'Mandrake' was heavy in the water, taking the rolling swells on her starboard shoulder. Bannon waited as the boat swooped down into a yawning trough between waves, and felt his knees buckle as the old timber boat clambered gamely up the rising face of the next crest.

The deck beneath his feet canted back, and he caught a sudden smudge of sky the color of old bruises through the thick glass.

Bannon opened the throttle on the big diesel engine, setting the long-liner for the next wave the way a rider gathers a horse before the jump. 'Mandrake' took the rise bravely, her timber frame shuddering as the snub of her bow cleaved through the swell like a blunt axe. A burst of white water detonated against the wheelhouse windows and went surging back along the open deck.

The boat was forty miles offshore. Here, unrestricted by land mass or the continental shelf, the waves sweeping in from the vast ocean were lined up before them like a procession of marching mountains.

Bannon tore his eyes away from the windows to glance down at the bank of monitors arranged on the counter in front of the wheel. He shook his head. The internet screens that showed water temperature and weather information were frozen.

They had been offline for several days.

He picked up the white phone and pressed it hard against his ear. The phone was a direct line to shore, given a range of over fifty miles through an antenna and booster box mounted high in the rigging above the boat's flying bridge. Even in poor weather, there should have been a dial tone. The phone was used to contact fishmongers and local restaurants as the boat steamed back into harbor with its brine tanks filled with giant tuna, allowing the catch to be sold even before the tons of glittering silver fish were unloaded and packed in ice.

The line was dead.

Bannon dropped the phone back into its cradle, then spun the wheel hard so that 'Mandrake' met the next foaming, bursting wave, and the whole boat shook and groaned as though hit by a mortal blow. Bannon cursed bitterly under his breath.

They had been at sea for thirteen days, steaming well off the east coast, following the warm currents of water with every inch of the boat's twenty miles of long-line dragging behind her. The catch had been spectacular; it was shaping up to be the best season in almost a decade, and Bannon was reluctant to turn for home when the holds were heavy with fish, and the days ahead promised even more.

But fear gnawed at his guts.

An instinct. A feeling: a sense that something was wrong, swirling in the air like smoke. It was a feeling that was impossible to catch and hold up to cold logic or reason.

But it wouldn't go away, and Bannon could ignore it no longer.

He turned to the three men jammed into the worn vinyl seats around the saloon table.

"We're heading home," Bannon announced to the crew.

For a long moment no one spoke. The sea smashed against the old boat's hull, and the wind howled through the rigging. Bannon watched the men's faces. They were all younger than him, still filled with the energy of their youth and an enthusiasm that Bannon only remembered.

He was thirty eight, and after twenty years at sea – eight as a long-line deckhand and another dozen as the *Mandrake's* skipper – he no longer felt the thrill of the hunt, or the rush of adventure that had once tingled in his veins each time the boat had steamed out through the open arms of Grey Stone harbor's rocky break walls.

Bannon stared hard at the men. His eyes were calm, and intelligent, set within a fine web of wrinkles, and his face was tanned the color of leather. He was broad across the shoulders, his frame lean and honed by the work of a fisherman's life, and his curly hair had been gilded by endless days under the harsh sun.

"We've got eight tons of fish – it's a hell of a catch," Bannon said with finality. "It's enough."

John Sully cocked an eyebrow. He was a rugged, muscular man with dark malevolent eyes and a shaved head. "Enough? Man, we get a lousy eight percent of the take," he said, and he turned to

7

include the two other young crewmen on either side of him. "The more fish we haul up, the more money we make. If we turn for home now, you're costing us thousands." His tone was bitter and accusing.

Bannon rubbed his chin. He hadn't shaved in days, and the bristled shadow on his jaw crackled under the press of his fingers.

"I know that," Bannon said. "And it costs me money too, Sully. But we've been out of contact from the shore for two days. No phone, and no internet. We can't fish the warm current if the charts don't update. All we're doing is burning fuel."

'Mandrake' was an old boat, built back in the early 1980's. She had unlovely lines and a squat wheelhouse forward so that she looked like a boxer with its head tucked low between hulking shoulders. Her working deck was a tangled maze of hatches and lines and rigging.

And she was heavy.

With so much weight under her hatches, she had a cruising speed of just nine knots. Battering her way through the cold front that had swept down on the boat overnight had reduced that to six. She was eight hours from shore, and her monster engine burned through over one hundred and fifty gallons of diesel a day.

Sully's face wrinkled into a sneer. "So what?" he became belligerent. "We're fishermen. We don't need computer equipment to know where the fish are."

"We need the phones," Bannon said. His voice took on a hard edge. He turned his attention back to the wheel as *'Mandrake'* swooped down into another deep trough between waves. For a moment there was eerie silence as the sound of the wind and hiss of the ocean were blocked out by the surrounding swells, and then the fishing boat began to claw her way up the face of the next swell. The boat creaked and shuddered beneath his feet.

"Well it's wrong," Sully spat. "Man, I got debts."

"We all have debts," Bannon said without interest.

Sully swallowed a mouthful of beer and belched. The bottle was empty. He put his elbow into the ribs of the man sitting beside him. "Get me another one, Claude," he said.

The young man slid off the saloon bench and went obediently into the tiny galley.

"Not from the front of the fridge," Sully ordered the man. "Get it from the back where the cold ones are this time."

The crewman slid a bottle of beer across the table to Sully and he wrapped his big hand around it. He belched again and stared defiantly at Bannon.

"You're starting early, Sully," Bannon said mildly. "It's not even eight in the morning and you're on your second one."

"Two beers per man, per day. Right, skipper?" Sully's voice was insolent. "That's your rule, right?" He twisted the top off the bottle and raised it high in mocking salute. "Here's to a fucked up boat."

Bannon set the fishing boat to the next swell and then looked more sharply at Sully. He was a big man and he carried his weight across his shoulders and chest. His forearms were laced with an intricate pattern of tattoos and scars.

9

"You can always find another job," Bannon's mouth tightened into a thin line. "If you don't like the way things are done here, go and get work on one of the trawlers. There are plenty of deckhands looking for good pay. I'm sure I will be able to replace you. No trouble."

"I might just do that," Sully growled.

Bannon's lips curled up into a wry smile. *No you won't*, thought Bannon. *You're all talk. You're like the big savage dog that barks and growls and bares its teeth... but cringes away the moment it's challenged.*

There was a long minute of silence as the *'Mandrake'* swished her broad tail over the top of the next rolling swell and plunged down the other side. The empty beer bottle slid off the saloon table and fell to the floor, rolling along the wheelhouse deck. Bannon's eyes felt raw and full of grit. He rubbed at them with his knuckles and yawned.

Sully sat pensive and brooding, and he glowered at the men on either side of him. He emptied the contents of the beer bottle and wiped his mouth with the back of his hand. He slammed the bottle back down on the table.

"Why aren't you drinking?" he growled at the fourth man in the wheelhouse. "What's your fucking problem?"

Peter Coe glanced up at Sully and shook his head. "Later," he said.

"Later? There is no later. We're heading back to port. Didn't you hear our fearless leader?" Sully sneered with icy sarcasm. Then he turned back to Claude and his breath was foul in the young man's face. "Get him a beer, Claude. The man looks thirsty."

Claude started to scramble off the vinyl seat, but Peter stopped him. "I said later," he looked at Sully with his jaws clenched tight. "I'll have a drink when we get back to Grey Stone and unload the catch." He was younger than Sully and Claude, with a long drawn face and dark thoughtful eyes beneath a mop of sandy hair. He eased himself off the seat and went across to the wheel.

"Want me to take her for a while, skip?"

Bannon nodded. He picked up the white phone again and jammed the receiver against his ear. Nothing. His cell phone was clipped to his belt. They were still miles out of signal range but he glanced down at the phone's small display window anyhow. He had no signal.

There had been a time, thirty years before when the fishing fleet that worked out of Grey Stone harbor had all been connected to an operational base on shore through radio networks. In the 80's, there had been thirty trawlers and eight long-liners bustling in and out of the harbor. But the economy, and modern technology had rendered the base ineffective. Now simple cell phones to the boat's owner connected each skipper, and the fishing co-op had dissolved as every boat struggled for its own survival.

Bannon sighed. He was weary, and worried. He stepped back from the wheel and Peter took his place. "I'm going to sack out," Bannon said. "Keep her on course, and keep her speed down. Wake me in two hours." Then he turned round to Claude and Sully. "I want you two on deck. Make sure

11

everything is secure," he said. "We've got $40,000 worth of equipment back there and I don't want to lose any of it. So check it — then check it again. There won't be time to do it when we reach harbor. We'll need to get the catch straight onto ice until I can reach the restaurants and fishmongers." Then as an afterthought he singled out Sully. "And check the antenna and the booster box."

"I did. Yesterday," Sully said.

"Then check it again."

Bannon turned, swaying with the rolling pitch of the boat, and ducked into the skipper's cabin. The room was narrow with space for just a couple of bunk beds and a small set of drawers. The top bunk was piled with clothes and his wet-weather gear. He stretched out on the bottom bunk and was asleep within moments.

Chapter 2.

"What do you think?" Sully dropped down heavily into the skipper's seat and threw a big muscled arm over the padded backrest. The seat was old and grimy. The vinyl had been torn so that yellow foam stuffing poked through the tears and the edges were frayed like an old coat collar. He turned his head and glanced out the port side windows, and then studied the broad back of Peter Coe who was hunched over the boat's wheel before him.

Peter didn't turn around.

"About what?"

"What do you think about us turning for home when we're on a winning streak, just because the fuckin' phone doesn't work?"

Peter shrugged, but said nothing. Sully's eyes narrowed.

"Hey?" He poked the young man in the ribs with his thumb. "I'm talking to you."

Peter's head snapped round and there was a flash of anger in his eyes. "Fuck off, Sully," he said, then paused as the fishing boat went nose-first through the crest of a swell and the windows blurred under a discharge of white seawater. "There's no choice. If we can't reach the fishmongers, and we can't get in touch with old Gino to do it for us, then we're stranded out here. It won't matter how many more fish we hook. The whole catch will spoil, and it won't be worth a dime."

'Mandrake' went down into the next trough. "And where would you fish?" Peter's voice was accusing. "We don't have internet. That means we don't know where the warm current is. Hell, we don't even know what's blowing up behind us. We could sail into the teeth of a storm and not know it."

Sully shook his head, and his lip curled in an expression of disgust. "Faggot," he said. He hawked a thick gob of slime into the palm of his hand and then smeared it across the back of the seat. "We're supposed to be fishermen," he said. "If you ask me, the skipper has gone soft. Fucking soft as cream. He ain't got what it takes to run a boat like this anymore. He's lost his edge," Sully's eyes were dark. "Ain't no way we're going to make good money on this boat with a skipper who wants to play it safe and won't take a risk once in a while."

Peter stared at Sully and raised an eyebrow in challenge. "Then quit," he said. "Like the skipper told you. Find another boat – instead of moaning and groaning to everyone else all the time. Man, I'm fucking sick of hearing you complain."

Sully's eyebrows knitted together and he scowled darkly into Peter's face. His features became red and swollen, and he lunged off the seat so they stood toe to toe. Sully jabbed his finger hard into Peter's chest. "You watch your mouth, boy," he growled with menace. "This is a big boat. Accidents can happen. Nasty accidents with hooks and knives and gaffs when you don't expect it." He pushed past the young man, and stormed across to the galley, then spun back.

"Maybe I will quit. And maybe I'll take Claude with me. That would fuck Bannon up nicely," Sully

14

smiled, and his eyes were shifting and cunning. He seemed to calm then, the anger disappearing as quickly as it had boiled. He lit a cigarette and blew a long feather of blue smoke that swirled around the low ceiling.

Chapter 3.

Bannon slept like the dead, and it was only the altered motion of the boat that finally woke him. He sat up with a start and checked his wristwatch, then swung his legs off the narrow bunk. He had been in that black death-sleep of exhaustion, and it took him several seconds to push back the curtains of his fatigue and come fully alert.

He knew that he had not slept long enough, and he swayed on his feet as he slid open the cabin door and thrust his head out into the wheelhouse.

Bannon could feel the throbbing pulse of the *'Mandrake's'* big engines vibrating up through the deck. Out through the wheelhouse windows he could see gentle rounded swells – the ocean still the color of steel, but the rage and strength of her mighty power somehow subdued.

Bannon went to the wheel and Peter nodded at him.

"We're about twelve miles out of Grey Stone," Peter said as he stepped away from the console and yawned. "I've pushed the old girl up to eight knots."

Now the boat was inside the continental shelf, the huge rolling swells of the open ocean had been suppressed so that the fishing boat's motion became sedate. She was cleaving through the cold water with the bustling thrust of a workboat, and her heavily laden bilge tanks pushed her down deep in the water and gave her stability so that she ploughed through the sea with stately purpose, no longer tossed and heaved by the untamed wilds of the deep ocean.

"Good man," Bannon said. He slapped Peter on the back and rested his hand on the wheel.

He had been asleep for almost four hours – much longer than he had planned. He narrowed his eyes and scanned the far horizon, and saw the dark mark low on the skyline, like an ugly black scar above the swells.

Grey Stone.

Bannon stared at the horizon for long seconds, as the fishing boat rocked and swayed beneath him, and then he glanced at Peter, his expression clouded.

"Something's not right."

For twenty years Bannon's first sight of Grey Stone had always been the same; the low dull grey blur of shape, away in the far distance, that gradually took on height and detail as the boat nudged her way closer to shore. But the dark smudge on the skyline he was gazing at was different.

Bannon felt something cold and ominous uncoil in the pit of his gut: a sudden sense of foreboding.

He snatched up the white phone and pressed it to his ear. The line was still dead. He turned to Peter.

"Did Sully check the antenna and booster box?"

Peter nodded. "He and Claude are still on deck. They're just finishing up with the lines and gear. Everything is stowed ready for unloading when we reach the dock."

Bannon nodded, but he wasn't listening. He frowned, and then tugged his cell phone from the clip on his belt. He held the phone up and saw the

17

tiny screen light with strong reception. He grunted with relief.

"Stay at the wheel, Peter," Bannon said. "Push her up to nine knots."

The young crewman nodded and Bannon turned away and stabbed the quick-dial on his phone for Gino Ginopolous, owner of the *'Mandrake'*.

Old Gino was a Greek immigrant who had come to America with his family as a young boy and who had worked the fishing fleets along the east coast until he had saved enough to buy his own boat and move to Grey Stone. That had been almost forty years ago, and for a decade the fishing industry from the little harbor flourished. In the 1980's, Gino replaced his old boat with the *'Mandrake'*, and skippered the vessel himself for several years until his age eventually caught up with him. He was a big man with a big booming voice. He had skin the color of old leather, deeply lined with wrinkles, but his eyes were clear and sharp. Bannon heard the line connect and waited. The phone rang out. He stabbed at the buttons and dialed his wife's cell phone, as the ominous sense of unease that had wrapped around him began to constrict like a python around his throat and squeeze his heart.

He heard the line connect to his wife's phone and then the echo of the ring tone.

"Come on, Maddie. Pick up…" he muttered.

There was no answer. He thumbed the buttons and dialed twice more, his concern turning cold and ominous.

"Dammit!"

Bannon snatched up the binoculars and slung them around his neck. He went out through the wheelhouse onto the stern deck. He saw Sully and Claude look up in surprise. The two men were gathered around the wire cage that held dozens of bright orange plastic bubbles. When the boat was working, the bubbles were marker buoys along the boat's long line.

"Skip?" Claude asked warily. "What's up?"

Bannon ignored the men and clambered up the narrow ladder to the flying bridge.

The flying bridge was a wide open space forward of the boat's mast, with a control console for steering as the boat was leaving and entering the harbor, and a stowage space for the twelve foot aluminum dinghy. Bannon strode forward and glanced down at the wide blunt bow cleaving through the water, then stared hard at the horizon line and pressed the powerful binoculars to his eyes.

For long seconds the magnified image flicked and wavered, and then Bannon swung the glasses across the skyline until the black scar filled the lenses. Bannon blinked, then felt a sudden stab of ice-cold dread snap-freeze the blood in his veins.

"Oh my God..." he said softly.

Bannon dropped the binoculars and spun on his heel. He scrambled back down the ladder and burst into the wheelhouse.

"Push her all the way!" he barked at Peter, his voice urgent. "Open the throttles and give her everything she's got."

The young man looked confused. Then he saw Bannon's terrible expression. His face was like a mirror breaking, twisted with anxiety and fear.

"What?" Peter was seized by sudden dread. "What's wrong?"

Bannon stabbed his finger at the wheelhouse window. In the far distance, the black scar of smoke was spreading like a cancer across the skyline. "It's Grey Stone," Bannon said, his face the color of ash. "The whole town is on fire."

Chapter 4.

The *'Mandrake'* vibrated under the terrible strain of her engines so that she sounded like she might tear herself apart as the big screw beneath the boat's hull thrashed out a wide trailing wake.

Bannon was up on the flying bridge clutching tightly to the binoculars, Claude and Sully close beside him. They were all infected by the tense strain as the coastline became clear, and the high rocky cliffs that bordered Grey Stone's southern break wall bared their jagged teeth.

The boat bore down on the headland, running up from the south so that for long agonizing minutes there was only the smudge of oily black smoke to be seen.

Bannon urged the boat on, seething with impatience and fear. The headland stood like a silent sentinel – a rocky hunched shoulder that stood over the sleepy little harbor and sheltered it from the great storms that swept up the coast. But now it masked his view of the little town, and he cursed with bitter frustration.

He strained forward and ran the powerful lenses of the binoculars across the dark shape of the cliffs. At their base, white water was boiling as the swells from the ocean came sweeping towards the harbor mouth in rolling grey humps only to collapse into chaos as they rushed over the shallowing entrance and dashed against the outstretched arms of the break wall.

Bannon lowered the binoculars and his expression was bleak. The men stared into the distance, silent and tense.

"Claude, go down and tell Peter to come up. Let him know that I have the wheel."

Claude nodded and scurried down the ladder into the wheelhouse. Bannon reached for the control console built into the port side of the flying bridge and toggled the rudder control, turning *'Mandrake'* slightly to bring her around the bulk of the headland. The boat ploughed on purposefully, but running at this new angle brought the trailing ocean swells hard under her stern so that she began to buck and wallow. Bannon's mouth drew into a thin grim line, as he stared fixedly ahead.

He heard scuffled heavy steps behind him, but did not turn. He sensed the rest of the crew gathered on the deck, subdued to silence as the scene began to unfold before them.

'Mandrake' reached the edge of the headland, still a mile beyond the foaming wake of the harbor bar, and as her heavy hull heaved and dipped on the rolling swell, the swirling veil of smoke opened like a theatre curtain, and Bannon got his first sight of Grey Stone.

It came as a shocking, horrified fusion of sight and smell.

The wind off the land was warm, hazed with smoke and made heavy by a cloying rancid stench that flared in Bannon's nostrils. It was the putrid stink of corruption and rotting flesh, and it was thick in the air like a nauseous taste in the back of his throat. He gagged, and then spat over the side of the boat. He scraped the back of his hand across his mouth, and then his senses were overwhelmed by chaos and destruction as the fishing boat cleared the headland and lined up for the run into the harbor.

"My God..." Bannon heard Claude breath, the young man's voice appalled and shocked. "The whole town is burning."

Bannon narrowed his eyes. He turned to the others, white-faced with rising horror.

"Peter, fetch the rifle." He handed the young crewman a key from his pocket and pressed it into his palm. "Go, boy. Right now!"

There was a .22 rifle aboard. The weapon was stored below, and the firing mechanism and ammunition locked away separately in an iron safety box beneath the bottom bunk in the skipper's cabin. Some of the big fish hooked on the boat's long line were the size and weight of a man, and it was common practice to have the weapon assembled and on hand when the catch was being reeled in. Such huge fish were impossible to haul on deck – often they were still alive and thrashing their mighty tails against the timber hull – and Bannon would lean out over the boat's rail and fire into the fish's head before the beast was hauled aboard.

Bannon heard Peter's heavy booted steps as he swarmed down the narrow ladder. He turned to the others. "On deck," he said grimly, then stared back at the shoreline as the harbor entrance opened up before them.

The line of rough water was drawn clearly across the ocean, the abraded deep sea scarred and furrowed by the talons of the wind while beyond the break wall the water within the harbor mouth had a calm oily gloss to it, like shimmering velvet.

'Mandrake' seemed to sense the refuge of still water and she bustled towards it.

Bannon snatched up the binoculars again.

Black smoke billowed across the harbor, swirling on the breeze and rising high above the burning buildings that lined the wharf. As Bannon watched, a sudden storm of sparks erupted and he heard the sound of a roof collapse. He swung the binoculars quickly, and each time he paused a new horror seemed to fill the lenses. Everything was veiled in smoke, but through it he caught horrific snatches of destruction. He saw a yacht at its moorings, burning fiercely as the flames licked up the mast and the fabric of the furled sails burst alight. He saw dark lumpen shapes floating in the water, and he saw the sky filled with raucous birds. He set the binoculars down and rubbed at his eyes. Everything was hazed and cast in an eerie orange glow as the smoke filtered the sun to the color of blood.

Bannon heard Peter's footsteps. He had assembled the boat's rifle. He set it down beside the flying bridge console and stared aghast at the unfolding nightmare spreading across the harbor.

"Is it loaded?" Bannon asked. Peter nodded numbly, gaping in horror, and then he flung up his arm and pointed, his voice suddenly rising with fresh alarm.

"Look!" he gasped. "There's a boat."

Bannon saw it. A gleaming white sailboat suddenly burst through the boiling mask of smoke, running out between the break walls towards the

'Mandrake'. The boat was not in the deep water channel, and as it cleared the shelter of the headland, the wind came hunting through the rigging so that the boat's sails collapsed and flapped in sudden chaos.

"Jesus!" Peter whispered.

Bannon felt himself suddenly tense. "Tack," he muttered under his breath, somehow trying to will the boat to respond. Then he said louder, his voice somehow hollow and heavy with despair. "She's not going to make it."

The boat lost its way and veered towards the massive boulders that formed the southern break wall, then at the last possible moment, she spun her nose away and the jib burst full and bulging with air. The boat careered across the mouth of the harbor and reached the open ocean. She met the first swell gamely, but then dug her shoulder into the cold grey water and as the next line of waves rushed down to meet her, the boat swung in a wild turn until she was broadside.

The boat reeled as the green hissing wave exploded against the hull and swamped her. Bannon heard a sound like artillery fire and saw the mast ripped away in a tangle of sails and rigging.

"Christ!" Bannon breathed. He watched in cold dread as the next wave raced down on the wallowing boat and drove her back onto the submerged teeth of the break wall. The rocks gouged at the boat, tearing a ragged hole in her bottom timbers, and then the sound of terrified panicked screams carried clearly to Bannon on the gusting wind.

Bannon snatched the binoculars up to his eyes and trained the powerful lenses on the shattered boat. A woman was hunched down in the cockpit, clinging to the figure of a young girl. The woman's face was a white mask of horror. As Bannon watched, another opaque wall of green water came sweeping over the sailboat's deck with the crushing force of a hammer blow.

Bannon swung the 'Mandrake' around, pushing her across the open mouth of the harbor.

"Peter. Get the dinghy ready."

The fishing boat nosed onto her new course, taking the ocean swells under her stern quarter, her motion rolling and drunken, as Bannon raced down on the stranded boat and the 'Mandrake's' big diesel engines growled.

Over his shoulder, Bannon heard the grind of the winch as the aluminum dinghy was attached to the boat's long boom arm. He turned his head, saw the little tender ready to be swung over the side. The tiny craft swayed like a pendulum, rocking on its cables, and Bannon cut the fishing boat's speed so suddenly that the big boat plunged nose down in the water like a heavy stone, the energy and momentum gone from her in just a few brief moments.

"Now!" Bannon cried out. He toggled the rudder control to swing 'Mandrake' broadside to the swells so that her broad bulk would shelter the tender as it was lowered into the choppy sea, and then he seized Peter's arm in a fierce grip.

"Take her," he said urgently. "Get her in as close to the rocks as you can and hold her there."

Bannon swarmed down the ladder and raged across the fishing boat's cluttered deck. There was a stowage locker hung with safety gear near the long-liner's massive deck winch and he snatched up two safety vests.

"Sully," Bannon snapped. "You're coming with me."

The two men scrambled down into the dingy and Sully unfastened the line to the boom. The outboard motor started the first time, and the big burly crewman swung the little boat around in a tight arc towards the dying sailboat and opened the throttle.

There was just forty feet of heaving ocean between the tender and the sailboat. Bannon sat forward, straining with anxiety as the aluminum hull of the tender slapped and bashed across the hissing chaos. He felt each wave with a bone-jarring thump that vibrated all the way up his spine.

The little tender dipped and bucked, and sea spray filled the air. The sailboat was twenty feet away. Bannon felt himself tensing. He glanced back at the *'Mandrake'* and saw a dirty belch of smoke erupt from her exhaust stack, as Peter gunned the big diesels and turned the long-liner away.

Bannon's eyes flicked to Sully. The man's face was drawn tight, his features frozen. "Get me alongside," Bannon had to shout above the fierce roar of the outboard motor. "I'm going after the woman and the kid. As soon as I get on deck, bear away until I signal you."

Sully nodded. His eyes were narrow slits against the wind and the driving spray, but Bannon sensed the young man's rising tension.

27

The sailboat was in its final death throes. The ocean's relentless pounding had shattered her hull below decks, grinding her timbers between the break wall's jagged jaws until the wrecked hulk of her was impaled and being hammered to pieces. The boat's broken deck was streaming with water, so heavily canted that the woman could no longer maintain her balance. She saw the dingy racing towards her, but as she got to her feet and frantically waved her arms, another great rush of grey water burst across the boat and she fell screaming to her knees. She was still clutching the girl's hand, the child's face contorted and crying out in terror. The woman heaved herself to the rail and took the child in her arms – then hurled the screaming girl over the side of the boat into the surging hissing maelstrom of angry surf.

"Christ!" Bannon breathed. He turned back to Sully and saw his own horror reflected in the other man's appalled face. "Get her!" Bannon cried. The girl's body vanished below the hissing vortex of white water.

Sully speared the dingy forward, waiting until the seething suck of the waves was on the ebb before committing the little tender to the narrow breach. The boat surged forward, the outboard motor roared, and then they were slammed hard against the boat's hull with the impact of a colliding car. Bannon got to his feet and launched himself. He wrapped his hands around the boat's stainless steel railing and heaved himself up onto the forward deck. Another wave came rushing in and he clung to the rail and bowed his head as the ocean heaved the aluminum tender high and then smashed hard against the crippled boat. The wave came aboard in a hissing bursting torrent that ripped at Bannon's grip and tugged at his legs. It swept over him and the weight of it was crushing. He felt the wind driven from his lungs and the strain on his shoulders burned like fire, until at last the ocean's energy was exhausted, and it began to suck and claw at him as it receded. Bannon's feet went from under him and he fell to the deck. He felt the solid crack of something smash into his ribs and he groaned aloud. Then, for brief precious seconds the deck was clear, and he raised his head and saw the woman's horror-stricken face, staring at him, frozen with fear.

Bannon crawled to the woman. She was young, her eyes huge and terrified. She was clinging to a tangle of the boat's ruined rigging. There was blood on her hands and streaming down her arm.

"My baby!" the woman screamed. "Save my baby!"

Bannon stole a glance over his shoulder. Sully was hurling the dingy around in frantic tight turns, his body hunched, his head craned over the side of the tender, searching for the little girl. The surging ocean hissed and roared as it detonated against the break wall, and the air was filled with rain-like spray. The woman was hysterical, her eyes wild, gasping through ragged breaths and sobs of dread. She flailed her arms and clawed at him like a wild cat. Her nails raked livid welts of skin from his cheek and her face was savage and horribly haunted. "You must save him for me!" She pointed at the dark opening of the hatch. "He's down there!"

Bannon's features collapsed with fresh horror. He stared down into the blackness. The hull was filled with black oily water. He could see debris being tossed about, as the ocean sucked and surged through the mortal rents in the boat's hull.

Bannon lunged towards the opening and then lost his footing. He went tumbling down into the ice-cold darkness and his head went under the water. He felt something graze his back and then he surfaced in the darkened hold, his hair streaming with water, slicked down over his face and into his eyes, and he gasped to fill his lungs. He scraped hair away from his face and reached out, groping blindly below the surface, feeling his desperate panic mount with every dangerous second he searched, trapped within the dark pit.

The cabin was more than half-flooded. Bannon stared down into the oily blackness that sloshed and splashed as the boat was remorselessly pounded. Another wave struck the shattered hull and Bannon heard the terrible rending tear as the sailboat twisted and tore to pieces. The vibration of her agony shuddered the length of the boat's fractured splintered spine. Bannon took a deep breath and slid beneath the water. His hands flailed. He felt more debris bash and graze against his knuckles, and the sound of the boat's dying agony was magnified like an echo in his ears. He burst back up through the surface, coughing and gasping, his lungs on fire and the despair and helpless frustration was like a lead weight on his shoulders.

Then, quite suddenly, Bannon saw a pale blob of flesh, just a few feet ahead of him, seeming to drift and ebb with the motion of the dying boat. He threw himself forward, blundering desperately and snatched at it. It was a hand – a baby's hand – the skin soft and translucent, perfect and pale and lifeless.

Bannon felt the heavy punch of shock and sorrow. He felt down into the dark water, touching the child's face, and then his fingers explored further until he realized the baby's legs had been trapped by a solid weight he could not see. The black water sloshed across the dark hull again and Bannon reluctantly let the dead child's hand go, let it be swallowed by the watery depths forever.

He turned and waded back towards the square patch of daylight at the cabin's entrance. The ice-cold sea was as high as his chest and he moved with desperation, clamping down on his panic until his feet felt the narrow cabin steps and he emerged on the deck.

The woman was gone.

Bannon's eyes swept the boat, and then darted to the aluminum dingy. Sully was there, holding his place just a few yards away, working the motor and tiller with fierce concentration to keep the boat from being hurled onto the rocks.

"The girl?" Bannon shouted.

Sully shook his head.

The sense of helpless despair was crushing. Sully screwed his eyes tightly shut. The fatigue of failure consumed him, robbed him of the last of his strength. He shook his head dully – and then finally saw the woman.

She was lying amongst the huge heavy boulders of the break wall. A wave rushed down and smashed hard against her. Bannon saw her fingers move weakly, as she tried to claw for a handhold. Then the wave sucked back and surged in on her again. For a brief moment the wall of water hung suspended over the break wall. Then it burst upon the woman with a sound like thunder, so that the very air seemed to shake. The woman was smothered by the swelling green surge, crushed to pulp. When the wave withdrew her body was no longer moving, but instead lay broken and crumpled, her bloody legs and arms at impossible angles and her neck twisted so that her dead vacant eyes were turned towards where Bannon stared on in pale horror.

The next wave swept the body away, leaving the rocks gleaming and glistening.

Bannon looked away. The sailboat was breaking up. He felt the deck beneath his feet crack open, and the violent shudder roused him from the spell of his despair. He reached the rail just as another swell burst over the boat and smothered him.

Sully dashed the tender in, close to the wreckage. Bannon shouted something that was lost in the booming crash of the next wave against the rocks, and when the grey wall of water and blinding spray cleared, Bannon stood poised to jump the gap of frenzied sea that separated the two vessels.

Bannon waited until the wave was seething back from the break wall and then he dived into the foaming white spume.

He plunged into the murderous stretch of water and came up, gasping for air, just ten feet away from the tender. The little boat was being thrown around like a cork in a washing machine, and Sully was no longer able to keep the dingy steady. He gunned the outboard and the engine flung the boat forward into the surging gap, while over his shoulder the next great crashing wave reared high.

Bannon saw the boat, saw Sully's pale white face. He flailed his arms and struck out gamely, but there was a heavy weariness in his body, a leaden sensation that clawed and dragged him back towards the rocks. He felt like he was swimming in glue, and within moments he knew he would not – could not – possibly swim the few desperate feet to safety.

Sully sensed it too. He was aware of the next swell breaking over them. It came rushing down on the tender and Sully had just a split-second to react. He spun the boat hard, swinging her tail round in a tight circle that brought the boat closer to the rocks, and gave her a sudden burst of speed. He leaned out over the side of the boat and dragged one massive muscled arm in the water, still giving the boat power to make headway, and he knew he had just one chance.

"Grab my arm!" he yelled.

The boat's nose bobbed and bucked. The wave began to break apart, her crest boiling, the momentum and crushing weight of the smooth green face beginning to curl and collapse.

Sully turned the bow of the tender to face the heaving sea, and swept past Bannon with only seconds to spare. Bannon threw up his hand. Sully's fingers caught him around the wrist and his grip was like iron. He heaved with all his strength and the muscles and joints in his arm caught sudden fire. He heard a crack, felt something deep

33

within him tear, as he plucked Bannon from the water just as the wave lost the last of its scimitar shape and began to explode upon the rocks of the break wall.

The tender's bow burst through the white-water crest, throwing her high, and for an instant she was weightless. Then the aluminum hull crashed down hard onto the back of the boiling maelstrom as the wave's energy burst against the broken hull of the sailboat and tore it to pieces.

Chapter 5.

Bannon stood in the wheelhouse of the *'Mandrake'*, shivering violently from the shock and the icy water. He hunched over and retched, then clutched at the console to support himself as a spasm of coughing racked his body.

He wiped his mouth with the back of his trembling hand.

"Thank you, Sully," he said, his voice hoarse, his throat raw as if it had been sandpapered. "I owe you."

Sully said nothing. He sniffed and looked away.

Claude came from the skipper's cabin with a towel and spare clothes. He dumped them on the saloon table.

"What about the tender, skip?" Claude asked.

Sully shook his head. "Fuck it," he growled. "Cut it loose, Claude. We haven't got time to bring it aboard."

The crewman raised his eyes in surprise, but Bannon never saw. He spun round to Peter.

"Something made a woman risk her life, and the life of her two young children trying to flee Grey Stone in a boat she couldn't sail. Now they're dead," Bannon's voice crackled like electricity. He clutched fiercely at Peter's arm and his eyes were suddenly blazing. "Get us into that harbor, Peter. Right now."

Chapter 6.

The *'Mandrake'* was seventy-five foot long and twenty-five feet wide: she came in through the harbor entrance at four knots, her blunt broad bow pushing a white wave of wash across the surface of the water. Boiling black smoke billowed, thick as fog, and Peter hunched over the flying bridge controls, peering blindly into the haze, as the big boat crept past the last green channel marker and coasted cautiously into the wide basin of Grey Stone harbor.

Bannon changed quickly, standing in the middle of the wheelhouse deck. Through the forward windows he could see little beyond the haze of smoke. He ran out onto the boat's wide deck and saw Sully and Claude leaning over the starboard rail.

The water was black, covered in a thick coat of ash, swirling with oil and debris. Sheltered from the ocean breeze by the massive headland, the air here was still and heavy with the stench of rotting corruption. It seemed to swirl in the smoke and permeate their clothes and skin like a coat of reeking grime.

Bannon stared aghast into the mist. He could see the faint shape of capsized motorboats, stranded and abandoned, their hulls crusted in green slime and barnacles, bobbing lazily in the fishing boat's wake. And he could hear the frenzied cries of the birds as they wheeled overhead in vulture-like flocks.

"What the hell has happened...?" Claude muttered in disbelief.

Bannon shook his head. He heard something scrape against the side of the boat's bow, and then a moment later he saw a corpse in the water. The body was ballooned by trapped air that had caught within its clothing. It bobbed in the ripples of the boat's bow wave, floating face down.

"Sully. Gaff it."

As well as the .22 rifle, the fishing boat carried two enormous gaffs, each with a razor sharp hook at the end of a ten foot long pole. The gaffs were used to hook the big fish before the crew hauled them aboard. If the fish was still thrashing and flailing on the deck, it was beaten over the head with an aluminum baseball bat. Sully brought both back to the side of the boat. He held the long gaff in both hands and passed the baseball bat to Claude.

Sully swung the gaff and its stiletto hook snagged into one of the arms. He tugged, and the body rolled over onto its back. It was a man. The face was old, a man of maybe sixty or seventy. His head was almost severed from the neck, and the chest had been torn open. But there was no blood. The ghastly wounds were washed and puckered white – the whole body bled out.

In fascinated horror, Bannon watched on as Sully dragged the body close to the side of the boat. He stared down into the wide lifeless eyes, and beside him he heard Claude cough and then retch. The young man vomited explosively, and the muck of it spattered over the deck and across his boots. Claude spun away, gasping for fresh breath. Sully held the body close against the boat and looked up into Bannon's sickened, horrified eyes.

"You know him?"

Bannon frowned then nodded. "It's Sam Kinkade."

"Kinkade?"

Bannon nodded again. "He did some deck work for one of the game fishing boats during the high season." For a long moment his voice trailed off, and then he asked in a whisper, "What the hell could have happened to him?"

The corpse was horribly mutilated. The dying expression fixed on the white face was one of sheer horror. "He looks like he's been torn to pieces."

Sully held the body so that it nudged gently against the hull for a few more seconds, then he unhooked the gaff and the corpse drifted away into the fishing boat's burbling wake. Instantly, a dozen gulls appeared, turning and hanging in the air. They landed on the body, hopping and flapping raucously as they squabbled over the eyes and soft flesh of the nose and lips. Others tugged and nipped at fingers so that the body seemed to twitch and move. Bannon turned away, appalled and numb with a creeping rise of revulsion. He went to the ladder and clambered up onto the flying bridge.

"I've got it," Bannon said grim-faced, striding to the control console. Peter stepped aside. He bent and picked up the .22 rifle. It was a bolt-action weapon with a ten round magazine. The law prohibited semi-automatic weapons aboard. Peter pulled back the bolt and chambered a round.

Bannon cut the big boat's speed until she was barely drifting on the calm oily water of the harbor.

The huge piers of the main jetty loomed out of the smoke, and Bannon saw the wide rust-streaked stern of a fishing trawler, tied to the wharf.

"Bow and stern ropes," Bannon called down to the crew. "And don't fuck it up."

The *'Mandrake'* coasted closer to the pier. Bannon put the engines in reverse and gave the big diesels a pulse of power. The last of the boat's speed bled away and she scraped gently against the huge black rubber tires hanging from the pier posts. Claude and Sully tied the boat to the jetty and Bannon cut the big engines. A final belch of black exhaust mingled in a sky hazed with smoke – and then the whole world seemed enveloped and choked by heavy silence.

It was eerie: unnatural. There was only the lap of gentle waves at the boat's hull and the shrill raucous cries of the gulls as they scavenged and squabbled. Bannon swept his eyes along the waterfront.

A complex of tourist buildings, each one newly constructed, but carefully built to create the charming atmosphere of an old fishing village, fringed Grey Stone harbor. The cafes, restaurants and tourist shops were all low wooden structures with quaint windows displaying antique nautical items.

Bannon narrowed his eyes warily through drifting tendrils of grey smoky haze. He concentrated his attention on the doors of each building.

"Claude, Sully, arm yourselves with those gaffs. Peter, take the .22 up to the bow and cover those buildings."

Bannon swarmed down onto the main deck and snatched at the aluminum baseball bat. He hefted it over his shoulder like a club and clambered from the boat onto the jetty.

For long seconds Bannon stood perfectly still, every fiber, every sinew in his body drawn tense. He could hear the roar of blood in his own ears and feel the thump of his heartbeat exploding within the cage of his chest. He took a dozen cautious steps along the jetty, and then paused – some instinct screaming at his senses in shrill alarm.

The jetty was streaked in spatters of fresh blood. It lay on the concrete in dark puddles, like an abstract artist's nightmare. The stench of death and decay was thick and cloying in the back of his throat. He tore his eyes away from the menace of the shop front doors and caught a glance of Peter, kneeling at the high canted bow of the *'Mandrake'* with the rifle sighted.

Behind Bannon, Claude and Sully scrambled onto the jetty. Bannon dropped onto one knee and the two crewmen came to where he paused.

"What the fuck…?" Claude's voice had a panicky edge to it.

Bannon shook his head, but said nothing. He pointed wordlessly at the door of a café that opened up onto a paved promenade area directly ahead of where the three men hesitated.

The café had been destroyed. The door hung from its hinges, and the long window that had given patrons a view across the harbor had been shattered. Black smoke billowed from the interior, rising up into the sky and smudging their view of the building.

"Something inside moved," Bannon whispered hoarsely at last.

He came up off his knee and the three men moved in cautious crouches along the jetty, narrowing the distance until they stood at the edge of the promenade. There was a narrow nature strip of bushy shrubs between the men and the building. Bannon felt a tremble of unaccountable fear. He turned, stared back over his shoulder. Peter had left his position and was running along the jetty towards them. Bannon spat a curse under his breath and clenched his jaw.

Beyond the waterfront, the town of Grey Stone was burning. Houses along the main street were blackened, charred shells. Bannon could see shapeless clumps on the blacktop and on the front lawns of homes that he knew instinctively were dead bodies. Buildings had collapsed. Others had burned to the ground. The road, and the waterfront parking lot were choked with crumpled, smoldering vehicles.

"Are we at war?" Claude gasped.

Bannon shook his head. "I don't know," he confessed. "I don't know what the fuck is going on."

Sully leaned in close, his voice tight and urgent. "What the fuck do we do?"

Bannon shook his head again. Nothing made sense. He felt himself reeling. "I've got to get to my wife," he said, with a terrifying coldness settling on his chest, the coldness of heavy dread.

Beyond the waterfront shops, beyond the manicured lawns and the parking lot, and beyond the two lane road that led into town, was the apartment complex where Bannon lived. His mouth formed itself into a thin bloodless line and he felt a surging sense of resolve drive down the trembling fear and swirling confusion. "I've got to get to Maddie," he said again.

He fisted his grip on the baseball bat and stepped from behind the dense wall of shrubs. He felt his feet find the hard paved surface of the promenade. His legs were trembling. He stood for a moment, exposed and vulnerable, and the panic came back upon him as a heavy lead weight in the pit of his gut. He could taste the acid tang of fear in his throat.

And then someone shouted.

Bannon swung around, his head spinning, his eyes wide and wild. Behind him Claude had burst through the bushes and was running towards the smoldering ruins of a restaurant. He had the boat's gaff hoisted high above his shoulder and there was a crazed berserker shout in his throat.

Bannon cried out, the sound impossibly loud and shrill in his own ears, as Claude went pounding across the promenade twenty feet to his right.

"Fuck!" Bannon swore. He took uncertain steps towards Claude and then froze.

From within the café directly ahead, a woman suddenly appeared. She came shambling through the doorway, lurching into the bright sunlight with her whole body seized into a contortion of unnatural movement. Her legs were stiff, her back arched as though she was racked with terrible pain. She swayed on her feet, her eyes sightless, and then her chin sank slowly onto her chest and she howled at Bannon in a grotesque shriek.

Bannon stared, aghast. Sudden fear sparked tiny fires of panic down the length of his spine. The woman raised her face and the dark eyes slammed into focus. There was fresh blood and gore on her chin and painted across her chest in grisly streaks and spatters. She stared feverishly at Bannon with red-veined eyes, her mouth opened in a deep snarling.

Bannon stood transfixed, horrified. His mind went white – became blank for long dangerous seconds as the grotesque figure rocked from side to side as though infected with madness.

"Jesus," Bannon's terror was raw in his throat.

What remained of the woman's hair trailed to her shoulders in unkempt clumps. The long satin nightdress she wore was stained with blood, and hung from her skeletal frame in scorched, blackened tatters. Clots of charred flesh had peeled away from her body, leaving open wounds of putrefied rotting slime.

The woman leered at Bannon, her rictus grin seething with a vicious spasm of hatred and rage. She hissed – and the sound in her throat was a harsh guttural grate like gravel.

She lashed out for him, the hand a claw of blackened gristle. The woman's rotted lips peeled back and corrupted into a vicious snarl.

Bannon took a faltering step back. He felt the rasping hot breath of Sully close behind him.

"How the fuck could she be alive?" Sully croaked.

Bannon shook his head. His mind began to thresh feverishly. "She *can't*," his senses reeled in disbelief. He felt his jaw unhinge and the hard line of his mouth became slack with astonishment. "*She can't be alive.*"

Sully's voice shot up an octave, and he seized Bannon's arm in a vice-like grip. "Well how the fuck do you explain that, man?" He thrust a finger at the woman as she took a sudden lunging step towards them.

Bannon shook his head, his gaze haunted.

Then the woman attacked.

In an instant, the burned revolting figure exploded into movement. A wild mindless snarl ripped the fragile silence apart as the woman flailed at Bannon's face with hands seized into claws. Instinctively, Bannon swayed away, losing his balance and staggering backwards. He threw up the baseball bat to protect himself and the woman snatched at it with impossible strength. Bannon felt a lance of pain wrench in his shoulder. The woman howled, her eyes shining with triumph and piercing spite, and a gout of dark brown gore gushed from her mouth and oozed like slime down her chin. She hunched her body, swayed and undulated with a bizarre kind of insanity. She rocked her head from side to side and her tongue slithered from the wretched slash of her mouth and flickered at the air as if she could taste the scent of the man's revulsion and fear.

Sully swung the gaff. The giant hook was stainless steel with a wicked razor barb. The point buried itself in the woman's neck and she shrieked and thrashed and flailed her body as the force of the blow flung her on her back to the ground. Sully bunched the muscles in his arms and chest, pinning the woman to the pavement like a giant spider as she convulsed and thrashed to free the gaff hook from her neck. She rolled and heaved, and Sully was pulled a staggering step off balance. Bannon watched on in horror. Sully's face was drawn tight, his mouth snarling, his features swollen. There was some kind of ferocious gleam in his eyes. Sully recovered his balance and took three quick steps to where the woman lay. He crushed his boot hard down on the woman's chest, freed the gaff, and then swung the weapon again, this time crashing the hook into the woman's head. The point of the brutal weapon crushed in the woman's skull and buried itself somewhere behind her crazed eyes.

The woman convulsed once more – and then lay still.

Sully flung down the weapon and reeled away, his chest heaving, the air sawing across his throat, rasping like sandpaper. He hunched over, braced his hands on his knees, and retched.

Bannon got dazedly to his feet. He picked up the baseball bat and prodded the inert body. The woman didn't move.

"She's dead," he hissed.

"Are you *sure*, man?" Sully glared, his face grotesque with a compound of outrage and horror. "Are you sure she's really fucking dead this time?" He scraped the back of his trembling hand across his mouth and then spat.

Bannon nodded – then turned and ran.

Claude's agonizing shriek of pain seemed to fill the still air. Instinctively, Bannon sprinted towards the sound. The restaurant was a dozen paces away. There was a covered awning out front of the structure, the pylons charred and smoky.

Bannon pulled up short as he plunged under the darkened awning and his eyes struggled to adjust to the gloom.

"Claude!" he cried out. "Where the fuck are you?"

There was a crash of noise from within the darkened cavity of the restaurant – the sounds of a frantic and desperate struggle. A piercing scream of horror slashed the stillness. Bannon edged himself towards the open doorway just as the restaurant window suddenly exploded outwards in a thousand glittering daggers of jagged glass.

Claude's body landed heavily on the promenade pavers, the sound of the impact a meaty thump as his body rolled several times and then lay prone. He was lying on his back. His face and arms were shredded with bleeding cuts, and there was a gaping wound in the center of the young man's chest. Bannon and Sully went towards him, reeling in horror. From the corner of Bannon's eye, he saw a flicker of movement in the mid-distance. His head spun, and he saw Peter carrying the .22 rifle. The young man was standing at the end of the jetty, his face bloodless white, his mouth open wide in a silent scream. Bannon's eyes snapped back to where Claude lay. Blood was pooling out across the promenade from beneath the young crewman's body, spreading like thick treacle.

Bannon went down on one knee beside the young man. Claude's body had been torn open, the hideous wound surrounded by tattered flaps of livid flesh. Bannon saw the ghastly, blackened shape of a torn fingernail embedded on the edge of the maimed puncture.

He crushed the palm of his hand over the wound in a futile gesture, pressing down with all his strength to staunch the bleeding. He felt the scald of tears in his eyes and a sudden sense of unaccountable despair. Sully gripped his shoulder.

"Leave him, boss," Sully's voice was unnaturally compassionate, gentle. "He's dead."

Bannon cuffed away tears with the back of his bloodied hand. There was a choking lump in his throat, but when he raised his eyes at last, the grief had begun to give way to something colder and darker.

He stood slowly, his eyes fixed on the menacing shadows of the restaurant. He felt his jaw clench until his teeth ached and a slow rising mist of rage seemed to cloud his eyes. He felt for the cold comforting weight of the baseball bat and glanced across at Sully and then over his shoulder at Peter.

"Whoever did it is in that building," Bannon said grimly. "I'm going to make them pay."

He took a single purposeful stride towards the restaurant, and then suddenly a cold and clammy hand seized his ankle. Bannon froze for a mind-numbing instant, and then stared down into the crazed, maddened eyes of the young man who had just died.

Claude hissed. Gushing blood had turned his face to nightmarish hatred. His eyes were wide and white, the pupils impossibly small, like sightless pinpricks. His grip was fierce so that Bannon grimaced as a lance of pain shot through his ankle. Claude's face became a grotesque distorted mask. His skin turned the color of ash, the corded purpling muscles in the young man's neck and arm bulged beneath dead flesh like thick braids of rope. He rolled onto his side and snapped thrashing maddened jaws at Bannon just as the man tore his leg free.

"Holy fuck!" Sully gaped in white horror. The men reined back in numbed fear as the young man's dead body writhed in sudden diabolical seizures. Peter threw up the rifle and slammed the butt into his shoulder, his eyes huge, his lips trembling with raw fear. He thrust the wavering barrel down into Claude's snarling face.

Bannon jumped back. He felt cold terror wash through him and turn his blood to ice. "Wait!" Bannon shouted. He knocked the weapon away impulsively. "We need to know what we're dealing with."

"Are you fucking crazy?" Sully snarled with scorching contempt. He had the boat's gaff in his hands, the barb still dripping blood, the handle slick and slippery in the grip of his sweaty palms.

Bannon stared at the big man defiantly.

"We've got to kill the fucker!" Sully blazed.

"Not yet," Bannon insisted. "He's not dead."

"Bullshit," Sully roared. "He fucking died! You saw him die, dammit. This isn't Claude anymore. This is some crazy fucking insane..." Sully's voice faltered as he groped to find the right word. "...undead fucker!"

The creature that had been Claude suddenly raised itself onto its haunches, and then sprang to its feet. It stood there, swaying and staggering, vicious demented hunger burning in its crazed eyes. It turned towards Peter and there was a clotted choking shriek in the back of its throat.

The sound of a single gunshot splintered the silence, the retort jarring and violent as it beat an echo against the smoke-filled sky. Bannon spun and stared in shock.

Peter reloaded the rifle, his movements mechanical, his eyes over the sight of the weapon wide and glazed and edged with hysteria.

The undead staggered and fell, Peter's bullet tearing through its thigh and shattering the bone. Thick brown slime oozed from the wound. The ghoul snarled in a spasm of virulent hatred and rage, and tried to claw itself forward, dragging the mutilated limb stiffly behind it.

The three men jumped back.

"Are you fucking happy now?" Sully's face was swollen in rage. The words shot from him like bolts.

Bannon stood, frozen in disbelieving shock. Sully didn't wait for an answer. He swung the gaff like a mighty axe, arching his back and bracing his legs so that the blow was delivered with every ounce of his energy and strength. The hook tore the undead's skull open and buried itself deep inside the head.

From inside the restaurant a new figure emerged into the sunlight. It was a man. His face and hands were grey, his skin withered, blemished and puckered as if rotting.

The man's guts had been torn open – a gaping hole of brown organs and entrails. Bannon could smell the reeking stench of corruption and see exposed bone and ragged white shards and fragments – as if the man had taken the full impact of a heavy caliber shot to the body.

The man moved in ungainly lunges, dragging one leg behind him and trailing dark ooze that leaked onto the ground. Then the undead snarled, and the red-veined eyes in the dreadful face rolled up until only the dull whites showed.

Peter reloaded the rifle and fired a snapshot that caught the ghoul in the shoulder, spinning the figure off balance so that it staggered backwards and crashed against the brick wall. Sully heaved the gaff hook free of Claude's infected body and closed on the undead figure as it came remorselessly to its feet. From somewhere further to their left, Bannon heard the restless rumble of rising voices, undulating and coalescing together so that the sound was like a menacing tremor, and his eyes hunted through the billowing clouds of smoke in alarm.

Bannon backed off, taking tentative steps away from the sound. It was like the very distant rumble of a train, a noise that seemed to hang in the air in wavering peaks and troughs. He frowned, confused and uncertain, yet sure that there was danger here. The air seemed to thicken, a rising stench of fetid corruption that burned in his nostrils and in the back of his throat.

The undead man against the wall spun away from the flail of Sully's gaff and lunged past the big seaman, snarling with mindless fury. He slammed into Peter just as the young man fired again, the bullet sailing wide, and the two figures collapsed to the ground with Peter crushed under the undead man's writhing weight and maddened momentum.

Peter screamed – a blood-curdling shrill cry of raw terror as the undead clawed bloody shreds from his face and throat. Peter struck out blindly, pummeling his fists as the frenzied ghoul tore the life out of him.

Too late, Bannon swung the baseball bat, striking the undead in the side of the head. The sound was gruesome, and the shuddering impact vibrated through the aluminum and all the way up to Bannon's shoulders. The undead ghoul seized rigid and then turned its monstrous snarling face to Bannon, its mouth gaping, Peter's blood dripping from its gnashing jaws. Bannon swung the bat again, crushing the side of the undead figure's head. It toppled slowly off Peter's body and rolled away, laying motionless.

Bannon swung the bat again and again, hysteria and rage merging into a flurry of brutal blows until all that remained of the undead's head was a bloody mash – a pulp of bone fragments and brain and gore. He threw the bat down, breathing heavily, his chest heaving and his lungs on fire as the madness and the fear slowly receded.

Peter lay, clutching at his neck as bright red, arterial blood pumped from between his fingers and splattered across the pavement. There was a keening hoarse choking cry in the back of his throat as the air hissed from his lungs and became his last dying breath. His eyes grew huge and terrified – and then slowly glazed over as the life faded from him.

Bannon stared down at the young crewman in horror. He saw Peter's eyelids flicker. A sudden spasm seemed to grip the body and then the mouth gaped open, tongue twitching between its lips. A thick clot of saliva spilled out of the dead man's mouth and dribbled down his chin. Suddenly the dead man opened his mouth wide and shrieked – a razor-edged cry of agony that stripped at Bannon's nerve endings so that he had to glance away, overcome with revulsion.

The body twitched, and spasmed into bucking convulsions that arched the spine. The dead glassy eyes filled with bloodshot veins and began to turn feverish yellow. Peter's skin turned grey.

Bannon gagged. He fought down the waves of nausea that rose up into the back of his throat.

Sully shook his head, numb and overwrought with incredulity. The world had become a place of nightmares. Bannon wheeled around suddenly and listened in silence.

"Can you hear that?"

Sully shook his head.

"Listen!" Bannon hissed.

Sully frowned – and then a slow transformation seemed to come over his face as the sound on the air drifted closer, and then was snatched away again. He nodded uncertainly, his heavy brows knitted together with foreboding.

"I hear," Sully said. "What the fuck is it?"

Bannon shook his head. "I don't know," he hissed, "but it's coming this way, and I don't want to be here when it arrives."

"And Peter?" Sully glared down at the dead crewman's body, watching it warily.

Bannon shrugged with helplessness. "He'll turn any second – turn just like Claude did. We can't help him. Grab the gun and let's get away from here – before it's too late."

Chapter 7.

With Sully close behind him, Bannon ran through the smoke towards the complex parking lot. The sounds of danger faded under the ragged heavy slap of their footsteps across concrete, but never completely became silent. At the edge of the parking lot was a low border of shrubs and Bannon dropped to his knee.

Ahead was fifty feet of flat landscaped grass and then the thin ribbon road that led into and out of town. On the opposite side of the road Bannon could see his apartment complex. Tendrils of grey smoke were drifting out through shattered windows. Sully fell to the ground beside Bannon. His breath was sawing in his throat, his chest heaving. His face was beaded with the perspiration of exertion and panic.

"I've got to get to Maddie," Bannon said again, his eyes fixed on the block of apartments.

"What if she's...?"

Bannon's eyes slammed into Sully's. "What if she's what?"

Sully shrugged. The man gnawed at his lips as though biting back words. "What if she's... not there?"

"There's nowhere else she could be," Bannon said firmly.

"She might have made a run for it."

Bannon shook his head. "Run where?" Everywhere Bannon looked, the town was burning. "Where could she possibly run to?"

Sully said nothing. He went through the motions of making sure a round was chambered into the rifle. The palms of his hands were slick with sweat. He scraped them down the front of his shirt and then nodded. "Okay," he said. "Ready when you are."

Bannon counted silently to three and then exploded to his feet and began to dash across the manicured lawns towards the road. He could hear Sully's pounding steps, heavier and more labored than his, over his shoulder.

There were bodies sprinkled across the lawn – inert figures that lay sprawled in grotesque attitudes of death. Everywhere Bannon looked the ground was soaked and stained in blood. He jinked past the corpse of an elderly woman who lay on her back, staring sightlessly up into the sky. The flesh had been flailed from her skin, clawed away in clumps, and the cage of her ribs cracked open. The woman's guts had been spilled across the lawn. Nearby was a middle-aged man. Both his arms had been gnawed away from the shoulders, and his legs chewed to stumps. Bannon saw the furry humped shapes of rats feasting on the dead body's blackening flesh, and the ripe stench of putrefaction was a thick and sickly taste that coated the back of his throat as he raced on.

He reached the edge of the road and paused for a single instant – just long enough for Sully to catch up. The big man was gulping for breath. He dropped to the ground behind the illusory cover of a straggly bush and scraped the back of his trembling hand across his brow.

"Did you see them? All the bodies?"

Bannon nodded. Said nothing.

Sully's eyes were haunted. "They weren't just killed," he croaked. "They were mutilated, man. They were butchered in some kind of a fucking frenzy."

Bannon nodded again, and then numbly shook his head. "I've never seen anything like it. It's like the whole world has gone to hell."

He swept his eyes ahead, torn between the instinct for caution, and the compelling need to get to his wife.

There was a silver hatchback in the middle of the blacktop, slewed sideways across both lanes. The car was a burnt out shell – a gutted blackened carcass. The front of the vehicle had been crushed in. The windshield had been shattered. Broken glass lay across the road, winking and glittering under the bright blue morning sky like diamonds. Wisps of grey smoke drifted in the air, carried on the breeze with the stench of burnt flesh and smoldering rubber. Bannon glared suspiciously at the blackened shape and then edged his way towards it. A swarm of flies buzzed angrily into the air, and Bannon saw the mutilated shape of an arm, lying in a stain of dry blood in the middle of the road.

Bannon stood over the limb and prodded it with the toe of his boot. It was a woman's arm: there were rings on three of the fingers, the nails polished pink.

"Where's the rest of her?" Sully grunted.

Bannon shook his head slowly, and then cast a furtive glance back over his shoulder towards the burning harbor. The undulating, haunting sound of menace reached him, and somehow the noise was made even more ominous. He felt vulnerable and exposed.

Bannon's instinct was to run. He raced across the road and up the paved driveway to the apartment complex.

An air of desolation seemed to hang over the two-story building. The apartment complex seemed totally deserted, silent and abandoned. Bannon stopped running – broke into a purposeful stride as he reached the double door entrance and braced himself for what lay inside.

Bannon pulled the doors wide open and Sully leaped across his path with the rifle on his hip, swinging the weapon into the arc of gloom. From somewhere inside the burned out building they heard the raucous bickering cry of birds.

"I'm going up," Bannon said grimly. "Stay close behind me and cover the stairwell."

Sully stepped aside and Bannon took the stairs two at a time as they turned back upon themselves until they reached the first floor landing.

Bannon hammered his fist on the front door of the apartment, and heard the sound of his blows reverberate through the room beyond. Beside him, Sully stood with his back to the door and the rifle poised.

Bannon rattled the door handle and beat upon it once more.

"Maddie!" he cried out. The door was made of heavy timber, solid in a steel frame. He pounded on the door one last time and pressed his ear hard against the wood.

Silence – not a comforting silence. It was a stillness that seemed filled with menace and foreboding.

"Don't you have a key?" Sully hissed.

Bannon shook his head. "Still on the boat," he said.

Sully's tone was seething. "Well you're making enough noise to bring every one of those undead fuckers down on us," he hissed.

Bannon clenched his jaw in frustration and helplessness. He took two steps back and lashed out, impulsively crashing the heel of his boot against the door.

The impact jarred his ankle and sent a shudder up his thigh, but the big door broke against its lock. Wood splintered, and Bannon flung his shoulder against the door. He burst inside and then paused on the threshold for many seconds. Sully came in behind him, shuffling backwards. Bannon took a deep breath and then took several tentative steps into the gloomy interior of the apartment.

The living area was spacious, but the drapes were all drawn tight so that Bannon was overcome by a sense of claustrophobia. He scanned the darkened interior quickly but sensed it was empty. On the opposite side of the room was a long passage leading past closed doors towards the main bedroom. Bannon went down it, nudging each door open as he passed.

When Bannon reached the main bedroom it was enveloped in semi-darkness and he paused to let his eyes adjust, becoming aware of a low noise. A murmured buzz of insects seemed to fill the room.

It was a sound fraught with menace, and Bannon felt a rash of prickles break out along his forearms.

"Maddie!" he rasped, and the sound in the room rose to become a buzzing. He felt something repulsive brush against his cheek and then crawl towards the corner of his eye. He slapped at it and felt a horrid shudder of revulsion. He went to the big bedroom window and with trembling hands pulled the drapes wide open. A shaft of brilliant blinding sunlight filled the room.

A woman lay on her back on the bed, her eyes seeming to stare in accusation directly at Bannon.

Flies crawled over the woman's body. They swarmed into the gaped cavity of her mouth and across her chest and arms. Bannon recoiled in hideous shock. For one staggering moment he felt the floor tilt beneath his feet and a burning rise of gorge scalded the back of his throat. The woman had slashed her wrists and bled out on the bed. Beside the body was a short-bladed kitchen knife. The mattress was stained dark red and big black flies crawled and feasted delightedly in the open wounds. The air was rancid, thick and choking in Bannon's throat. He swallowed hard and took a reluctant loathing step closer to where the woman lay.

The bedroom filled with flies.

He knew the woman. Her features were swollen, the body bloating with gasses and distorted, but still he recognized her.

"It's Evelyn," he said, glancing over his shoulder. Sully stood in the bedroom doorway, his face a grotesque mask of loathing. "She lives on the top floor."

Sully flinched and then shrugged his shoulders. "What the fuck is she doing in your bedroom?"

Bannon shook his head. "Maybe she came looking for Maddie," he guessed.

Sully grunted. "She's not one of these undead fuckers, is she?"

Bannon shook his head again. "Looks like she's been dead for a couple of days," he said softly. "She cut her wrists."

Sully grunted again. "No Maddie."

Bannon straightened and moved slowly away from the bed. The angry swarm of flies gleefully returned to the putrid body. "No sign of Maddie," Bannon repeated. His voice was heavy and desolate. He cast a bewildered glance around the bedroom as though maybe Maddie was there and he hadn't noticed her. He felt hope punched from him like a last desperate breath.

They checked every room in the apartment for a second time until Bannon stood disconsolate and devastated once more in the living room.

"I told you she wouldn't be here," Sully said. He shook his head. "I told you this was a waste of time."

The words seemed to drift around Bannon without ever registering. His eyes were blank, staring sightlessly at the walls for long seconds. Suddenly he sighed heavily as though he had been holding his breath for many minutes. His shoulders slumped and he lowered his head. "I need to check upstairs," he said flatly.

Sully's temper flared, bitter with fatigue and frustration. "Are you fucking kidding? We need to get the hell out of here, man."

Bannon shook his head and there was some low rising sense of resolute determination in the gesture. "Evelyn slit her wrists and died in our bedroom," Bannon explained. "For all we know Maddie might have made it to one of the upstairs apartments. She might be hiding somewhere right now, waiting for me."

Sully felt his fingers tighten on the stock of the rifle. "She's not here!" his tone became exasperated. "Let's just get the fuck out of here while we still can."

Bannon raised his eyes slowly. They were black and empty and cold. "Go if you want," he said. "But I'm going upstairs to look for my wife."

He went out the apartment door and paused on the landing, eyes cast upwards to where the internal staircase led to the next floor. He felt the bulk of Sully's body close behind him but he didn't turn, and he didn't look. He just lifted his eyes into the darkened gloom, straining some instinctive sense, as though he were trying to feel for Maddie with his mind.

One of the landing windows had been smashed and there were spatters of dry blood on the carpet and on jagged shards of glass. Dust motes hung in the air, seeming to be suspended in the silence.

Bannon clamped one hand on the railing and began to climb the stairs.

He felt himself holding his breath. Each step was a new torture of tension. He heard a creak of movement and the sound set his heart pounding in his chest and drew every nerve in his body taut to the point of snapping. His ears became acutely sensitive to the slightest sound – the rasp of his own breath: the muffled tread of every step on the worn carpet, the rustle of Sully behind him, until he felt his jaw clenched so tightly that his teeth ached.

Suddenly Bannon stopped on the stairs and paused, as though his will had suddenly deserted him. He could smell the odor of his own fear and strain. His palms were clammy, sweat trickling down his spine and soaking the armpits of his shirt. He wished for a weapon – anything to protect himself. Standing in the darkened narrow confines of the stairwell he felt exposed and vulnerable. He cursed himself for not picking up a knife from the kitchen, and for one blinding moment of white terror, he considered retracing his steps, and fleeing the building. Maybe Sully was right – maybe Maddie had run for her life – abandoned any hope that he would come for her...

No. He shook his head, casting off any uncertainty. Maddie would wait for him if she could. She would know in her heart that he would find a way back to her. He screwed up his resolve and forced himself to take the last few steps to the top of the landing.

The second floor – the top floor of the apartment block – was a narrow hallway with three doors: three apartments. As Bannon crept warily towards the closest door he heard the squawking bickered cry of birds from inside. He paused. The apartment door was ajar. He stole a glance over his shoulder at Sully.

"Mr. Hardigan," he gestured with his head. "He's an old guy – maybe in his seventies. This is his place."

Sully prodded at the door with the barrel of the rifle and then flung the weapon up to his shoulder in anticipation. He paused, frozen for several seconds with the sound of his breath loud in his ears and his heart thumping in his chest as the door swung back in a low arc on creaking hinges.

"Nothing," Sully hissed.

Bannon went into the apartment.

The floor plan for all the units in the building was exactly the same. Sully glanced around the living area. There was shredded newspaper strewn across the floor, and a sofa had been overturned. He went down the hallway and when he reached the first bedroom, he stepped into a ghastly nightmare.

Ted Hardigan was slumped, sitting against the foot of the bed. The man's face was ashen, his features collapsed into wrinkled and distorted pouches of loose flesh. His eyes were still open, the expression filled with unspeakable terror. His chest had been torn open and congealed blood soaked down the old man's shirt and into his lap. He had a pistol in his lifeless hand. The fingers still seized the weapon in a fierce grip. Two black crows were perched on the sill of a broken window, watching the men with curiosity. The room was a chaotic shambles, and Bannon tried to imagine the horror as the old man struggled and thrashed for his life. Sully came into the bedroom behind him and his face was grim.

"Is he dead?"

Bannon turned his head slowly. "He's dead," he said.

Sully's eyes were filled with suspicion. "Yeah, but is he *really* dead?"

Bannon went to the body and crouched. His knees cracked. He reached for the old man's hand and the flesh was ice cold. "Come and find out."

Sully shook his head, restrained by wary reluctance. "Why hasn't he turned into one of those undead fuckers?"

Bannon wrenched the pistol away from the dead man's fingers, and felt the comforting weight of the weapon heavy in the palm of his hand. He leaned over the body and carefully drew the old man's eyelids closed. "I don't know why he hasn't turned," Bannon shrugged. "By the look of the wound, it seems like he took a shotgun blast in the chest." He shook his head and then narrowed his eyes thoughtfully. "Maybe the undead didn't do this," he speculated. "Maybe the old guy was just murdered by some desperate crazy bastard."

Sully nodded his head like that explanation made simple sense to him. "Yeah," he kept nodding. "Maybe it's like an infection thing, y'know? Maybe it's like a virus that you only get in your blood if they bite you."

Bannon made a face. He couldn't argue because he just didn't know. He got to his feet, glanced once more around the small room, and then went back out into the hallway.

He thrust the pistol out ahead of him, arm fully extended and together the two men searched the rest of the old man's apartment. It was empty.

Bannon led Sully back out onto the second floor landing and they crept forward to where the next closed apartment door seemed to loom in the menacing silence.

"The Roses," Bannon said. "They're a young couple."

He stretched out a hand and tried the door. It was locked. He looked over his shoulder at Sully as though it was a good sign. "Maybe they've survived this...," he shrugged, "...whatever it is," he said.

"Apocalypse," Sully said softly.

Bannon blinked, surprised by Sully, but he said nothing. He bunched his fist and rapped loudly on the door. Close behind him, Sully winced as the sound seemed to echo off the walls.

Bannon pressed his ear to the door and frowned. There was a sound – the slightest, merest hint of a rhythmic noise from somewhere inside the apartment. He tried to concentrate – tried to ignore the pounding of his blood through his veins. After long seconds, he turned back to Sully.

"There's something..." his voice trailed away.

"Something... or someone?"

Bannon didn't know. He bashed his fist against the door again and then impulsively cried out. "Kate? Jerry?"

"Fuck!" Sully hissed, and felt himself physically cringe. "You're going to get us killed."

Bannon trapped his bottom lip between his teeth and narrowed his eyes thoughtfully. That sound...

"Break it down," Bannon said.

Without hesitating, Sully slammed his body against the door and it burst open at the impact of his shoulder. The door crashed back against its hinges and Sully took four staggering steps into the apartment's living room before he regained his balance. He pulled up short, with a gasp of shock choking the back of his throat. "Jesus!"

Bannon crowded into the doorway and the two men stood, horror-struck.

Jerry Rose lay on his back on the living room floor, his arms flung out wide, his legs spread apart. He was lying in a pool of spreading gore. His eyes were open, gazing sightlessly at the ceiling. The man's shirt was awash with blood and the fingers of his left hand were tapping in a nerveless spasm on the polished floorboards as his young wife crouched over the body, feasting on the tender flesh of her husband's throat. She was hunched, feral and primitive on her haunches, dipping her head over her husband to tear away chunks of flesh with greedy relish.

"Kate?" Bannon called incredulously.

The woman looked up suddenly. Her long blonde hair was matted to her head with blood. Her features contorted into a malevolent mask, and her tongue lolled wolfishly from her mouth to lick at the gore that was spilled across her chin.

Bannon stood rooted in paralyzing shock. "Kate?" he called again.

The woman's eyes glinted as though with some sly secret amusement and then she wrenched up a keening shriek, the sound rasping and raw in her throat. She glared at Bannon.

The macabre scene seemed frozen into timeless immobility. The stench in the room was like a slaughterhouse and Bannon felt his senses recoil. The ghoul that had been young Kate Rose came slowly to its feet and it bunched its shoulders as though poised to lunge at the men. The undead raised its loathsome head. It was twitching violently, its jaws frothing with blood and spittle.

Bannon took a staggering step backwards as though recoiling from some unclean evil force. He threw up the gun – leveled it at the ghoul's twisted face, and his knuckles were strained into jagged white-topped ridges. The woman's gaze became one of virulent hatred. Its mouth gaped and it hissed again – then impulsively attacked.

Bannon crushed his finger against the trigger of the pistol and at a distance of just a few feet the impact of the bullet striking the woman in the middle of the face was horrendous. A thunderclap of sound filled the room and slammed off the walls, and Bannon felt his arm punch back with the heavy recoil of the weapon. The undead woman was flung to the floor as though struck by a mighty and invisible fist. The bullet smashed through its teeth, tore up through the palete of its snarling mouth, and went on through the back of the zombie's skull, splattering brains and gore against the far wall of the room.

Bannon stood frozen, rooted to the floor, his eyes filled with the enormity of what he had done. He stared down at the body, peered at the disfigured head that had collapsed into bloody oozing mush as it had been ripped apart. There were clotted fragments of skull and tufts of hair splashed across the floor. Somewhere in the distant recesses of his mind he felt Sully tugging frantically at his arm and the faraway sound of the man's voice. Bannon shook himself, his eyes still transfixed on the motionless body that had been Kate Rose.

"What about him?" Sully hissed. "The fucker will turn any minute now."

Bannon turned his head in a slow daze.

Sully pressed his face close. "We need to finish the guy off," his lips curled into a snarl.

Bannon blinked, and then reality came crashing back through the haze. He nodded. "Yeah," he said.

Sully leaned over the body of Jerry Rose and pressed the muzzle against the man's broad forehead. Blood still pumped from the grotesque gouges across the man's throat, and the rising stench of his tortured death began to drift on the still air.

Sully stared down into the dead man's face as the color drained away from its features and the flesh seemed to turn grey and brittle before his very eyes. He pulled the trigger and the rifle pulsed in his hands. The bullet blew through the dead man's skull and the sound of the shot was like the peal of a bell.

Sully turned to Bannon, his face grim. "Now what?"

Bannon sighed. He felt unaccountably heavy. There was a weary lethargy in his arms and his legs, and an invisible pressure of strain around his chest that seemed to shorten his breath. He lifted his eyes to Sully and it seemed that even that small gesture required effort. "Evelyn's apartment at the end of the hall," he said.

Sully's expression darkened to belligerence. "We ain't got time!"

Bannon seemed not to hear. His face stayed remote. He went back out through the apartment door and stood in the hallway. Sully came after him. He seized Bannon's arm and shook him.

"We don't have time for this," Sully's voice became strident. "We've made enough noise to wake the fucking dead – and the dead are already awake! We need to get as far away from here as possible, before the whole fucking apartment complex gets overrun."

There was a moment's pause and then suddenly Bannon snapped. In an explosion of movement he threw a short jabbing punch, left fist bunched like a hammer that caught the big crewman under his jaw and crushed his teeth together. Sully staggered back two paces, his grip on Bannon's arm loosening. There was an instant where his eyes became glazed and then they refilled with a malevolent menace. The big man stood, shoulders hunched, his chest filling as he took gasping long breaths of rage-filled air. He ran his tongue across his teeth. There was the warm coppery tang in his mouth. He turned his head and spat blood against the wall.

"You shouldn't have done that," Sully's tone was filled with low warning. His lips pared back into a snarl as he touched a finger to his jaw. He could already feel the tender flesh swelling. "That wasn't a smart thing to do."

Bannon glared at him in silent defiance and the two men faced each other like gunslingers for long tense seconds.

"I'm going to check the last apartment," Bannon's voice snapped with new authority. "I don't care what you do."

He turned on his heel and walked down the passageway towards the last door. There was no need for stealth – Sully was right – they had made enough noise to alert anyone or *anything* still lurking in the building. Bannon stopped outside the closed door of apartment 2C.

The light in the hallway was gloomy. There were no external windows at this end of the building. Bannon pressed his ear hard against the door, with the pistol raised so close to his face he could smell gun oil and the odor of the round he had fired, still lingering on the short barrel. He reached out slow tentative fingers for the door handle and turned it with infinite care.

The door was unlocked.

Bannon pressed the palm of his free hand against the door and it swung open on creaking hinges that jarred the silence. He winced, felt his breath jam in the back of his throat. He stood on the threshold until the door was hanging wide open and the sound had wrung through the stillness, then faded. He thrust the gun out in front of him, clutched in a double-handed grip, his arms outstretched, his eyes hunting feverishly for any sign of movement.

The living area was empty. He took three shuffling, wary steps into the room and swiveled from his hips back and forth like a macabre dance, as he brought the weapon to bear on the deep dark holes of shadow in the corners of the room. He felt the first trickle of his breath escape from his lips as the sound of blood throbbing at his temples overwhelmed his hearing. His hand was shaking. Bannon clenched his jaw as the tension wrung beads of sweat from his brow. He was overwhelmed by a sense of dread – a premonition of disaster that was like a heavy weight in the pit of his guts. Keeping the pistol aimed down the length of the empty hallway, he stepped lightly across to the open kitchen area and stole a quick glance around.

There were rancid scraps of molded food spread across the kitchen counter, and a saucepan on the stove. Bannon peered at the contents and then recoiled violently as the stench of something foul filled his nostrils. He grunted. He snatched open the refrigerator; the cloying stink of rotting vegetables thickened the air so that he gagged. He closed the door again and moved towards the hallway.

The carpet in the passage was stained with wild spattered patterns of muddied footprints and blood. Bannon felt his grip on the weapon tremble. His palms were sweaty, the pistol unaccountably heavy and he crept closer to a doorway.

It was a bedroom.

Bannon nudged the door open an inch with the toe of his boot, and then leaped back in anticipation. The door swung with creeping slowness, gradually revealing the ghastly nightmare of the scene beyond.

"Christ!"

Bannon felt a scald of nausea burn the back of his throat. He slapped a hand across his mouth and nose and reeled away until he was slumped against the far wall of the passage.

Inside the bedroom, furniture had been thrown across the floor in some kind of pathetic barricade. The bed was upturned: a chest of drawers and an old wardrobe lay on their side. There was splintered timber strewn across the bloodied carpet and the stale, stuffy air was thick and reeking with the stink of decay.

Bannon felt the gun in his hand waver, then drop to his side. His face was glistening with sweat, his features twisted into a sickened expression of revulsion.

The bedroom was sprayed with the kind of frenzied splatters of blood that Bannon had only ever seen in horror films. It had drenched the floor and dripped down the walls. It was streaked across the ceiling, and it had run in rivulets across the broken furniture. The bedroom was a charnel of chaotic murder.

Bannon doubled over at the waist, and then vomited explosively. He scraped the back of his trembling hand across his mouth and gasped for breath. His eyes watered from the abattoir smells that seeped through the door.

He forced himself upright – and lurched into the room.

He counted three bodies, torn apart so that the pieces of them were scattered across the floor. As far as he could tell, the dead had all been male. He gaped at the carnage with incredulous shock. His mouth hung slack and open, as though unhinged from his jaw as the terrifying reality of the slaughterhouse scene closed in around him.

He went reluctantly to the first corpse and stood over a body that was slumped, sitting upright, against the opposite wall. The face had been torn from the man's skull. The nose was chewed off, the eye sockets just black empty holes that seemed to glare at Bannon in accusation. The soft flesh of the man's lips had been ripped away from the mouth, exposing yellowed rotting teeth and the decaying flesh of gums. The man's shirt had been torn to shreds, and there were deep bite marks in his chest as though a voracious pack of wild animals had savaged him. The flesh was pale as marble, dark blue veins of clotted blood showing clearly through the translucent layers of decomposing skin.

Spread across the floor was the corpse's entrails; thick bloodied ropes of small intestine and other organs, scattered around the body. The soft pouch of his stomach had been clawed open and the contents of his guts spilled across his lap. Fat white maggots slithered in the rotting cavity so that the slime they feasted on seemed to pulse and slowly writhe.

The man's legs lay stretched out before him. Below the knee of the left limb, the body had been gnawed back to bare bone. There were shreds of denim and slivers of fleshy gristle hanging in tatters from the ankle.

Bannon reeled away from the corpse, and stumbled backwards. His foot tripped over the body of another victim.

The man had been torn in half, severed at the torso as though the gnashing jaws of some prehistoric monster had cleaved it apart. The torso of the body laid facedown, head turned, cheek pressed to the blood-drenched carpet. The eyes in the white face were wide and staring in sightless trauma. The rest of the body had been thrown over the edge of the bed, legs hanging limp from mutilated hips, dangling internal organs that were swollen and bloated with gases.

There was blood everywhere.

Bannon was overwhelmed by the carnage – the mindless madness of the savagery. He shook his head in slow bewilderment and shock. This was not murder – this was the frenzied and feral butchery of blood-lusting animals.

He closed his eyes, felt his senses swimming as though he might teeter off balance and collapse. He swayed until he steadied himself, clutching at the wall to keep his legs from buckling beneath him and fighting to rein back his revulsion.

The creeping sound of a footstep brought Bannon jarringly alert.

He snapped his head around and peered at the open bedroom door. The noise had come from beyond the room.

But from where?

There were two other bedrooms and a bathroom further down the hall...

Bannon raised the pistol with painstaking silent slowness, his jaw clenched so tight he could feel the nervous throb of his own pulse. The barrel of the weapon wavered in small circles as he struggled to control the leaping nerves along the length of his arm.

He crouched down behind the cover of the blood-spattered mattress and exhaled a breath he hadn't realized he had been holding. Slow agonizing seconds ticked by. Bannon mopped the sweat from his forehead with the sleeve of his shirt then wrinkled his nose. Above the sickening stench of the corpses, he could smell his own fear.

Narrowing his eyes, Bannon tried to *feel* the silence – compelled himself to concentrate all his attention, anticipating the slightest sound. His body was drawn tensed like a bow about to be loosed, with every nerve drawn unbearably taut and his instincts screaming.

He heard a soft indistinct scrape – a noise like a foot being dragged, and then a distorted hulking shadow crept along the hallway and leaped across the wall through the open bedroom doorway. Bannon felt his guts twist into knots. He took up the pressure on the trigger, feeling the tension of holding the unfamiliar weight of the pistol outstretched begin to burn at the muscles of his shoulder. He was trembling; juddering nerves made his thigh twitch and he could not control the reflex.

A sudden blur of movement – a strained explosion of sound – and Bannon felt himself flinch and then recoil with shock...

...and then relief.

Sully swung through the doorway, the barrel of the rifle held low on his hip, his eyes wide and wild, his mouth wrenched into an ugly snarl to mask his own dreadful fear. The big crewman's muscled frame seemed to fill the opening as his head snapped reflexively to every corner of the room, taking in the macabre gruesome scene of slaughter in an instant, searching for threats.

Bannon stood slowly, appearing from behind the shelter of the mattress. Sully swung the gun onto him instinctively – and then relaxed.

"What are you doing here?" Bannon's voice was tight.

Sully shrugged. "Watching your ass," he said, as though he resented it.

Bannon's eyes hardened. "Nobody's forcing you."

"Nobody's given me a better option either," Sully said as he took a long incredulous look at the carnage of bodies. "Jesus..." he said in a voice that was hushed to a whisper by his horror.

Bannon grimaced. "There's a third one. He's over here, behind the bed."

"Maddie...?"

Bannon shook his head, a mixture of relief and hopelessness. "No sign of her, yet."

Sully shouldered the rifle and stepped delicately around the gored bodies until he was on the far side of the room, standing alongside Bannon. The two men stared down at the corpse at their feet, dismayed and sickened by what they saw.

The body had been mutilated almost beyond belief. The head of the man lay severed from the shoulders, the flesh gnawed and shredded at around the neck, and the soft tender flesh of his throat torn open. The face was bloodless, mouth wide agape. The tongue was swollen and purple, protruding from the thin desiccated lips almost obscenely.

The head was sitting in the dead man's lap.

He was propped with his back against the bed. The stump of his neck had gushed arterial blood down the front of the body, soaking the clothes, the head and the carpet. The body's legs were splayed, the arms limp at its side almost as if the victim had been arranged in the pose after death. Bannon crouched down on his haunches and stared at the decapitated head. The man's face seemed younger than the others that lay dead around him. Bannon frowned. The eyes had rolled up into the skull so that only the whites showed. The features of the face had been made gaunt by decomposition so that the cheekbones protruded through dead flesh that had turned the withered color of dusty parchment.

As Bannon watched, something dark moved within the gaping mouth. He narrowed his eyes, leaned forward and a little to the side to allow more light to spill over the body. He saw the shadow of small movement again and his instincts screamed a warning. He was reaching for the pistol – aiming it at the corpse and rising to his feet with a cry of warning in the back of his throat... when a spider crawled from between the man's drawn lips and crept up his face before disappearing again inside the cavity of a nostril.

Bannon recoiled from the body with a skin-creeping shudder. Cold tingling fingers shuddered down his spine. He shuffled away from the body warily and forced himself to focus.

Sully nudged him with the point of his elbow. "You know these people?"

Bannon shook his head. "I've never seen any of them before."

Sully frowned. "Strangers?"

"To me," Bannon said. "But maybe not to Evelyn. They might have been family or friends who came to visit," he shrugged his shoulders.

Sully grunted. He cast a long last look at the scene of heinous atrocity, and then his expression became peculiarly blank – as though a shutter had come down behind his eyes.

"Let's finish searching the apartment," the big man said gruffly. "The sooner we get this done, the better."

Bannon nodded. They left the bedroom and closed the door quietly behind them.

The bathroom and two remaining bedrooms were empty.

No sign of Maddie.

No signs of violence.

The bed in the main bedroom was made, as though it had never been slept in, and the rest of the room tidy. There were still racks of women's clothes hanging in the wardrobe, and perfume products on the night table. It was if there had been no thought – or no time – to flee before the undead terror had struck.

Bannon stood in the living area of the apartment and felt the crushing weight of his own despair. Until the very last moment he had clung to the belief that his wife was here – waiting for him, and somehow hidden from the horror that had swept through Grey Stone. Now he had to accept the reality that she was gone – or dead.

Or undead.

Bannon's desolation was like a heavy sickening weight in the pit of his stomach. He felt suddenly very tired. His mind was numb, his arms and legs felt leaden.

His last flickering tendril of hope had been extinguished, and with that dark reality came a despondency that left him hollow and gutted. He stared at Sully, and his eyes were haggard wells of pain. "You were right," he muttered grudgingly. "She didn't wait for me. She didn't think I would come back for her."

Sully shook his head grimly. "Maybe she didn't have a choice," the big man's voice became strangely sympathetic. "Maybe she *couldn't* wait."

Bannon grunted.

What difference did it make? Maddie had fled, or been killed... and he hadn't been here to protect her.

Sully dropped wearily down onto a sofa and draped the rifle across his lap. "We need to take a minute," he said. "Before we go anywhere else."

Bannon's eyes hardened. "What?"

Sully became brusque. "You heard me, man. We need to figure out what the hell is going on."

Bannon slumped against a wall and folded his arms across his chest. His expression was wry. "Ever since we docked, you've wanted to get out of town as quick as possible. Now you don't."

Sully's expression darkened. "I told you coming here to look for your wife was a waste of time – that's all," he said. "But the fact is that we've sailed into some fucking nightmare and we don't know shit about what's going on."

Bannon paused for a long moment before he said anything. Bitterness and desolation were raw in his voice. "We're fucked," he said in a tone that no longer cared about consequences. "The whole town has been overrun. We're gonna be next."

Sully looked up in sharp alarm. "Hey, maybe it's not just Grey Stone. Maybe the whole east coast is…" he shrugged. "You know."

"Undead?"

"Yeah, undead," Sully said. "Crawling with those crazy fuckers." He shook his head. The enormity of the possibility was too appalling for him to absorb. "How can something like this happen?"

Bannon grunted. "Maybe it's some kind of a virus," he guessed. "Something highly contagious that consumes the infected people with an insane blood lust."

Sully did not look convinced. "Those fuckers we saw on the waterfront weren't infected," he said belligerently. "They were dead. They fucking died, and then got up again."

Bannon nodded. "But maybe that's *because* of a virus," he went on, doing nothing more than speculating. "Maybe the virus spreads from one person to the next through bites or blood. The wound kills the person, and then the virus does something to bring them back to life – except they're not alive as we know it."

Sully stared off into the distance. He was frowning as though thinking required some monumental effort. "We might be the only ones left alive – anywhere," he said and then his voice trailed off into silence.

Bannon shook his head. "No, I don't believe that," he said. "No virus can spread that quickly. It can only be a matter of a few days since this nightmare started – maybe somewhere around the time when we lost internet and phone contact at sea. That would make sense," he said, and then went on again quickly. "There will be plenty of people still living, Sully. We just need to find them. Maybe the government is already fighting back," he shrugged. "Or maybe this whole thing started right here in Grey Stone and it has already been contained by the military. For all we know, they have the town blocked off."

The big crewman didn't look convinced. "Then what are they waiting for?" he challenged. "Why aren't there soldiers on the ground?"

Bannon looked sad. "They might not have a cure," he said. "They might believe that containment is the only option."

"Containment?"

"Yeah," Bannon pushed himself away from the wall and went to stare gloomily out through the windows that gave a sweeping view of the burning harbor. "Maybe they're waiting for everyone to become infected. You saw the ghouls at the marina, for Christ's sake. Their flesh was literally rotting away from their bodies. They're decomposing. So maybe the army is standing back behind some defensive line and simply waiting for the virus to run its course."

Sully looked grim. "You mean they're waiting for everyone to kill each other."

Bannon nodded his head. "Maybe."

Chapter 8.

Bannon and Sully went down the staircase slowly. Sully led the way, a big bulky frame of brawn and muscle like a human shield, while Bannon trudged disconsolately behind him. When they reached the murky foyer, Sully pressed his nose against the cold glass doors of the apartment complex and studied the world beyond.

Past the paved driveway that ran alongside the building, was a high wooden fence and a fringe of garden that separated the apartments from the next building – a single story holiday home that was rented by visitors to the area throughout the summer months. Smoke was rising from the home, billowing through broken windows. Sully grunted and glanced over his shoulder at Bannon.

"No movement," he muttered, "but I can't see much from here. What do you want to do?"

Bannon looked blank. "Do?"

"Go?" Sully's voice became hard. "Where do you think we should go, damn it?"

Bannon's eyes were glassy, his gaze distant and remote, as he drowned in his own despair and gut-wrenching loss. Sully reached out and shook him brutally. "Hey!" he shouted into Bannon's face. "Fucking wake up! I need you, man."

Bannon flinched and slowly closed his eyes. He took a deep shuddering breath, and when he opened them again his gaze was cleared, less clouded. He looked like he was waking from a dream...

... or a nightmare.

"Forget the harbor," Bannon said, thinking furiously and talking at the same time, playing out possible options and then discounting them just as quickly. "There's no way we could get *'Mandrake'* back out through the heads."

Sully cut him off. "What about my boat," he said abruptly. "She's tied up at the end of the far jetty, alongside the game fishing boats. We could make it through the wreckage with her. She's only twenty foot…"

Bannon thought about that. A small cruiser like Sully's fishing boat might be able to navigate the carnage and floating debris they had seen as they cruised through the heads. He was about to agree, and then stopped himself.

"No," he said, frowning thoughtfully. "The foreshore is going to be too dangerous. Remember that sound? That fucking noise that we heard?"

Sully nodded, like he remembered, but wasn't happy about the decision. "So?"

"So I'm not risking the chance that we might run into a whole horde of these fuckers," Bannon spat with sudden conviction. "We need to get as far *away* from the waterfront as we can – not move towards it."

"But, we *saw* nothing!" Sully's temper flared ferociously.

Bannon shook his head. His expression was grim, his mouth set in a hard, determined line. "Where there's smoke, there's fire," he went on gravely. "They're over on the waterfront, Sully. I know it. And besides, the harbor will be a minefield of wreckage by now. You saw all the boats burning. You saw them drifting from their moorings. No boat is going to get safely in or out of Grey Stone for a very long time."

As if to confirm Bannon's warning, there was the sudden percussive sound of a shattering explosion that boomed in the air and shuddered up through the ground. Both men flinched and ducked their heads instinctively. The roar of the blast seemed to linger on the breeze for long seconds, and then they heard the distant sound of crackling flames. Sully edged the glass foyer door open a couple of inches and stared, aghast.

"Holy mother of God," he gasped in a voice filled with incredulous shock. "The whole fucking complex has just exploded."

"The buildings?

"Every one of them," Sully croaked. "The restaurants, the café... everything along the marina has just been destroyed."

Bannon pushed past Sully, standing in the driveway as though drawn into the open against his will by his fascination and astonishment. He stared gaping towards the harbor, the entire scene embroiled behind a screen of black ruptures of smoke.

Slowly, Bannon turned his eyes back to Sully. "The propane tanks?" It was more of a question than an explanation. There were two huge propane tanks in a bricked off area discreetly concealed by trees, near the loading dock of the marina complex.

Sully shrugged his shoulders, awed to silence by the sheer magnitude of the explosion and the devastation it had wrought. All along the waterfront, leaping flames flickered through dense smoke as the buildings burned in an inferno.

"There's nowhere safe to hide," Bannon shook his head, his tone definite. "And there's only one road out of town. We need to find a car."

At the rear of the complex there were six parking spaces – one allotted to each unit of residents who lived in the apartments. Bannon and Sully ran.

There were only two cars parked within their spaces: Maddie's compact green hatchback sat forlornly in its allotted space, the car low on its springs, the paintwork faded. At the other end of the lot was a silver SUV, parked in the space given to Evelyn's top floor unit.

Sully went for the SUV.

Bannon went towards Maddie's weary old hatchback.

"This one!" Sully barked. The SUV was just a year or two old with dark tinted windows and large chunky tires. There was a steel nudge bar fitted to the front of the vehicle. Sully reversed the rifle and smashed the driver's window open with the butt of the weapon. Shattered glass sprayed across the upholstery.

Bannon cried out to him. He was flinging the door of the hatchback open. "This one!" he insisted. "I know where Maddie kept the spare key."

Sully wavered. The SUV was the better choice, but it was no good at all if he couldn't get the vehicle started. He stared for one more lingering second of hesitation... and then turned and ran towards the little green car.

From around the corner of the building a shambling shape suddenly appeared. Sully saw the figure from the corner of his eye and in an instant his mind made the calculations – he was too far away from Bannon to reach the car before the wavering undead shape could cut him off. He slowed... then stopped running. His heart was pounding in his chest. He threw the rifle up to his shoulder and turned to confront the dark figure. From the corner of his eye he saw Bannon slide into the driver's seat of the hatchback and an instant later he heard the little engine cough and splutter to life in a belch of blue exhaust smoke.

The undead ghoul came shuffling out of the shadows, into the harsh daylight with a malevolent snarl thick in its throat. It was a man. He was drenched in blood. It stalked closer to Sully until the big man could see the yellow-tinge of infected madness in its eyes and smell the rotting carrion stench of it. The ghoul was decomposing. The flesh of its face was rotting, rippling with the movement of a thousand maggots so that the air became foul, putrid – almost poisonous. Sully gagged, and felt the acrid taste of his own fear in his mouth. He let the undead zombie come closer – so near that the barrel seemed almost to be reaching out to prod the figure in the chest.

It was just ten feet away, and hunting him with a peculiar predatory mindlessness that Sully found utterly unsettling. Sully took up the pressure on the trigger and raised the rifle until it was aimed between the ghoul's frenzied eyes.

The moment became burned into Sully's memory. The sounds of the shuffling, staggering feet, the appalling stench that thickened the air – the fine details of that infection ravaged face, distorted gruesomely by the decay and the incensed fury that seemed to compel the undead. Sully heard the engine of the little hatchback finally settle into a throaty roar and flicked his eyes for an instant to where the vehicle was parked. Bannon's face was a white blob behind the windshield, glaring at him. The passenger door of the car had been thrown wide open. He need only to run to the car to escape.

If he could only get to the car...

The moment he looked away, Sully knew he had made a dreadful mistake. The ghoul erupted into frenzied attack, an explosion of violent rage as the sound in its throat rose to a triumphant snarl. It flung itself at Sully, jaws gnashing as the desiccated claw-like fingers gouged at the flesh of Sully's arm and chest.

A scream of horrified shock died in Sully's throat as the ghoul crashed against him. The crack of the rifle shot was loud in his ears, but his arm had been flung high and the bullet flew wide. Then it was too late – too late for anything other than a furious desperate fight for his very life.

The ghoul was a fury of flailing arms and lunging jaws. Sully threw his hands up to protect his face, but the zombie shredded at the flesh of his shoulders and Sully screamed in sudden pain. He lashed out with his fist: felt his knuckles connect meatily against the side of the ghoul's head but it was in vain. The ghoul was voracious, threshing and snapping at Sully's throat until, finally, its jaws bit deep, and Sully felt a single white–hot moment of panic... and then crushing despair.

Blam!

The sound of the shot was cruel against the silence – a roar so loud that for an instant everything seemed frozen in shock.

Sully could hear his panted ragged breathing. He could feel his blood gushing from the savaged wound in his throat, spilling down his shirt and splattering the concrete. He was laying on his back, knees drawn up to protect his guts, with the ghoul heavy on top of him, crushing the last of his breath from his lungs. But quite suddenly the zombie was seized rigid – an inert weight without energy. Slowly, the undead toppled over and fell, unmoving, to the ground.

Sully blinked his eyes, and stared up at the silhouette of Bannon, standing astride him. The pistol was heavy in the man's hand, and there was a grim, bleak expression on his haggard face.

Sully clamped a hand over the savaged wound torn across his neck. Blood oozed through his fingers. He felt his vision begin to blur and despite the radiant warmth of the parking lot on his back, a creeping cold seemed to seep through his body. He gazed up at Bannon and saw the terrible torment etched into his expression.

"It's okay," Sully whispered hoarsely. He felt an eerie sense of calm acceptance, and there was resignation and peace in his eyes. He was dying.

Bannon stood over Sully's body and leveled the barrel of the pistol so that it was aimed at the broad expanse of the man's forehead. He grimaced, watching the flickering spark of life slowly fade from Sully's blank expression, taking up gradual pressure on the trigger so that the instant the big man became one of the undead, he could fire.

Bannon waited. Sweat beaded across his brow and ran in trickles down his back. Sully gave one long last gasp of breath – made a final gasping, gurgling sound, like the croak of a piteous soul suffering the final tortured moments of life...

... and then lay still in a growing pool of his own blood.

Bannon tensed. The chaos around him seemed to fade into the distance. The sounds of bedlam, of death and destruction blurred and then were washed away, as if carried on the wind until it felt as though the world had become eerily still.

Sully's dead body began to alter. It was an imperceptible change at first, almost like a trick to the eye. The skin around the gaping wound began to ashen and as the flesh died, the pulse of blood slowed and began to congeal, turning dark muddy brown.

Sully's eyelids fluttered.

Bannon leaned over the body and pressed the cold steel of the barrel against the dead man's forehead.

Sully's eyes opened.

And then he spoke.

"Don't shoot," Sully said softly. "Please, don't pull the trigger."

Bannon recoiled in alarm and incredulous disbelief. He snatched the pistol away, but still held the weapon extended, finger tensed on the trigger. "Sully?"

The crewman sat up slowly. His body seemed to creak and groan. He felt a heavy lethargy in his arms as if they were loaded with lead weights. He stared fixedly into space – and the view he saw of the world was somehow now tinged yellow and blurred out of focus. He screwed his eyes tightly and then opened them again, slowly lifting his face to Bannon's.

"Say something," Bannon growled, with an almost superstitious sense of eerie shock. He held the pistol at arm's length, just a few inches from Sully's head.

"That fucking hurt!" Sully groaned. He tentatively pulled his hand away from the lacerated flesh of his throat and held it up, inspecting his own blood that trickled through his fingers like thick oozing paint. He stared for a long time, frowning with bewilderment.

Bannon felt the gun in his hand waver a little.

"You're supposed to be fucking dead," he hissed. "When Peter and Claude got bitten, they turned within a few seconds. You're supposed to be infected."

Sully nodded his head slowly. His senses swam, his mind in a torpor of lethargy. He took a deep breath, feeling his lungs fill with air, and then slapped his bloodied hand across his heart.

"I still have a heartbeat," he said in wonder... "But I... I can't smell anything... and my eyes – they're glazed or something. I can't quite seem to get them to focus." He rubbed his forehead and eyelids with his fingers. "And I can't feel my legs."

Bannon took a cautious step back, away from Sully, putting space between himself and the big crewman, still not trusting, not believing...

"What's your name?"

Sully's head turned slowly. "Huh?"

Bannon's finger took up the pressure on the trigger. "I asked you what your name is."

"Sully," the man said clearly.

"First name?"

"John."

"And what do you do for a living?"

"I'm a crewman on your fucking fishing boat," he snapped irritably. He got slowly to his feet and took a testing step. Bannon backed away one more pace.

Sully's balance was there, although his legs felt somehow numbed, almost like they were prosthetic. He stared down at himself, and shook his head with disbelief. He had lost a lot of blood – too much for a man to survive. His shirt and jeans were awash with it, and there was a dark stain on the concrete around where he had fallen. He stared down at the ground and then shifted his eyes to the undead ghoul that was crumpled at his feet. The contents of the zombie's skull had been blown out the back of its head and sprayed across the parking lot in clumps of stringy hair and dead maggot-infested flesh.

Bannon scraped his hand down the side of his face, feeling the roughened stubble on his jaw crackle. "Why didn't you die?" he asked. "And why didn't you turn into one of them?" He thrust his finger out at the grotesque disfigured corpse on the ground.

Sully shook his head. "Don't sound so fuckin' disappointed," he growled.

Bannon felt his expression begin to crack and crumble. He seemed to regret the words, for he went on quickly. "I didn't mean it that way," he frowned slightly in sympathy. "I just don't understand it – how you didn't... aren't..."

Sully's eyes went blank for an instant and he cocked his head to one side. For long seconds he stood unmoving, as if his body had frozen. When the light of recognition returned to his gaze, he was frowning and guarded.

"Trouble," he said in a wary whisper, the words so soft that Bannon barely caught them.

Bannon looked doubtful. "Can you hear something?"

Sully nodded his head.

The sound of glass breaking brought Bannon's head snapping round. He glared over his shoulder and froze, his body tensing with alert awareness. He heard vague shuffling sounds, and a heavy thump. He glanced at Sully, then turned warily towards the corner of the apartment complex and threw the pistol up in ominous expectation.

"Get to the car," Bannon whispered harshly.

"What about the rifle?"

"Take it."

Sully bent for the weapon and then began to move, his steps uncoordinated as though he had spent the day on a bar stool drinking. Bannon followed him, measuring each pace carefully, holding his breath and wincing at soft rustled sounds of his clothes as he moved, and the scrape of his boots on the tarmac. He felt his body coiling like a spring, the tension compressing him so that he was poised and ready to explode into movement at any instant.

A great black dog stalked around the side of the building, its head rocking from side to side and its slathering jaws gaping. The coarse hair along the dog's back bristled like barbed wire.

When it saw Bannon, the animal went stiff for an instant, and then its head swung low between the bunched muscles of its shoulders. It saw Sully move but ignored him. Instead it padded closer to Bannon, its eyes yellow and rolling – demented within the snarling face. Its snout was stiff and stained with dry blood, and there was more blood on the dog's paws and caked in the coarse hair across its broad chest. The beast growled and thick ropes of foaming saliva drooled from its gnashing jaws. The lips of the dog were peeled back, revealing jagged teeth. The dog slinked forward two more creeping paces.

Bannon froze, sensing the slightest movement would provoke the infected animal to attack. He could hear the thumping race of his heart trying to break out of his chest. He could feel the blazing heat of the afternoon sun, as sweat trickled down his brow and into his eyes.

Sully had reached the hatchback. He raised the rifle, drawing a bead on the dog.

Bannon risked a step towards the car...

The dog lunged.

The beast exploded upon Bannon like a savage avalanche of black snarling muscle. It seemed to hang in the air, and then flinch as though punched sideways by an invisible fist.

Then it struck Bannon full in the chest, the crushing impact of its momentum hurling him off his feet so that he collapsed to the ground with the weight of the maddened animal crushing the wind from his lungs. He screamed in panic and fear and desperation. He thrashed his fists at the animal, twisting his head away from the putrid stench of the dog's gaping jaws. He kicked out, and felt the toe of his boot dig deep into the animal's unprotected ribs.

The dog didn't move.

The dog didn't bite him.

The dog was dead.

Bannon lay on his back for long seconds while his breath rattled painfully in his chest. The beast's inert weight was like a bag of cement. He struck out and shoved it off him. He got to his feet, his legs trembling uncontrollably and his hands shaking so badly that he could not feel his fingers. He stared wide-eyed down at the dog, and then slowly turned his head to where Sully waited by the car. The big man was re-loading the rifle.

"Good shot for a guy with blurred vision," Bannon said dryly, but though he tried to sound calm, the words squeaked horribly in his throat.

Sully said nothing for a long moment, and then set the weapon aside. "You're assuming I was aiming for the dog..." he said with an acid growl.

Bannon threw himself behind the wheel of Maddie's little car and slipped the handbrake. The hatchback leaped forward and he crunched through the gears, swerving the vehicle nimbly around the corpses of the dog and the ghoul, then gunning the engine as the car raced down the narrow driveway. Without braking, he swung the wheel hard as the car slewed sideways onto the blacktop, clipping the burned out shell of the vehicle they had seen as they crossed the road from the waterfront, before yawing on tired suspension. Bannon felt himself thrown around inside the car. It was fishtailing uncontrollably. He spun the wheel against the roll and tapped the accelerator. The hatchback's tires

93

churned in a squeal of blue rubber. Bannon wrenched the wheel to the opposite lock and the car settled, and then lunged forward bravely.

"Where are we going?" Sully asked. His voice sounded muffled and rasping in his own ears.

"Out of town," Bannon was grim. His hands were white-knuckled on the wheel. There were dead bodies littered across the blacktop. He kept his foot down, squeezing the gas pedal until it felt like it was pressed hard against the firewall. The car crunched over the corpses like they were speed bumps.

"If we can get across the bridge, we might have a chance," he said. He flicked his eyes to the rear view mirror. The burning foreshore was gradually dwindling in the distance, pillars of grey smoke spiraling into the hazy sky.

Bannon felt the racked tension ease momentarily – enough for him to at last despair.

"Maddie didn't make it out," he said with a heavy voice.

Sully shot him a hard look. Bannon was shaking his head.

"She would have taken this car," Bannon went on. His tone had an air of finality. "When I saw her car in the parking lot, I knew. I knew she never made it out of town before... before everything went to hell."

Beside him, Sully had the rifle resting across his lap. He lowered the passenger window and thrust the barrel out, as though he were riding shotgun on a wild west stagecoach.

"She could be hiding," Sully offered.

Bannon shook his head again. "There's nowhere to hide, Sully. You saw those things. They're relentless. I can't think of anywhere that would be safe from them."

The township of Grey Stone was an isolated oasis community that had sprung up around the early fishing industry. A wide river spilled into the harbor, meandering through miles of wooded valley contours as it journeyed down through the mountains. Bannon's last hope for his own survival was that the bridge on the fringe of the settlement was still intact...

He held his breath. The car went round a long sweeping bend, past isolated homes set well back from the road and a sprinkling of trees.

The bridge was still there.

Bannon saw the arched hump of its shape rise in the far distance, ethereal and remote through smoke haze. He gritted his teeth, feeling the tension come back into his muscles. The hatchback was speeding along gamely, juddering around the corners on old tires and then pouncing forward again every time the road straightened. The car nosed down a dip in the road and as it climbed up the far rise, the clouds of smoke opened up before them like a vast curtain.

The road was clogged with destroyed and abandoned vehicles that stretched for a mile back from the bridge. Bannon slammed his foot down hard on the brakes and stared through the windshield with a crushing weight of despair.

He could see wrecked vehicles of every shape and size. Some of them had been burned out. Others had simply been abandoned. Car doors were flung wide open, swinging eerily in the sudden wind. Black crows wheeled in the air, their cries like a harsh gloat.

Some of the cars were still smoldering. Others had roof racks piled high with family possessions. There was glass and debris and clothing scattered across the roadway.

And bodies.

Hundreds of bodies.

They were bloated ugly shapes, distorted and hideous with gases. The figures were blackened, burned by the merciless heat and the fire that had scorched through the carnage. The grass on either side of the road had been turned to scarred ashes. Bannon covered his mouth and nose with a hand. The vile sickening stench of death was nauseating. As he watched, a big dark bird winged delightedly down and landed on the stomach of a dead child, laying by the side of the blacktop. It was a girl. Her legs were splayed wide, her arms stretched out so that it looked like she had been staked out in the sun. She was wearing a pink dress. The bird hopped onto the girl's chest and craned its neck forward to feast on the soft flesh of her face.

Bannon got out of the car and stood gaping at the carnage like he was living through a slow-motion nightmare. The closest car was a big black sedan. There was sleeping bags and camping gear stuffed in the back seat. The rear window had been smashed and there was spattered blood on the trunk.

The vehicle had collided with the car ahead of it. The front of the sedan was horribly crumpled, and there was the lingering smell of oil and gas still in the air. Everywhere he looked there were horrific scenes of panic, and desperation.

And death.

Bannon heard a car door creak open slowly and turned to see Sully clambering out of the hatchback. The big man moved stiffly. Sully stared at the bridge and then turned until he was looking back towards Grey Stone.

"Do we walk from here?" Sully asked.

Bannon nodded. There was no other choice.

Sully frowned. He narrowed his eyes like he was concentrating and Bannon became instantly alert. He recalled Sully's expression back at the apartment complex parking lot. It was as if he had sensed the danger of the maddened dog's presence, well before it had appeared from around the side of the building. As Bannon watched the big man's tensed grey face, he felt a shudder of eerie superstition.

"You hear something?"

Sully said nothing. He turned slowly in a full circle and then closed his eyes. It was as if he was feeling at vibrations in the air. His eyes flashed suddenly wide open and they were filled with urgency.

"They're coming," he said with an air of finality. His voice was bleak and flat, lacking any inflection of fear... which made the warning all the more chilling to Bannon. "The undead. They're pouring out of the town. I can hear them – hear their breathing. They're coming for us."

A rash of dread crept up Bannon's spine. He peered back past where Sully stood, staring fixedly into the dense writhing smoke. He could hear nothing – nothing at all.

"Are you sure?"

Sully's expression darkened. His lips stretched taut into a savage grimace and his voice was edged with spite. "Do you want to wait around to find out?"

They ran.

The road to the bridge was a tangled maze of dead, ravaged bodies, mangled cars, and debris. Both men ran doggedly, jinking around obstacles, their plodding feet slapping hard and heavy on the blacktop. The bridge seemed to come no closer. Bannon felt his lungs begin to burn and his breath saw painfully across his throat. He ran with the despair and desperation of the hopeless and the hunted.

By the time they reached the foot of the bridge, Bannon was a lather of sweat. He collapsed against the hood of a wrecked car and hunched over, retching air and gasping to refill his lungs. Sully had fallen paces behind him, the bigger man's steps unnaturally heavy and stiffened. Bannon threw his head back and stared up at the afternoon sun. There was at least a couple more hours of light before dusk.

Sully reached him. The man's face was grey, made all the more pale by the peculiar yellow blaze of his eyes. He barely drew a breath.

"I'm leaving the rifle," Sully said. "It's too heavy. Throw the pistol away. Anything that doesn't need to be carried gets left here. Right here."

"I must keep the pistol," Bannon protested.

"Then you'll die within the hour," Sully snapped with a brutal flare of impatience. "They will run us down."

Bannon hesitated for long seconds of indecision. He peered back at the curtain of heavy smoke that hung like a veil across the road. The tendrils of grey seemed to writhe above the ground, changing shape and darkening into ethereal coils that crept towards the bridge, gradually engulfing the mangled wreckage that was strewn across the road.

Bannon could see no sign of pursuit... but there was blurred sound in the air: a vague hum of noise like the buzzing swarm of bees that was so indistinct it had no definition.

He threw the pistol reluctantly over the roadside guardrail. Then they began to run again.

They went up the incline of the bridge, Bannon running stiffly alongside Sully. The bigger man moved with a shamble of legs and arms that was uncoordinated and awkward, but measured into a relentless cadence. Bannon matched the bigger man's pace, no longer sprinting with panic, but controlling his stride – and his fear.

At the arch of the bridge, Bannon slowed and then came to another stop. His shirt was soaked with sweat and he could feel a heavy weariness in his legs that made them tremble. He slumped against the side of an abandoned car, sucking in deep breaths. He looked back from the rise.

"I think they've given up," he sounded relieved, peering back down along the road into town and the heavy pall of smoke that hung over the harbor.

"Maybe," Sully did not sound convinced. He stared back along the way they had come for several minutes before he suddenly gave an angry grunt and pointed.

"There! Coming through the smoke about a hundred yards before the bridge. Can you see them?"

"Shit!" Bannon hissed. A wavering dark line of shapes began to materialize in the haze. The line was undulating, writhing... and coming closer, gaining definition with every moment they stared.

"How many do you think?" Sully asked. He had sensed them – knew how close the undead were – and yet curiously he could not see them with clarity.

Bannon hawked a glob of thick slimy phlegm onto the ground at his feet. "At least a hundred," he guessed. "Maybe more."

Sully nodded, said nothing.

Bannon took several deep breaths, and took stock of himself. He was a lather of sweat, and there was cramping fatigue in his legs. He wasn't accustomed to running. There wasn't much call for it on a fishing boat. His mouth was dry and gummy with saliva. More than anything, he wanted a drink.

There were wrecked cars cluttering both lanes of the bridge. The vehicle closest was a small blue Japanese sedan. All four doors of the car were wide open and the trunk hand been sprung. The windshield was cracked and smeared with blood. He went to the vehicle and rummaged around on the back seat. The car had been piled with family possessions – blankets, clothes, and a cardboard box of tinned food. He found a can of soda. It was warm. He drank thirstily, then carried the can back to where Sully stood.

"We need to go," Sully said, without taking his eyes from the dark line of undead that were in pursuit.

Bannon nodded. He handed the soda to Sully but the big man shook his head.

"They've sensed us," he said bleakly.

"Are you sure?"

"Take a look for yourself," Sully grunted. The line of undead had reached the foot of the bridge, breaking apart like a wave around rocks, as the chaos of crashed and mangled vehicles fractured the line into small clusters of undead. About a dozen of the pursuers had torn free of the horde, running with more purpose than the others.

"They're probably the fresher ones," Sully guessed. Bannon frowned curiously. He watched the knot of blood-covered shapes come closer until he could see detail and definition in every figure. Most of the pursuers were men.

"How do you know that?" Bannon snapped. His sense of panic was beginning to rise again. Their lead had been squandered away by the need to rest. Now the pack was perilously close.

Sully didn't answer. Instead, he turned and gazed at the road ahead.

They were standing on the humped back of the bridge. The slope down was a gentle fall, and then the road ran in a straight line all the way to the horizon. Along the black ribbon was the littered carnage of destruction. On either side of the road lay undulating lush green farm fields, speckled with small dark lumps that were bodies.

"We need to go," Sully said.

They ran again, their steps given momentum by the gentle undulation down the back of the bridge. Their feet slapped in unison on the blacktop, slipping into a monotonous rhythm. When they reached the bottom of the bridge and the road flattened out ahead of them, Bannon lengthened his stride, feeling a renewed fearful need to gain distance.

Sully barked at him. "Slow down!" he spoke in broken pants as they continued to run. "You'll burn out if you push too hard. Keep a rhythm."

Bannon restrained himself. He fell back into stride with Sully, running with his mouth open, his jaw slack and gulping for air until his arms and legs began to lose co-ordination and he felt himself beginning to stumble. His calves were cramping. He winced in pain, screwed his face up against the biting agony... and then went tumbling painfully to the road, rolling over and barking skin from his elbows and knees.

"It's no use." It took Bannon a full minute to gasp out just those few words between ragged shuddering breaths. He felt himself on the verge of collapse. He lay on his back, staring up at the sky as it filled with the first colors of sunset. The cramp in his leg knotted and he grimaced. He curled up his toes and then snatched at his knee, grunting.

Sully stood over him, hands on hips, his eyes open but his expression somehow vague and vacant. He turned back to face the bridge and stood rigid.

"They're closer," he said darkly. "Can you see them?"

Bannon sat up. He blinked stinging sweat from his eyes and peered back at the crest of the bridge. He saw wavering movement.

"Yes," he said. "They haven't given up."

Sully nodded. "They won't."

"Then we're fucked. It's just a matter of time." Bannon heaved himself to his feet. Long shadows were stretching across the ground and a gentle breeze carried on the air, chill against his sweat-drenched shirt. "I should have kept the pistol," he said bitterly.

Sully shook his head. "If you had, they would have caught us already."

"If I had," Bannon snapped, "We could have fought our way out of this instead of running. There are only a dozen of them. We would have stood a chance."

Sully turned his jaundiced eyes to Bannon. "There are at least a hundred more behind those chasers," he reminded.

Bannon looked longingly at the abandoned cars jamming the road. "Let's take our chances in a car," he growled. "I can't run any further."

Sully looked incredulous. "The fucking road is jammed!" he seethed. "A car is useless without clear road."

Bannon nodded absently, but he wasn't listening. He limped to a nearby car and peered in through the driver's side door. It was a yellow Lexus. The keys were in the ignition. Lying slumped back in the passenger seat of the vehicle was a young woman. The body was limp, arms dangling across her lap. The woman's eyes were open – wide and staring, her head turned slightly to the side, chin resting on her chest. There was a single bullet hole in the center of her forehead, and a thin trickle of blood had run down her face. Bannon opened the driver's door, and the sudden rotting stench of the corpse made him recoil and retch.

"Get in!" he choked at Sully.

Sully stared, defiant. He flung his arms. "The road is fucking blocked!" he flared. "What's the point? You're going to drive twenty feet and then what?"

Bannon shook his head. "I'm not going that way," he glanced down the road. "I'm going that way." He turned his head and stared at the open fields. Cross country."

Sully shook his head. "No good."

The embankment at the shoulder of the road was raised several feet above the level of the surrounding fields. A drainage ditch, overgrown with grass and mud, ran alongside the blacktop like an ancient moat.

"You'll tear the guts out of the car before you even reach the fence line," Sully said.

"Maybe," Bannon said grimly, "but I'm going to try." He shot a furtive glance back to the crest of the bridge. The undead were coming on relentlessly. Two of the ghouls were running ahead of the others, narrowing the gap quickly. Both of the undead chasers were men, their features contorted infernally. One of them wrenched up a keening shriek of fury, and the sound carried clearly to where Bannon stood. He flung the driver's door of the Lexus open, and then paused for one last instant. "You coming?"

Sully said nothing.

His face had become blank, the gaze sightless, so that for one terrifying split-second Bannon thought the big crewman had finally turned and become another one of the undead. Then the yellowed eyes opened slowly, and they were clear... and somehow still human in the grey death-like face.

"A helicopter," Sully said. "Coming this way."

He turned, and then turned again. He was frowning with deep concentration, his head bowed but his body alert and quivering with some sensory strain.

He stabbed a sudden finger into the air. "There!" he shouted.

Bannon stared up into a sky that was becoming golden with the first colors of sunset. Hanging low, suspended above a distant forest, he saw a small dark speck. He gaped. He could hear nothing, but as he watched the dot grew in size gradually as it came closer.

Only then did he hear the very distant *thwack-thwack* of rotors beating at the air.

Bannon forgot the car. The helicopter was skimming the contours of the ground, rising and dipping as it hopped over hillocks and wooded clumps. It was coming in fast from the north, sunlight reflecting off the cockpit canopy.

Bannon started running.

"Come on!" he cried hoarsely to Sully. He scrambled across the road and slid down into the drainage ditch. Thick mud sucked at his boots as he waded back up to firm ground. There was a farm field ahead of him. He ducked through rusted strands of barbed wire fencing and ran into the open grass, waving his arms frantically over his head.

Sully was behind him, moving stiffly, on limbs made awkward. Bannon streaked ahead.

For long agonizing seconds the helicopter flew on a straight course that would take it directly over Grey Stone. Bannon could see the shape of the chopper clearly now – see the harsh angles of the hull and the bulbous nose of the beast. It was military – blotched in camouflage paint and bristling weapon pods beneath short stubby wings attached to the fuselage.

Bannon scampered across the field until his legs ached and the pain in his chest flared like a furnace. He cried out as he ran, screaming until he could not hear the sound of his own voice above the crushing clatter of mechanical roar that seemed to shudder the very air.

Then – when he had given up all hope and began to stagger in despair – the helicopter seemed to tilt and then jink, lurching almost onto its side to veer and dive towards him.

Bannon waved his arms and cried out in relief. He turned and glanced over his shoulder. Sully was just scrambling through the wire fence, and close behind him came the undead – snarling and howling like a pack of ravenous wolves.

The downdraft from the helicopter's massive scything blades flattened the grass and swayed the nearby trees. The air flailed at Bannon, kicking up dirt and mud so that he threw up his hands to shield his face and turned his head away. The sound was a roaring cacophony that beat against his eardrums. He felt himself cowering against the violent noise as the helicopter swung suspended in the sky, almost directly overhead.

Through tightly squinted eyes, Bannon looked up and saw the monstrous belly of the beast, hanging from the blurred disc of its giant rotor. He saw a cargo door open and then the distorted helmeted face of a crewman appeared. Bannon dropped to his knees and felt all the strength finally fade from his body. The sound in his ears became a throbbing roar, a rushing hissing bellow.

The crewman's body appeared, and then hung suspended from the helicopter, dangling in the air like a spider from a delicate strand of web. The man dropped closer, and Bannon dragged himself to his feet. The crewman hit the ground, his legs buckling to cushion his landing. The helmet and visor made him look other worldly. He shook Bannon's shoulders and felt him sway, as though his bones had turned to jelly. The crewman harnessed Bannon to his chest with the quick efficiency of someone trained in the art, and then signaled urgently with a thrust of his right hand. Bannon felt himself become weightless. His head lolled to the side. He was hanging limp in the air, twenty feet above the wind-whipped ground. He saw Sully, still running doggedly across the field, and the undead all around him. Bannon opened his mouth and shouted at the crewman, but the crushing roar of the rotors and the whine of turbines wrenched the words from his lips before they could be heard.

Bannon watched Sully slow despondently, and then stumble. The big man stopped, his head thrown back, watching as Bannon was dragged inside the belly of the beast.

Then the air was suddenly ripped apart by the shattering roar of machine gun fire.

Sully staggered. The helicopter was pivoting on its axis, spitting gouts of flame as a hail of bullets stitched the ground. Clods of earth were flung into the sky. The bullets caught three of the undead and ripped their bodies apart, shredding them mercilessly. Sully turned and lurched away. The undead paid no attention to him. The helicopter spun again and the sound of machine gun fire in Sully's ears was like a stick being dragged along a fence of corrugated iron. He felt the air around him rupture with the brutal flailing shred of bullets.

Then the helicopter was rising and tilting, moving off to the south quickly, and fading from sight on the dwindling clatter of its rotors.

John Sully stood forlorn and abandoned in the field and stared warily at the undead ghouls that mindlessly milled all around him.

Part Two.
Chapter 1.

Something shadowy flittered across Bannon's face, darkening his vision for an instant before moving away like a tenuous veil. He heard himself groan softly, and then his eyes fluttered open.

There was a man hovering over him.

Bannon blinked in confusion. He swept his gaze past the man. He was lying on a narrow uncomfortable cot. There was a tube in his arm connected to a bag of clear fluid, hung from a steel stand beside where he lay, and a lamp glowing above his head. The walls and ceiling around him were white. He narrowed his eyes and frowned for long seconds. The air smelled of antiseptic.

He turned his gaze slowly back to the man. He was sitting hunched on a chair beside the cot, leaning over Bannon with a kindly expression. The man was wearing army fatigues, but Bannon could see no insignia – no identification on the uniform at all. The man had haggard, worn features, his dark eyes set deep into his face and surrounded by spiders webs of fine wrinkles.

"Welcome," the stranger said in a calm, friendly voice, "to Camp Calamity. Glad you survived your ordeal."

Bannon licked his tongue across dry parched lips. His mouth felt thick, as if stuffed with cotton wool. He felt his vision come gradually into focus. He tried to lift his hand to rub at pain that stabbed behind his eyes, but his limbs felt unnaturally heavy. He grunted and his head lolled to the side.

There were other people in the room, standing back against the far wall of the infirmary in a shadowed cluster beyond the reach of lamplight. They were faces without definition, gathered on the periphery of his vision, standing quietly and unmoving. Bannon sensed they were all watching him with some kind of strained anxiety.

"Where am I?" he asked.

The man leaning over the cot gave Bannon a benevolent smile. "You're safe," he said. "You're at Camp Calamity. One of our recce helicopters plucked you out of a field just outside of Grey Stone. Do you remember that?"

Bannon remembered.

The horrific memories came slamming back with a rush; he saw the dead bodies scattered across the lawns of the harbor foreshore, the undead ghouls that had attacked as the boat had docked, the macabre slaughter room in the top floor apartment. He saw it all again in chilling detail that made his skin crawl. He nodded his head slowly.

The man beside the cot seemed pleased and relieved. He patted Bannon's shoulder in some kind of reassurance.

"Can you tell me your name?"

"Bannon. Steve Bannon."

The man nodded like he already knew. "And what did you do, Mr. Bannon?"

"Do?"

"Your work?"

Bannon swallowed. There was a dry hard lump in his throat. "Skipper," he said, his voice nothing more than a soft croak. "I was the skipper of a fishing boat. The *Mandrake*."

110

"What kind of fishing boat?"

"A fucking big one," Bannon said gruffly. "A seventy-five foot long line boat that operated out of Grey Stone harbor."

The man turned and glanced over his shoulder at the shadowy figures standing at the back of the room. He nodded his head, and another man suddenly stepped forward, peeling away from the dark shapes. He was a tall thin man, wearing a long white lab coat. The man had a narrow, drawn face, and thick dark-rimmed glasses framed his eyes and bushy eyebrows.

The man didn't sit. He stood at the foot of the cot and his voice was clinical, devoid of compassion or emotion.

"Mr. Bannon, how do you feel?" the man asked with the kind of perfunctory tone that suggested he didn't much care about the answer.

"Like shit," Bannon said. He felt a groggy lethargy holding his body down and wondered whether he had been drugged. The pain behind his eyes was like a brutal stabbing blade.

"Good," the man in the coat said, as if he hadn't heard. "Do you feel up to answering some questions about your ordeal? They're important, and time is of the essence."

Bannon started to nod his head, and then stopped himself. He tried to sit up, but couldn't move. He frowned.

"Am I paralyzed?"

The man in the coat shook his head. "Restrained," he said bluntly. "Your hands and feet are bound to the cot," and then went on quickly as he saw the sudden alarm flare in Bannon's expression. "It's a security precaution only, I assure you."

Bannon flinched. "Precaution against what?"

The man in the coat shrugged, as though the answer was obvious. "Against infection," he grunted. "In case you are carrying the virus."

Bannon laughed suddenly, but it was a cynical and bitter sound, edged with something close to hysteria. "If I was infected, you fuckwit, I would have turned undead within twenty seconds. I assure you, I'm fucking normal."

The uniformed man sitting behind the bed cut across the conversation smoothly. He put a restraining hand gently on Bannon's shoulder and flashed a silent message to the other man with the glare of his eyes. "Of course you're right, Mr. Bannon," the soldier said to mollify him. "We've had you here under observation for a couple of hours. You don't actually have a scratch on you. Apart from dehydration and exhaustion, your vital signs are steady."

"Then untie the fucking restraints," Bannon snapped. The two men at either end of the bed exchanged another meaningful glance, and then the man in the white coat shrugged his shoulders and nodded his head reluctantly. The uniformed man unfastened the strap around one of Bannon's wrists and then paused, as though the skipper might suddenly explode into furious attack. When he didn't, the man let out a breath, like a sigh of relief. He reached across and loosened the other wrist restraint. Bannon sat up, massaging the abraded skin and flexing his fingers until he felt the tingle of renewed circulation.

"How long have I been here?" Bannon asked. There was restrained resentment in his voice.

"Two hours," the soldier replied.

Bannon nodded. He felt his temper cooling. "What about Sully?"

"Sully?"

Bannon nodded again. "John Sully. The other guy in the field. He was running with me. Did you send helicopters back for him?"

The man sitting beside the cot studied Bannon's face with a curious, intrigued expression. He leaned closer to the bed, watching Bannon's eyes with minute fascination. He said nothing for a long time, and it looked to Bannon as though the man was choosing his words carefully when he spoke at last.

"Mr. Bannon, there was no other man in the field. There was just you, running from about a dozen zombies."

Bannon shook his head and his voice tightened. "There was another guy," he insisted. "He was one of my crewmen from the fishing boat. His name is John Sully."

The soldier sat back, his eyes narrowed to appraising slits. He glanced past the tall man in the lab coat and seemed to be frowning at someone else, who was still a part of the shadows. He turned back to Bannon slowly and leaned forward until his face was close.

"We played the tapes back," he said quietly. "The recce chopper recorded the whole incident. That footage shows you running across a field and several of the undead chasing you."

Bannon screwed his eyes tightly shut and let out a long weary sigh. "Sully wasn't entirely undead,"

113

he said. "He got bitten, but he didn't turn. The infection... or whatever it is... didn't kill him. He was still alive."

The uniformed man's eyes went wide with sudden shock and he recoiled as though Bannon had bitten him. He stared incredulously at the skipper on the bed for long seconds, his mind a whirl. Finally the man got up from the chair and disappeared into the shadows at the far end of the room. Bannon could hear hushed urgent voices, but the words were indistinct and muffled. He pressed his fingertips to his temples and massaged at the ache that lingered behind his eyes. He felt as though he was swaying. He slumped back down on the bed and stared at the ceiling.

The uniformed man came back to the bed, but something in his expression had altered. His eyes were dark and penetrating, the friendly demeanor now hidden behind a furrowed brow and a thin-lipped scowl.

"Mr Bannon, tell me again the name of the man who you allege was bitten, but did not become infected."

Bannon fixed his eyes on the uniformed man. "First, tell me who the fuck you are."

The man flinched. For an instant he paused and Bannon saw something dark and dangerous shadow the stranger's eyes. It was there for just an instant, and then gone again, like a passing cloud across the calm green surface of a lake.

The man smiled without warmth. "My name is Smith," he said stiffly. "Army intelligence."

Bannon said nothing and in the silence the soldier made a half-hearted gesture to the man standing at the foot of the bed in the lab coat. "And this is doctor Jones. He's army too. He's with USAMRID, the United States Army Medical Research Institute of Infectious Diseases... which is why we always just use the anacronym," the intelligence man muttered dryly.

Bannon arched a taunting eyebrow. "Smith and Jones?" he repeated dryly. "And who are the rest of the goons, cowering back there in the shadows?"

"The von Trapp family, from *'The Sound of Music',*" Smith said without any hint of humor.

Bannon got the message.

Who those people are is none of your fucking business.

The intelligence officer turned the chair around and sat down, straddling the seat with his arms draped over the backrest. He leaned forward into the soft light of the overhead lamp.

"The name of the man?" he prodded.

"Sully," Bannon said and spelled it out. "John Sully." He heard the scuffle of footsteps in the shadows and then a door open and close again.

"And he was a crewman aboard your fishing boat?"

"Yeah," Bannon said.

"Did you know him well?"

Bannon shrugged. "I guess," he said. "Sully worked the boat with me for about the last three years. He was casual – I called on him when I needed him."

The intelligence officer looked thoughtful. "So he wasn't on board the fishing boat every time you went to sea?"

"No. Not every time. I rotated the crew."

The man nodded. "How old is this Sully?"

Bannon didn't actually know. "Twenty-four, maybe twenty-five," he guessed.

"Physical description?"

"Big, muscular guy."

"Anything else? Any distinguishing marks?"

"Tattoos on his forearms, and a shaved head," Sully said. "Oh, and now he has a massive gouge bitten out of his fucking neck."

The intelligence officer frowned in disappointment. He sighed. "I don't think you're taking this line of questioning with the seriousness it deserves," he said stiffly. "Your description of John Sully could help your country. What I am talking to you about tonight are matters of national security."

The man's stare was like ice and slowly Bannon felt the edge come off his temper. He felt bone-weary, wrung out by the endless hours of unbearable strain he had endured. He let his tension go in one long wretched breath.

"Sully is about six-two, maybe six foot three. Brown eyes. A couple of scars on his left arm."

The intelligence officer nodded. Over his shoulder, Bannon saw the infirmary door open again and someone stepped stealthily into the room. The uniformed man heard the noise of the door and glanced over his shoulder. A young woman emerged, her face pale and plain, her dark hair scraped back severely from her face. She was wearing some kind of a uniform. She handed a piece of paper to the intelligence guy and then faded back out of sight.

The man called Smith studied the page for long seconds and then turned it around for Bannon to see. It was a police report.

"Is that John Sully?"

Bannon frowned. The quality of the image was poor – so dark in places that the shadows were inky black patches. Bannon looked carefully. "It's him," he said, "but he's changed since this photo."

The army officer skimmed the page with his eyes. "This is a police report from about four years ago," he said. "Sully was arrested on a breaking and entering charge." He read through the details of the report and then scowled at the photo image. "How has he changed?"

"The hair, for one thing," Sully said. "His head is shaved now, like I told you. And his face has filled out more."

The intelligence officer's frown deepened. He turned his head and spoke into the shadows.

"Do we have anything else on the guy, Stephanie?"

"No, sir," a woman replied. Bannon guessed it was the same young woman who had handed across the report, but he couldn't see her now that she had stepped away from the glare of the lamp.

The man named Smith grunted, like he had taken a solid punch to the guts.

"Mr. Bannon, what was the time delay between when Mr. Sully became infected, and when you were rescued by the helicopter?"

Bannon thought about that. The entire day had been one of such intense chaos and fear that he couldn't possibly be certain. He shrugged his shoulders. "Maybe an hour," he guessed. "Give or take thirty minutes either way."

The intelligence officer's expression stayed blank. "And what – exactly – was the nature of Mr. Sully's wound?"

"The nature?"

"Yes. How did he become infected?"

"He was bitten," Bannon said, and resentment began to creep back into his voice. "We were standing in the parking lot of the apartment complex I lived in. We had just been through all the units looking for a sign of my wife – searching for her," Bannon's voice became thick and then choked off. The intelligence officer waited patiently. The room was eerily silent pulsing with a sudden tension.

"When we came down to the parking lot, one of the undead fuckers suddenly appeared from behind a corner of the building. It rushed at Sully. Sully went down. The ghoul hit him hard and they both fell to the ground. The thing bit him. It gouged his shoulder as he tried to protect his face, and then it tore a chunk from his throat."

"A chunk?"

Bannon nodded. "Like it was a wild fucking animal. I shot the ghoul, but I was too late. Sully was lying on the ground bleeding out. He had his hand over the wound, but it didn't help. Then, he faded."

"Faded?"

"Yes," Bannon said solemnly. "His eyes faded, went dull. Then he died. I put the barrel of my pistol against his forehead. We had lost two other crewmen earlier in the day. Both of them had turned into undead killers about ten seconds after breathing their last breath. I expected the same thing to happen to Sully. I had the gun ready – waiting for the instant he turned."

"But he didn't, right?"

Bannon shook his head. "He did begin to turn. His skin became grey like the color of the sidewalk, and the blood from his bite wound seemed to thicken and then turn brown. Then he opened his eyes. They were yellow."

"And then what happened," the intelligence officer was leaning close to Bannon, and there was a blaze of intensity in the man's expression.

"I had pressure on the trigger. I was about to fire. Then he spoke to me."

Bannon heard someone in the shadows gasp. The intelligence officer looked incredulous. "He *spoke* to you?"

"Yes."

The next voice Bannon heard was from someone in the back of the room. It was a deep, powerful man's voice – the bark of someone who was accustomed to command. The words slashed across the stunned silence.

"Was his speech affected? Was he able to communicate with you clearly?"

Bannon squinted his eyes, hunting the origin of the questions. "He was perfectly lucid, and had no trouble talking."

"Son of a bitch!" someone breathed impulsively, their hushed tone filled with awe and astonishment.

The big voice boomed again in a snap of decision. "Right," he barked. "Get this man cleaned up. Shower, shave and something to eat. I want him in the Colonel's office in exactly three hours, and not a single minute later."

Chapter 2.

Bannon stood at the end of a long conference table and stared at the people seated around him. The lighting in the room was subdued, but there were spotlights nested in the ceiling. They lit the table and left the edges of the room darkened.

On the far wall was a clock. It was a few minutes past eleven at night.

At the end of the table was a large bull of a man. He had a blotched, ruddy complexion, and clear piercing eyes. His hair was grey, his mouth clamped around the stump of a cigar. He sat back in his chair, half hidden in the shadows, watching Bannon's every move, missing nothing. He was dressed in army fatigues. For all his imposing size, the man looked amiable. Bannon imagined, in a different life, the guy could have been a physical education teacher, or maybe a college football coach.

Beside the soldier was another, younger man. He was wearing a rumpled business suit. The man was unshaven, with a dark shadow of stubble on his jaw. He looked like he had slept in the clothes he wore. His eyes were dark and nervous. His gaze shifted fitfully to the last man in the room, sitting across from him. It was the intelligence officer – the man who had introduced himself as Smith.

Smith spoke first.

"Mr. Bannon, this gentleman across from me is Dan Lawrence. He works for the government. Mr. Lawrence has been sent to Camp Calamity from

Washington to monitor the outbreak and he has direct contact with the President."

The nervous man twitched his mouth into something closer to a grimace than a smile. He nodded at Bannon, then hunched back into his chair.

"And this is Colonel Fallow, commanding officer here at Camp Calamity," the intelligence officer went on. "The Colonel and his troops are at the pointy end of the U.S. Army's initial response to the crisis."

The big man leaned forward, propping his elbows on the edge of the table and then snatched the cigar from his mouth. "How you feeling, son?" The question was grudging.

"Like shit."

The Colonel offered no sympathy. "Well at least you're alive. There are thousands that aren't so lucky."

The intelligence officer flipped open a folder set in front of him, and the other two men turned to their own notes. For a moment there was heavy silence, then the man named Smith cleared his throat and looked up at where Bannon stood waiting.

"To be brutally honest about this, Mr. Bannon, we're not interested in you at all. We're actually interested in this John Sully – the man you claim was bitten by one of the infected, yet somehow survived the attack."

Bannon paid close attention to the intelligence officer's words. "He didn't survive – not completely."

Smith nodded. "That's right," he said, and then shuffled through several pages of information before plucking a single sheet from within the folder. "You actually claim that he was bitten, and then died, and then came back to life, but not entirely undead."

Bannon nodded. "Sully somehow survived. When he came back to life, he was actually alive."

The Colonel cut in. "Son, I'm just a farm boy from Idaho," he growled. "You wanna explain that last statement in full so someone like me can understand?"

Bannon stuffed his hands deep into the pockets of his jeans and paced across the room. His head was bowed and he was frowning in concentration. He paused by a wall and looked up. "When Sully turned, for some reason he didn't turn entirely. He had normal functions, but for all that, he also had some of the characteristics of the undead."

The government man interrupted, and his tone was almost cynical. "You are an expert in the field of undead characteristics?"

"Expert enough," Bannon's temper snapped. "I became a fucking expert this morning, asshole. My expertise was through close up encounters with the zombie fuckers – watching two of my friends get killed, and grappling with these frenzied killers for my fucking life. I got drenched in blood and gore. That makes me an expert." His voice became strident, and he wrenched his hands from his pockets suddenly and hammered his fist on the tabletop. The government man flinched, and then shrank back down in his chair. His eyes flicked furtively from face to face and then he gave a weak, wavering smile.

"Fair enough," he said in retreat.

123

Bannon took a deep breath. He was tired – impossibly exhausted, and his nerves were frayed. He rubbed at the pain behind his eyes, massaging his temples, and everyone in the room watched silently for long seconds. He waved his hand. "Sorry," he said. "It's been a long day."

"No apology necessary, son," the Colonel said abruptly. "We haven't got time for niceties because while we sit here getting pissed off with each other, more people are dying. So right now, I need you just to tell us everything – everything you know, or think about what happened to this Sully friend of yours." The Colonel paused to glare meaningfully at the government man. "We're listening."

Bannon nodded. There was an empty chair in the corner of the room. He dragged it across to the table and slumped down wearily.

"When Sully came back to life, he spoke to me, just like he was still alive, even though he was displaying the symptoms I had seen in my two other friends when they woke up dead."

"What symptoms?" the intelligence officer asked.

"I already told you," Bannon said. "Grey skin, congealed wound, yellow eyes…"

"What did he say? What were his first words?"

Bannon thought back. "Something about 'please don't kill me'," he replied. "Something like that. Then he sat up. He slapped a hand over his chest. He still had a heartbeat. He said he couldn't get his eyes to focus, and… and he couldn't smell anything."

The intelligence officer looked suddenly serious. He leaned towards Bannon and thrust his face into the light so that his features showed in ridges and deep shadow. "Are you sure about that?" the man asked. "He said he couldn't focus his eyes and he couldn't smell anything?"

"I'm sure," Bannon said. "It was one of the curious things that I noticed from that moment on – Sully's hearing... or his sense of hearing seemed greatly heightened. It was as if he could *feel* vibrations in the air. He sensed a dog approaching us before I saw it, and he could sense the undead chasing us long before I could see them. Jesus, he even sensed the helicopter long before I saw it, let alone heard it."

"But he couldn't *see* these things?" the government man cut in, this time his tone almost timid.

"Not clearly," Bannon explained. "When we were on the bridge, running from the town, he sensed the undead were chasing us, but he couldn't actually see them clearly enough to tell how many of them were hunting. The virus had affected his eyesight, I guess. But his instinct for hearing, or sense..." Bannon shrugged because he didn't have a better way to explain himself, "... well that was incredible."

The three men at the far end of the table leaned their heads close together and Bannon heard hoarse excited whispers. The government man wrote a note on the back of his folder and slid it across the table to Smith. The intelligence officer read the message and made a thoughtful face. He nodded slowly, then looked back at where Bannon sat.

"Tell us again why you and Sully went back to the apartment complex?" Smith asked carefully.

"Maddie – my wife," Bannon said. "I went looking for her."

"And John Sully went with you?"

"Yes."

"Why?"

Bannon shrugged. "He didn't want to," he admitted. "He didn't think Maddie would be in the apartment, but I was determined to look for her. I guess Sully came along because he figured the only safety was in numbers."

The intelligence officer narrowed his eyes. "But you didn't find your wife, did you?"

Bannon shook his head and his expression became tragic. "No," he said. "We searched the entire complex. Maddie wasn't there. I started to hope she had escaped before the town had become overrun... but her car was still parked in the lot. That was the car Sully and I used to get to the bridge."

"So your wife... you think she is still in Grey Stone?"

Bannon nodded. "I have to believe she is hiding somewhere, waiting for rescue."

There was a polite tap on the door, and the room fell suddenly silent and secretive.

"Come," the Colonel gruffed. A young soldier entered the office pushing a projector on a steel wheeled trolley. He turned the projector on and the room filled with weird glowing light. A patch of wall turned stark white. The soldier went back out through the door, pulling it quietly closed behind him.

The government man, Lawrence, got out of his seat and went to the wall. The white space exploded into black and white images showing an aerial view of the fields and river beyond the town of Grey Stone.

"This is the footage taken from the helicopter showing the moments before you were rescued," Lawrence said. The footage swung dramatically to a new view that picked up small shapes in the top left corner of the frame, running parallel to a road. "That's you," the man said. "You can see the distance between you and this second figure, and then the other undead closing quickly."

Bannon nodded. "That second figure is John Sully," he explained. He got out of his chair and went to the wall, watching his own nightmares play out with a macabre kind of fascination. He stabbed his finger. "Sully was behind me, and falling further behind. When I was already well into the field, he was just climbing through the fence. The undead – well I didn't know how close they really were until now."

The image paused and the intelligence officer began to play the scene through frame-by-frame. "Why was Sully so slow?" he asked. On the wall, the projector showed the figure at the fence moving in long lumbering strides.

"I think it was the infection," Bannon said, and then remembered something he had forgotten until that moment. "Sully said he couldn't feel his legs."

"When? When did he say that?"

"Right after he was bitten. I think the infection affected his co-ordination. He could move, but not quickly."

"Explain!" the Colonel suddenly barked.

Bannon sensed the soldier's urgency. "He moved with some kind of economy," Bannon struggled to find adequate words. "He could run, but he couldn't sprint. His movement was always awkward, but he never tired, never sweated. He never ran out of breath."

The image on the screen flashed back to white empty wall. Lawrence turned the machine off.

Colonel Fallow stood slowly and planted his big hands on the polished tabletop, thrusting his jaw out and searching the eyes of Smith and Lawrence. "Gentlemen, do we have enough?"

The two other men nodded. The Colonel looked bleak, but satisfied. "Very well," he announced. "Mr. Bannon thank you for your help. If you head out through that door, someone will be waiting to escort you to a bunk for the night. We appreciate your assistance. That will be all, for now."

Bannon shook his head slowly, and his expression became grim and stubborn. "No," he said. "That won't be all, Colonel. I'm not leaving this room until someone tells me what the fuck is happening."

Smith reached out for his arm but Bannon shook the man off with a snarl of defiance. "Fuck you!" he turned on the intelligence officer, and then whirled and stared hard at Fallow. "I've been up to my neck in blood and guts all day, Colonel. I've been chased and attacked... and I've seen my town burned to the ground and overrun by some... some kind of virus infected fucking zombie killers. I need to know what is happening! You at least owe me that much, dammit!"

The Colonel's gaze was like stone, smoldering behind his stare. He was a man unaccustomed to having his instructions questioned or his orders defied. The two men locked eyes and the tense silence stretched out.

Finally the Colonel nodded his head, and then slumped back down into his seat. He regarded Bannon carefully, as though he was choosing his words, striking a balance between what he could reveal, and what must remain confidential.

"Six days ago, medical staff in a town about forty miles south of Grey Stone reported a patient who had suddenly been overcome by a psychotic episode. They said the victim had gone on a rampage through the town, shooting several people before authorities could restrain him. The man was taken to hospital. Once in the hospital, the man just up and died."

"For no reason?"

"Apparently the man began retching violently. A nurse went into the room to attend to him. He must have concealed the vial in his mouth. Security vision from the room shows him vomiting something up and then crushing it between his teeth."

"And then?"

"And then the world started going to hell," the Colonel sighed heavily. "The man was a Syrian national. A thirty-three year old who had been in the country for exactly seven days."

"Syrian?"

The government man cut in smoothly. "It is our belief the man might have been a terrorist, sent to America as the most gruesome suicide bomber the world will ever know," Lawrence's voice lowered and became hollow. *"He was the bomb."*

"He stayed dead for just a few minutes, then seemed to come back to life and began biting and attacking medical staff in a mindless frenzy," the Colonel continued. "Those who were bitten died horribly, and then came back to life just seconds later, also now filled with the same mindless urge to murder and kill."

"How do you know this?" Bannon asked.

"Survivors," the Colonel said. "Two of the nurses fled the hospital and escaped. A handful of other residents made it out of town. But by the time the CDC responded, it was already too late. Within twelve hours the town was overrun and burned to the ground."

Bannon stared appalled. "What are we doing about it?"

The Colonel's voice was weary and heavy. "Trying to contain it," he growled. "So far the infection has spread to Grey Stone and three other towns along the coast. Maybe twenty thousand people already dead or undead... infected. The military has a perimeter line that we're holding – for now."

"For now... what does that mean?"

The big man mad a grim face. "It means that we have thrown every piece of equipment and every man available into a defensive line surrounding these towns and cordoning off an entire section of the state. At this point, contact at the line has been minimal."

Bannon felt suddenly very tired. "Minimal?"

"That's right," the Colonel said. "So far there has been a dozen isolated encounters along the perimeter, and each approach has been driven back. It seems that the infected are still milling around within the towns, not yet pressing our defenses. But that can't last forever. Sooner or later..."

"So it is an infection?"

The Colonel shrugged. "Or a virus," he said. "Truth is we don't goddamned know. Whatever it is, it's passed from person to person through bites and blood. Once bitten, there is no cure. The mortality rate is one hundred percent."

"Or it was," the intelligence officer cut in. "Until you told us your account of John Sully's apparent survival."

Bannon frowned and thought for long moments. "You said I am at an army base?"

"Camp Calamity," the Colonel nodded.

"Where are we – exactly?"

The big man's eyes narrowed just a little. "We're about twenty clicks north of Grey Stone," he said with some caution. "This installation is a temporary headquarters for the army's containment efforts."

"And is this virus being contained?"

"At the moment," the Colonel said guardedly, as though his confidence was somehow provisional. "We have all roads blocked off – effectively we've quarantined half the state, all the way north and south of the infected towns, right across to the coastal perimeter."

Bannon nodded. "So you're not going in, are you? You're not going to do a damned thing about rescuing people who might still be living and trapped."

Smith, the intelligence officer, cut across Bannon's question, sensing his rising resentment. "We can't," Smith said. He made a placating gesture with his hands. "The fact is that we don't have a cure. Sending the army into these townships is just offering up more bodies."

"So what happens?" Bannon became belligerent. "What happens to people like my wife?"

Lawrence, the government official, made an uncomfortable face and brushed at the wrinkles of his jacket with no effect. "We don't know for a fact that your wife – or anyone else – is still alive," he reminded Bannon. "As the Colonel rightly explained, the mortality rate for the virus is one hundred percent."

"So we leave them? We leave survivors to fend for themselves?" Bannon was incredulous. "What is the plan, if it's not to rescue the helpless?"

The Colonel's face turned rigid with indignity. He glared at Bannon and the words seemed to scald on his tongue as he spoke.

"We're in a containment phase," he said acidly.

"Containment?" Bannon bunched his fists and put them on his hips, "What does that mean?"

"It means we don't know what the fuck else to do," Smith gave the answer gravely. "Except hope and pray these undead infected bodies decompose quickly and the whole epidemic burns itself out."

Chapter 3.

Rough hands shook Bannon and he came awake with a start. "Sorry, sir," a young soldier was standing over the cot. "But the Colonel wants to see you. Pronto."

Bannon sat up. He felt groggy. He slapped a hand to his forehead and squinted his eyes. Sunlight was spilling through the window of the infirmary, painting a bright wedge of light onto the far wall. "What time is it?"

The soldier was standing at attention. "Oh six hundred, sir," he said smartly.

"Jesus," Bannon groaned. His few hours of sleep had been tortured by graphic all-too-real nightmares. He rubbed the back of his neck and stood stiffly. He had slept in his clothes. He glared at the fresh-faced soldier. "Where is the Colonel?"

"Waiting in his office, sir," the man's rely was crisp. "My orders are to escort you there immediately."

"Christ! Can I at least wash up first... or get a coffee?"

"Immediately, sir," the soldier said without any hint of sympathy in his voice.

Bannon grumbled. He shoved on his boots and followed the soldier down the hallway and through the infirmary door into bright morning sunshine.

The base was a hive of activity: troops were exercising between ranks of camouflaged tents, and in the distance he could hear the squeal and grind of mechanical vehicles somewhere below slow rising clouds of dust.

The Colonel's office was inside a large pre-fabricated building, broken into a hive of administrative and operational segments. Bannon followed the soldier down narrow corridors until they were standing outside the same room he had been escorted to the night before. The soldier tapped politely on the door.

"Come!"

Bannon stepped into the room.

The Colonel was seated at the end of the table, and Smith, the intelligence officer was beside him.

There was no sign of the government man Bannon had met the night before. He went to the end of the conference table and stood, waiting. The Colonel and Smith looked up at him. They were both bleary-eyed and somehow haggard so that Bannon wondered if either of the men had even left the room through the night.

The Colonel sat back in his chair and yawned. He scraped his hands through his hair and then propped his elbows on the edge of the table and laced his fingers together. It was a contemplative gesture, somehow made unsettling by the man's unnerving gaze. Bannon felt a sudden stir of foreboding.

"We have come to the conclusion," Colonel Fallow said like a judge about to pronounce sentence, "that we believe you."

Bannon frowned. "What?"

"We believe you about Sully," Smith cut in. "We've analyzed your information and made an assessment of the circumstances you described. It seems highly probable that you're telling the truth."

Bannon recoiled, and narrowed his eyes. "Well fuck you very much," he said dryly.

The Colonel's face darkened. "Son, you will watch your tone. Military or not, I don't like your attitude."

"Well how the fuck do you expect me to react, Colonel?" Bannon's voice kept its angry edge.

"Relieved," the Colonel barked. "Because now we believe you, we are going to send a team in to find this Sully and bring him out of Grey Stone."

Bannon shrugged. "So?"

The two soldiers exchanged glances. Smith gave an almost imperceptible nod of his head, and the Colonel swung his eyes back to Bannon.

"So, while the special team is in Grey Stone... they also have instructions to look for your wife – and rescue her."

Bannon said nothing. He felt a strange surge of euphoria – a rekindling of some emotion he thought he would never feel again.

Hope.

The Colonel snatched up a photograph that had been laying facedown on the tabletop. He held it up. It was an eight by ten inch black and white image of an attractive blonde haired woman. The photo looked slightly blurred.

"This is your wife, right?"

Bannon nodded, not trusting his voice.

"Last night a witness who escaped Grey Stone three days ago says he saw your wife, alive."

Bannon blinked. The surge of relief came sweeping over him so that he clutched at the edge of the table to support himself.

"Where was that photo taken?" he asked, his voice choked.

"We picked it up off some surveillance footage," Smith said vaguely, "and then verified it with the witness."

"Who?" Bannon felt his senses swimming. "Who is the witness? Can I speak to them?"

Smith shook his head. "Sorry," he said, his facial expression tight. "It was a local man, but he was evacuated last night."

The Colonel's voice interrupted before Bannon could speak again. The big man's tone was abrupt... and ominous.

"But there's a catch to all this," Colonel Fallow said.

Bannon flinched. "A catch?"

The Colonel pushed his chair back and stood up suddenly, as though his imposing size and weight would somehow lend persuasion to his next words. He walked the length of the long table until he was standing close to Bannon, staring at him.

"We want you to join the team."

"The rescue team?"

"Yes."

"And go back into Grey Stone?"

"Yes."

Bannon felt a sudden heavy sickness of fear slide around in the pit of his guts. "Is that necessary? You have a photo of Maddie..."

"But we don't have one of Sully," Smith said from the far end of the table. "Not a current one. You said that yourself."

"We need you with the team," the Colonel said slowly, measuring out every word for emphasis.

"You're the only one who can positively identify Sully."

Bannon closed his eyes for long seconds and felt something lurch in the back of his mind. He opened his eyes again, slowly.

"You bastards," he said in an appalled whisper. "Oh, you cunning, clever bastards!"

Colonel Fallow didn't move. Smith stood up from the table and came over quickly.

"You're playing me," Bannon said as the realization struck. "You don't give a fuck about Maddie. You're using her as bait – bait to get me to go back and identify Sully."

The Colonel's face remained impassive. "That's right, son," he said, and his voice turned suddenly cold. "We're giving you no option. If you want your wife rescued, then you join the team and you help us find John Sully. That's the deal."

"Why" Bannon snapped.

"Because we *need* Sully," Smith crowded close and thrust his face into Bannon's. The intelligence officer's eyes glowed with some kind of fanatical flare. "He's crucial to our nation's survival."

"How?"

"Because he is somehow immune from the virus. We need him in a lab, immediately. We need to know what makes him tick. It's America's only hope."

Chapter 4.

There were four soldiers and two men wearing flight gear waiting quietly in the conference room when Bannon answered a summons from the Colonel at midday.

Smith and the strangers were pouring over maps that had been spread across the long table, and pinned haphazardly to walls. The Colonel was nowhere to be seen.

"What's this about?" Bannon asked. He stood in the doorway, and his eyes were wary.

Smith looked up from a map. "We're planning the op," he said. "This is the team that is going into Grey Stone to get Sully and your wife... and these two men are helicopter pilots," the officer nodded. "I thought you would like to meet, and help with some local intel."

Bannon regarded the four soldiers bleakly. "Where are the rest of them?"

"Rest?" Smith lifted an eyebrow in question.

"The rest of the rescue team?"

Smith shook his head. "This is it."

"Just four men?"

"Yes."

"But... I thought you would send in a whole... like a hundred or more."

Smith shook his head. His voice was flat and emphatic. "This is the team," he said. "We can't spare any more men, or the equipment." He stepped away from the table and crossed the room. He took Bannon by the arm and steered him into a corner, away from the others. "Our best hope is to get in and get out again quickly. This has to be treated like a snatch, not an attack," he dropped his voice, so that Bannon alone could hear. "We believe it's the best chance of success. A larger force means more noise, more co-ordination, more elaborate communications... and use of choppers and hardware that, quite frankly, we just can't spare."

Bannon was appalled. "Four men won't be enough," he heard the bitter heaviness in his own voice. "They'll be overrun."

Smith's expression tightened. "Mr. Bannon, these men are JSOC – do you know exactly what that means?"

Bannon shook his head.

"It means they're the best," Smith said simply. "The Joint Special Operations Command teams are made up of SEAL's, Marine Special Ops and the Combat Applications Group... the new name for DELTA. They're the best in the world – and they've operated on missions like this before in hot-spots around the globe. They have to be enough, because there is no alternative."

"Then we're all fucked," Bannon snapped acidly. Suddenly he was shaking with anger. "Didn't you hear a damned thing I told you? These undead bastards have an incredible sense of hearing – they sense sound and movement before we can. As soon as they pick up the vibrations of your helicopter, they're going to start swarming towards the sound. When we set down, they'll come from everywhere!"

"I hope so," Smith said softly.

"What?"

"I said, I hope so," Smith's voice was unnaturally calm. "It's part of the plan. And so is fitting a speaker to the helicopter. We're going to fly over Grey Stone and broadcast."

"You're fucking what?" Bannon's voice rose sharply.

"We're going to circle the town and broadcast an announcement before landing."

Bannon said nothing. He felt the blood drain from his face and a creeping chill of shock.

Smith smiled mirthlessly and spoke with small sharp stabbing gestures of his finger for emphasis. "Sully is still part human. He hasn't turned. When we fly over the harbor we'll broadcast a message to him. We'll tell him we are a rescue force coming for him. We'll tell him where we are going to land. He'll meet us there. And so, hopefully, will your wife."

"And about a thousand fucking undead zombies!" Bannon hissed.

Smith nodded, conceding the point. "But we're sending *two* Black Hawks, and one team, Mr. Bannon. The second helicopter will fly over and land, then take off and land somewhere else – and keep repeating the process in a series of false insertions to lure the undead towards it... and away from the team. That distraction is going to clear most of the undead away from the LZ. And the team will take care of the rest."

Bannon sighed. He took a long deep breath. "What's an LZ?" he muttered with resignation.

"Landing Zone," Smith said. "In fact that's one of the reasons you are here right now. We want your local knowledge of Grey Stone. We need to locate a suitable site to set the chopper down. Somewhere with a clear field of fire, in case things don't quite

140

follow the script and we need to be on the ground longer than expected."

He took Bannon's arm again and led him towards the long table. The six assembled men stopped speaking and looked up. Their eyes were hard, and steady. The soldiers looked Bannon over with a veiled group hostility that was a reflection of their team's tight, closed bond. He was an interloper, an unwelcome intruder.

And an untrained civilian.

Bannon returned their frank scrutiny with a calm steady gaze, meeting each man's eyes, before moving to the next. The men were unshaven, dressed in an assortment of clothes and fatigues that gave them the unkempt arrogant air of men who did not readily conform to normal military regulations. Their faces were intelligent, their eyes alert, and they carried themselves with the unaffected confidence of elite athletes.

The group opened up grudgingly for him. Smith hovered in the background, excluded by body language, and made introductions.

"Mr. Bannon, this is Paul. He is the team leader."

Bannon shook hands with a tall muscular man who had square faced features and a jaw like an anvil. Bannon guessed the man to be in his early thirties. He was lean and muscular, with an unruly mop of dark curly hair. He had an inch-long scar on his cheek, the discolored skin puckered and in the final stages of healing.

"Howdy," the man said in a broad Texan drawl.

"And these other characters are the rest of the spec ops team," Smith's tone became amiable. He clapped a hand on one of the men's shoulders. "John, George and Ringo."

Smith did not introduce the two helicopter pilots.

Bannon gave Smith a dry, withering glare, and then shook hands with each of the special forces team. Smith went on quickly, snatching at a large map of the Grey Stone coastline and smoothing it out flat with his hands.

"Now – help us," he said. "We need to find a suitable LZ."

The special forces men gathered around either side of Bannon as he scanned the map, locating local landmarks. He stared at the marina complex, and stabbed at it with the tip of his finger.

"Those buildings along the waterfront are destroyed," he said. "Sully and I saw them explode. This whole area around the waterfront is chaotic, and was crawling with undead."

On the map, the harbor looked like the shape of a horseshoe, with the long arms reaching out into the ocean, and the marina complex built around the broad end of the bite. Bannon traced the line of the road, following it towards the coast.

"Here is the actual town," he said. "There are maybe fifty small businesses along this strip of road, and the ground rises as it nears the coastline."

The team leader leaned in closer and narrowed his eyes. "So the population base is along the contours of the coast?"

Bannon nodded. "It's about a mile from the marina to the business area," he explained. "The coast beyond the harbor to the south is rocky – lots of high ledges."

"And what's this?" the man Smith had named as Paul tapped a clear area of featureless terrain.

"That's the lookout," Bannon explained. "It's a high hill that overlooks the harbor. You can see the road into town branches off and leads to a loop at the top of the crest. It's a tourist drive for visitors that doubles back on itself."

"Wooded?"

"Some," Bannon said. "But the best place for a landing zone is between the rise of the lookout and the business strip. There is a sporting field right... here..." he tapped the map. The soldiers all craned forward, their brows furrowed with deep concentration.

"Tell us about it."

Bannon shrugged. "It's a sports field – a large flat area with a good line of sight to the road and the businesses, but it's also protected by the high cliffs on the coast side."

The soldiers all exchanged glances, secret messages sent with their eyes.

"What about the other direction – heading out of town?"

Bannon shook his head. His finger went back to the marina. "If you imagine the harbor being the center of Grey Stone, then it's about a two mile drive before you get to the bridge," he explained. "The river winds its way down from inland and spills into the harbor here," he scratched a mark on the map with his thumbnail. "But the bridge was built to cross the narrowest point in the river, so it's further away from the waterfront."

143

Smith hunched his shoulders and leaned over the map, studying it closely. "Is there any clear ground between the marina and the bridge?"

"No," Bannon was emphatic. "Houses mainly, some small clearings but not enough for your purposes."

"But enough clear ground to land a chopper?"

"Sure – but not enough clear land for a good field of fire when the zombie fuckers come to kill us."

Smith grunted. He turned to the two helicopter pilots. The men wore serious expressions. They poured over the map.

"Clearings along the roadside aren't going to work for the false insertions," one of the pilots stared at Bannon as he spoke. "Every tower and every road is a strike zone – too many wires, and too much risk. We need you to identify areas we can land a chopper between the marina and the bridge that are isolated from obstruction."

Bannon frowned. He went back to the map and thought for a moment, and then drew a circle with his fingertip. "That's a hill," he said. "It's a camping area."

The pilot who had spoken looked up at Bannon and fixed him with a withering look of contempt that every man in the room recognized. "I can see it's a hill, dumbass," the pilot said dryly. "I can read a map. What I want to know is whether it's a clear area or not."

Bannon nodded. One of the special forces soldiers grinned. Bannon felt his cheeks flush. "There's another clear area there," he pinched off the words, "but I imagine it would take some pretty precise flying. It's surrounded by trees."

Smith smiled to himself mirthlessly. "Don't worry about that, Mr. Bannon," he said. "These pilots are from 160 SOAR – the Special Operations Aviation Regiment. They're the best chopper pilots in the US military. It was helicopters from the 160th that flew our SEALS in to get bin Laden. Precision will not be a problem for them." Smith straightened slowly and glanced at the team leader.

"Paul?"

The big soldier shrugged his shoulders. "I like the sports field," he said. "We can come in from the ocean and drop down without overlapping the efforts of Chopper Two," he gestured with his flattened hand as if it were flying above the map. "If we set down in the middle of that clearing we'll have good sight lines from the two possible approaches – the marina, and the business district."

Smith nodded. "Concur," he said.

The men straightened. Bannon looked confused. "Is that it?"

Smith shook his head. "No, we need to work out the diversion," he said, then hunched back over the map. He stared for long seconds and then said slowly, "If Chopper Two circles the marina and broadcasts the announcement to Sully –"

"– And my wife…"

"And your wife," Smith conceded apologetically, "for about ten minutes, it's going to draw all the undead to this one area." He had a marker pen in his pocket. He scrawled a circle around the waterfront. "Then we'll have Chopper Two start to make a series of false insertions, firstly here… and then here…" he drew black crosses on the map in the small areas of clearing between the waterfront and the bridge that Bannon had indicated, "then finally here." Smith looked up, grimly satisfied. "Just like the Pied Piper," he said. "That should give Chopper One time to come in from the ocean and drop down for the pickup."

The soldiers nodded curtly. "Sounds like a plan," Paul agreed.

Smith threw the marker pen down and stood back from the map with a satisfied sigh. He folded his arms. "Okay," he said, "let's make it official."

There was a shuffle of movement in the room and then a kind of formal silence that somehow left Bannon feeling a sense of sudden exclusion. All eyes were turned to the intelligence officer.

"Gentleman, I'm Captain Smith and we will be conducting the mission brief at 1230 hours along with our time hack." The men in the room looked to their wristwatches. "It will be 1230 in thirty seconds..."

Silence.

"Ten seconds... five, four, three, two, one... hack." The men surrounding the intelligence office all synchronized their watches, and there was an instant of pause. Smith swept his eyes across the assembled men's faces. "Okay, let's get down to details. If you have any questions, save them until the end of the brief."

Bannon stood silently. Smith went around to the far side of the room and planted his hands on the edge of the big table, hovering over the map.

"Situation," he announced. "We have a male who has been bitten by the virus, but has not turned into one of the undead. We also have the possibility that at least one local woman is still alive in a hostile environment, possibly without food or water.

"Mission," Smith said, and then paused to glance down at the map one last time. "We are going in to Grey Stone to extract the infected male and any remaining civilians via two UH-60 Black Hawks and four spec ops personnel."

No one spoke. Bannon watched the men closely. Their expressions were concentrated, focused.

"Execution for this mission will be conducted by Flight Lead and spec ops command," Smith went on, and then gestured with his hand at one of the pilots. "Sam, do you want to take it from here?"

He was a tall man with short sandy hair and piercing blue eyes. "Weapons status for the mission is strictly 'hold', en route," the pilot began in a steady calm voice. "Once Chalk One is over the LZ we are weapons 'free' until extraction has taken place. We will use the same flight route as yesterday's recce and operate in trail formation until the separation point. Position and anticollision lights all the way."

The other pilot nodded, and Bannon saw a couple of the special forces guys nod as well.

"Administration and logistics have all been covered," Smith spoke across the silence, "and so has command and signal. Abort and bump criteria will be left to spec ops." Smith turned to the man he had introduced to Bannon as Paul.

"This is a priority op," the soldier said and his voice had the tone of someone accustomed to leadership. "So if Chopper One fails start, we are going to bump to Chopper Two and continue the mission. If Chopper Two goes down, the mission continues. If Chopper One goes down, the mission will abort," the soldier declared in a no-nonsense tone. "Understood?"

Everyone nodded. The soldier turned his attention to his own men, gathered next to him.

"Once we're on the ground we'll split – two men covering any approach from the business strip, and the other two covering the direction from the marina," he said. "We hold that perimeter until we see the subjects and get them onboard."

"Kit?" one of the other soldiers asked casually.

The team leader paused for a moment. "Light," he said, and then went on with assurance. "We go in light and fast. No body armor, no kit that won't kill zombies. We're there for a short time. This is a ten minute job. If we're on the ground any longer it will be because we're dead."

The soldier who had asked the question raised his eyebrows with mild surprise. "No body armor?"

"None," the team leader said again. "If we're on the ground and carrying a hundred pounds of gear, we're going to lose our speed. No point wearing body armor – we're not going to be taking fire."

One of the other men made a face. "What if they get close? Armor could come in handy."

The man named Paul shook his head. "If they get that close, it's already too late. We need to be able to avoid and evade – to bug out fast."

The rest of the team nodded. They were casual and calm. Bannon could see signs of tension and impatience in the way the soldiers carried themselves, as if they had been through this routine a dozen times before. Their expressions exuded a kind of arrogant confidence – repetitive familiarity mingled with an appreciation that every combat situation was inherently different.

"Speaking of bugging out..." the soldier who had asked about body armor prompted.

The team leader nodded. He leaned over the map, and his eyes were hawk-like. "Reconnaissance shows the buildings in the business strip ruined and burned – but they're not all destroyed, so if everything goes to hell, we make for those buildings. It's our best chance for cover and concealment. We get into the shops and offices and find an LUP for the night." The man turned his head slowly and found the intelligence officer with his eyes.

Smith nodded. "We'll have a bird back over the LZ at sunrise," he said.

Paul turned back to his gathered men. "That's fourteen hours we need to lie up for – so find somewhere secure, and then get back to the LZ before zero six hundred."

One of the men rubbed his chin. He didn't look convinced. "Those buildings are going to be crawling with tangos," his voice sounded dubious.

"That's possible," Paul conceded. "But there aren't other options."

Bannon spoke up suddenly. "What's an LUP?"

"Lying up position," Paul said.

Bannon nodded, then hesitated for a moment. "You could use the apartment complex – the place I lived," he offered uncertainly.

Paul looked suddenly curious. "Where is it?"

Bannon stabbed the point on the map with his finger.

The team leader shook his head. "Too far away from the LZ," he said, narrowing his eyes as his gaze swept over the details of the map, "and too close to the waterfront." He shook his head adamantly. "Guys, it's the buildings that form part of the business strip. That's the point we exfiltrate to. Clear?"

The rest of the team nodded. "Let's just hope it doesn't come to that," one of the men muttered. He stepped back from the table and yawned.

"What about me?" Bannon asked at last.

Smith turned, frowning. "What about you?"

"Well what do I do?"

"You stay on the bird," Paul cut in curtly, making the words sound like a barked order. "And you don't get out, under any circumstances. We need you to ID Sully. So stay out of the way and out of trouble. When he approaches the perimeter, we will bring him to you."

Bannon nodded, and suddenly the meeting had the air of being finalized. The tension in the room seemed to dissolve and the faces of the soldiers became more relaxed.

Smith looked at his watch. "You have less than four hours to prep, gentlemen," he declared. "Lift off is sixteen hundred."

Bannon flinched. "Whoooa! Hold on. You're doing this in *daylight?* Don't you guys normally do these special operations in darkness? What about cover and concealment?"

Smith shrugged. "What's the point?" he asked. "Daylight gives us the best chance to see what's coming after us... and the best chance to spot John Sully."

"And my wife, right?"

Smith made a little irritated gesture of weary acquiescence. "Yes, Mr. Bannon. And your wife."

Chapter 5.

The jacket Bannon wore was like a camouflaged hunting vest – covered in pouches of various sizes.

"Keep this on," Paul insisted. "It's a modular chest rig."

Bannon nodded. "Will it protect me?"

"No," the man said bluntly. "We just need you to be a packhorse in case we need extra ammo."

Into the pockets the special forces soldiers loaded spare magazines of ammunition, a medical kit containing bandages, tourniquet, aspirin and laxatives, a small black flashlight, a pocket knife and a compass.

And a small black box with a digital keypad on one side.

"Homing beacon," Ringo explained gruffly and then showed his teeth. "So we don't lose you if things get shitty."

"Is it on?" Bannon studied the device.

"No. You key in the code and that activates it. It's set on a military frequency. Once the distress signal is activated, everything – I mean everything – the US military has at its disposal comes a runnin'. I'm talking land, sea and air."

Bannon frowned at the beacon, twisting it in his hand and inspecting it carefully. It was about the size of a cigarette packet. "Wanna tell me the code?"

Ringo looked bored. He was a stocky man, younger than the rest of the team. He had massive muscled shoulders and a thick neck. His face was craggy with the pitted scars of adolescent acne, his eyes dark under even darker bushy eyebrows.

"Six, Zero, Two," Ringo's voice sounded like gravel in a cement mixer. "Just don't fuckin' lose it. If we run into trouble and need to tap out of the area for any reason, we're going to need that beacon."

"Tap?"

"Fuckin' run," Ringo explained the jargon. He jerked his head. "John there did some stuff with the SAS a few years back. It's a Pommy expression."

Bannon nodded gravely, then frowned. Fully loaded with spare magazines, the chest rig was heavy and bulky. "Do I get a gun?"

"No," Ringo said. "The last thing we need is an amateur running around in a firefight."

"What about a knife?"

"No," Ringo said again, and then sighed wearily. "If these fuckers get close enough for you to use a KaBar, boy, then you're already dead."

Smith, the intelligence officer, came up behind the team. "Gather round everybody," he said crisply. "I want you all to listen to this – it's the message we will be broadcasting from Chopper Two."

He had a small audio player in the palm of his hand. Bannon and the special forces team fell silent.

"Announcement. Announcement," the message had been recorded in a man's voice. *"This is the US Army with a message for John Sully and Madeline Bannon. We are a rescue team. Come immediately to the sports field below the lookout. We have a helicopter waiting to take you to safety. Carry something white for recognition and be prepared to identify yourself to US troops ready to evacuate you... Announcement..."*

Smith stopped the device. "Well?"

Paul shrugged. "It does the job," he said grudgingly. "It's not exactly eloquent, but it's specific enough."

The intelligence man turned to Bannon. "Your thoughts?"

Bannon nodded his head. "If Sully and Maddie hear it, I'm sure they will respond."

Smith smiled, satisfied. "Good. Now remember, this message will be broadcast over Grey Stone for exactly ten minutes before Chopper Two makes its first landing, and then begins hopping to each new designated false insertion point. You need to get in – and out again quickly."

The team was gathered inside a huge hangar on the perimeter of the base. They walked out into bright afternoon sunshine carrying weapons and kit. Two helicopters squatted on the ground, their rotors idling slowly.

To Bannon, the closest Black Hawk helicopter looked similar to the one that had plucked him out of the field, except forward of the open cargo door in the fuselage of the machine, he could see a heavy machine gun, mounted just aft of the flight deck. A crewman was checking the weapon, and there were two pilots in the nose of the chopper, watching the men approach.

Bannon scurried to catch up.

Ringo grabbed Bannon's shoulder just as he was about to climb aboard the helicopter.

"Have you ever been in a helicopter crash before?" the soldier had to raise his voice above the slow whine of turbines.

Bannon shook his head.

Ringo grimaced. "If it looks like we're going to crash, just tuck your head down between your knees, okay?"

Bannon nodded anxiously. "Then what?"

"Then you kiss your ass goodbye, because you're probably going to die!" The soldier laughed. He shoved Bannon in the back, and he climbed up into the belly of the beast.

The rest of the team was seated on metal benches that faced front and back on either side of the cargo door. Paul leaned close to the crewman and shouted. "Where's the other crew chief?"

The man at the machine gun looked over his shoulder at the other heavy weapon mounted on the opposite side of the Black Hawk. It hung loose from its mounting, and the seat behind it was empty. The man smiled at Paul grimly. "I'm the only one today."

"You're kidding!" Paul was stunned. He frowned. "Isn't it regulation to have two crew chiefs on every flight, unless it's a training run?"

The crew chief's expression was wry, almost ironic. "Regulation?" he grunted and shook his head bleakly. "We're going into action against zombies. *Zombies, for fuck's sake!* What part of this op is regulation?"

Paul stared. The man turned back to his weapon. Paul's lips were thin and pale. He turned his baleful eyes onto Bannon.

"Have you had a briefing about emergency procedures?"

Bannon nodded, still rattled. "Ringo just gave it to me," he said without humor.

Chapter 6.

Paul handed Bannon a headset. "Put these on," he said as the helicopter's big rotors began to gain momentum and the noise from the twin engines rose.

The four soldiers all wore them. The headset had light green ear muffs, joined by a black headband. A small microphone was attached to one of the muffs. Bannon fiddled clumsily with the set until the mike was positioned close to his mouth.

The electronic sound of Paul's voice filled his ears. "A combat UH-60 has practically no soundproofing," the soldier explained, pointing in a mime around the stark interior of the helicopter. "Once we're in the air, this is the only way we can communicate."

Bannon nodded. A few seconds later he heard another distorted voice through the headset.

"Takeoff is sixteen hundred hours and we expect to be over the LZ at sixteen-twenty hours, plus or minus thirty seconds." Bannon realized it was the voice of one of the pilots. "I'm going to isolate you now. If you need anything, signal the crew chief. Isolating." There was a split second burst of static, and then the headset went abruptly dead.

The two helicopters took off together, the front struts of the Black Hawks coming off the ground first, as the big helicopter hovered in the air, with its nose up and tail hanging for a couple of seconds. Then the pilot nosed the giant bird over and set course for Grey Stone.

Bannon felt his stomach swoop. It was like being in an elevator for a couple of seconds as the Black Hawk took to flight. Then, when the chopper had tilted, he had been pressed back into his seat, taken by surprise by the helicopter's aggressive acceleration. He sat, stony faced, and concentrated on not looking scared.

The helicopters followed the winding course of the river, skimming just above the canopy of treetops in tight formation. Bannon stared out through the cabin window as the ground below went rushing by in a swirling blur and deafening clatter of noise. The ride was bumpy. The helicopter rose and fell through minor thermals.

Five miles north of the town, the helicopters reached the release point and quickly separated. Chopper One heeled over and swung away towards the shimmering ocean on the far horizon. Bannon snatched at a hand-hold as the helicopter seemed to tilt on its axis. The special forces team didn't even seem to notice. They were slumped and relaxed in their seats, their bodies riding with the juddering changes in altitude and sudden course alteration. The men's faces were impassive, their gaze distant. Bannon felt a nervous twitch in the corner of his eye and wondered how any man could be so calm, flying into the face of imminent death.

Once they had cleared the coastline, the team went through a weapons check, the movements of their hands practiced to the point of instinctive habit.

"Locked and loaded," Paul said. The rest of the team repeated the expression. Paul glanced at his wristwatch and then Bannon heard sudden chatter through his headset. It was the pilot.

"We are four minutes from the LZ."

Paul was frowning, listening to the same message. He repeated the words to make sure everyone in the team had heard.

"Four minutes," he spoke into his mike, then held up four fingers and watched their faces until each man acknowledged. Bannon felt himself tense, and the atmosphere in the belly of the helicopter became suddenly strained. The helicopter swung in a tight turn, and then came racing back towards the smoke-hazed cliffs of the coastline.

Paul leaned close to Bannon. "Chopper Two has been circling the harbor for exactly six minutes," his voice through the headset sounded weirdly disconnected. The whine of the helicopter's turbines and the droning beat of the big rotors was numbing. "Let's fucking hope John Sully hears the message."

Bannon nodded. "How long do you think we'll need to be on the ground?" he spoke slowly and carefully back into the soldier's bleak face, measuring his words because he was unfamiliar with the mike system.

Paul shrugged. "Maybe two minutes... maybe five. As soon as Sully shows his face, we are outta there."

Bannon frowned. "What about Maddie? She might need more time."

The man's eyes became steely, devoid of any emotion. He stared at Bannon for long hard seconds and then said slowly, "We're not waiting for your wife," the soldier declared as the helicopter suddenly leaped a hundred feet higher into the air with a gut-wrenching swoop. "We're not even looking for her."

Bannon's face went white. "What?"

"We have orders to get John Sully. That's all."

"No!" Bannon shook his head vehemently. "Smith and Colonel Fallow said we were going in to get Sully *and* Maddie."

Paul's expression turned to granite. "Well that's not what they told me. Your wife is not part of this mission. We've only got orders to go in to get Sully."

"What?" spat Bannon, stiffening on the hard metal bench and turning his face to stare incredulously at the soldier. He felt a sudden suffocating tightness in his chest. His lips moved. He was deathly pale. His voice came out as a small croaking whisper, hushed by the sudden enormity of his realization. He had been betrayed.

"It was all a set-up," he gasped.

Suddenly the roar of the helicopter, the juddering jolting ride – everything faded into a swirling chaotic mist of confusion and desolation. Bannon's expression changed, utter dismay twisting his lips like his face was contorted in pain.

"What about the photo? The witness who saw Maddie?" his voice was strangled even through the tinny sound of the headset.

"All bullshit," the special forces soldier made an irritable gesture of dismissal, and then – almost as an afterthought – shrugged his shoulders apologetically.

Bannon stared dazedly into empty space, his lips becoming soft and slack. He felt himself somehow grow heavy. His shoulders sagged and his face felt suddenly cragged and etched with the deep lines of shock. He felt himself panting, his breath whistling and wheezing from his lungs. There was sweat on his brow. It trickled down his forehead and into the corner of his eye but he did not notice.

He had been betrayed.

The helicopter came in low over the ocean, its wheel struts seeming to brush the crests of the rolling swells that marched relentlessly towards the rugged coast. They were flying into the afternoon sun, and the interior of the chopper lit with bright golden light.

Paul was staring at his wristwatch intently, counting down the seconds. He looked up. "One minute!" he bellowed, and held up a single finger. The rest of the team shouted back the words, and then the helicopter seemed to rear up like a horse, swooping up the face of the cliffs and over a stand of dense trees before dropping like a stone towards the ground.

The special forces team snatched off their headsets and went tense, their bodies coiled like springs. Ringo reached out a hand for the fuselage door.

The pilot pulled back on the cyclic and lowered the collective. The nose of the Black Hawk rose up and Bannon felt himself sink back into his seat. The helicopter seemed to stop in the air as if it had hit an invisible wall. The sensation as the chopper plunged towards the ground was like being trapped in a falling elevator. Bannon felt his stomach churn. His eyes went wide with panic. He saw Ringo across the space of the cargo hold grimace at him mirthlessly. Then the pilot pushed forward on the cyclic control and at the last possible moment hauled up the collective to cushion the landing as the helicopter's forward momentum bled away. Bannon felt the nose of the helicopter draw level and through the cabin window the world suddenly flattened out as it rushed up to meet them.

The wheels of the chopper swished in long grass, then bounced and settled again with a gently jarring thud. Billowing clouds of dirt swirled in the air like thick smoke.

They had landed.

Steve Bannon had flown back into hell.

Part Three.
Chapter 1.

"Go! Go! Go!" the crew chief shouted. He sprang from his seat and crouched by the open door. Ringo exploded from the helicopter, and the crew chief slapped him on the back. "One!" he barked as the soldier went through the opening. Ringo hit the ground, cushioning the impact with bent legs and a grunt.

"Two!" the crew chief cried. He thumped George on the back as the man paused for a split-second at the breach, and then hurled himself down into the long grass of the sports field.

"Three!"

John went through the open door like he was leaping out of a plane. He hit the ground hard, rolled over on his shoulder and came up in a single fluid movement, bounding away with a curious lumbering gate, weighed down by kit and his weapon.

"Four!" the crew chief shoved Paul out of the helicopter. The team leader landed on his feet and went down in a crouch, goggles over his eyes to protect his vision against the swirling chaos of dust and noise.

Ringo and George were fifty yards to the north. They dropped down onto the ground, flat on their stomachs, side by side. Paul turned his head, saw John sprinting away to face the approach from the marina. He sprang to his feet and ran in a crouch to join him, snapping the goggles off his face and propping them atop his helmet as he ran.

Bannon stared through the open doorway. The crew chief was hunched down behind the machine gun, swinging the heavy weapon in a wary arc. The helicopter's rotors began to wind down, and the noise faded to a dull idling roar of background noise, like the rhythmic beat of loud music in a crowded bar.

The soldiers had formed a triangle, with the helicopter as the top, and the two teams forming the far points – one facing towards the shops and buildings of the business strip, and the other covering the approach to the field from the marina.

Bannon stared in dreadful fascination. The veil of haze began to thin, lifting like a morning mist, to reveal the unfolding danger.

Only there wasn't any danger.

The afternoon was ominously still.

Bannon studied the team covering the marina. He saw Paul cock his head to the side and focus with all his attention on a faint stench that seemed to carry like a whisper on the air. Bannon stared hard at the open ground ahead of the team, following the grassy field until it ended at a low wooden fence. Beyond the barrier was the road out of town. It crossed a narrow canal of mangrove and swamp, and then disappeared behind a stand of thick trees.

Nothing moved.

He turned his head and peered at Ringo and George. The soldiers were laying prone in the grass, automatic rifles pressed to their shoulders, sighting across the ground beyond the fence line of the sports field as it rose towards the strip of businesses. Buildings were smoldering, charred timbers like crisp blackened bones around collapsed brick and glass.

Smoke rolled down the slope and hung like a writhing curtain. Bannon narrowed his eyes, and felt his breath choke harsh in the back of his throat.

Through the roiling grey veil suddenly danced ethereal figures, spilling out of the narrow side streets and from within the wrecked shops, forming into clumps and then clusters, and then crowds as they rushed down the hill, howling shrieks of formless, furious sound that rose to a blood-chilling clamor.

There were at least a hundred of the undead, Bannon guessed, moving in an extended ragged line that had no cohesion. They came on like a churning sea, undulating and breaking apart, and then reforming again to become a solid driving mass of madness.

The closest zombies were almost on top of the soldiers' position. Incongruously Bannon noticed that most of the undead were women, flailing their arms and running down the gentle slope as though unable to control their legs. Some of the undead were dressed in tattered rags and many others were naked. Their bodies were streaked with blood, their faces contorted with the frenzy of their insanity. They howled and snarled with rage and the world filled with the roar of their hideous horror.

"Fire!" roared Ringo, and the urgency in his cry carried clearly to where Bannon watched in ghastly fascination. Then the air erupted, and the rattling sound of automatic fire ripped the horde apart. Smoke blotted out all Bannon's vision for an instant.

"Fuck it!" Bannon swore. He craned forward, hunting through the grey curtain with his eyes, desperately searching the haze of shadowy wraiths for a patch of brilliant white. Beside him, the crew chief opened fire with the heavy machine gun, and the helicopter's fuselage seemed to shudder and vibrate beneath him as an arc of white-hot shell casings spewed and clattered around his feet.

The roar of the weapon was deafening – the sound reverberating and hammering at his ears. Impulsively, Bannon leaped from the chopper and started to run.

"Hey!" the machine gun fell silent for a shocked second as the crew chief cried out to him. Bannon kept running. He felt unnaturally bulky wearing the heavy chest rig and his gait was lumbering. He reached the fold of ground where Ringo and George were, and threw himself face-down into the dirt.

A wall of zombies loomed ahead of him. Ringo and George were firing in controlled bursts, sighting targets through the smoke, working their weapons with precise economy. The undead line rippled and wavered like a field of wheat as the hail of automatic fire scythed them down. The ghouls collapsed in crumpled heaps, flung to the dirt as if punched by invisible fists. Ringo and George kept firing.

Bannon saw one woman take a burst of fire that juddered into her abdomen, tearing her almost in half. She went over on her back, thrashing her legs and with a shrilling scream gurgling in her throat. The ghoul rolled in the grass and then sprang back to her feet. Her guts had been torn open, ragged holes seeping thick syrupy ooze down her legs. The woman threw back her head and howled, her mouth wrenched into a hideous slash, before another searing hail of gunfire caught her full in the face. It blew the top off the zombie's skull.

The corpse fell backward, and the pulped yellowy mush of its head splattered over the shambling figure beside it. The contents of the skull hung in the air for an instant like a fine mist.

Still the undead came on. Bodies were piling up around the two soldiers, forming a gruesome wall of inhuman sandbags, and the grassy field became wet and slippery with blood and gore. George rolled onto his side, flung an empty magazine away and slotted a fresh one into his weapon. He saw Bannon hunched in the grass.

"What the fuck are you doing?" George asked in the split-second of relative silence. The soldier's expression was incredulous. He snatched a fresh magazine from one of the pockets of the vest Bannon was wearing. His face was blackened with dust and spattered with flakes of gore and guts so that his eyes looked like they were set in deep dark holes.

"Looking for my wife!" Bannon hissed.

George rolled back onto his stomach and opened fire again.

For a few moments of respite, the charging zombies seemed to lose their momentum. The ground was strewn with the dead and dismembered. Some dragged themselves closer, clutching at shattered limbs, the berserker insanity of their infection still blazing in their eyes. The soldiers picked them off with merciless precision.

Ringo stole a glance at his wristwatch. He was breathing hard. He licked cracked dry lips and wiped his sweating forehead on the sleeve of his uniform. His face was streaked with dust.

"We've been on the ground for two minutes," he said. He spat a thick wad of phlegm into the grass, then squinted up into the sun.

George shook his head, incredulous. "The fuckers just keep coming."

"We hold here for two more minutes, then start moving back," Ringo decided. "If this fucker Sully hasn't turned up by then, he ain't coming."

George nodded. Across the field Paul and John were in the process of reloading. The line to the marina was still clear.

The slope of the hill was a slaughter yard. Pale, blood-streaked limbs protruded stiffly from corpses that had been piled upon each other. The stench of death burned in Bannon's nostrils. It was a smell of guts and gore, of decay and decomposition.

He got numbly to his feet and peered past the break wall of infected corpses, his bloodshot stinging eyes searching the ground for a patch of white. He saw nothing, and the clutch of his despair gripped tight around his heart.

"Maddie!" he cupped his hands around his mouth and cried out. "Maddie Bannon!"

He took a couple of tentative shuffling steps forward. The smoke was being drawn down the hill by a gentle breeze. It rolled across the grass like an eerie ocean fog bank. On the edge of the haze, Bannon saw a sudden apparition of movement – a specter that lurched towards him. He felt himself hope against hope. He called out again, turning towards the approaching figure.

"Maddie?"

An undead woman came bursting through the tendrils of smoke with a crazed snarl of rage, and shrieking a demented scream. Her features were contorted into an infernal bloody mask. Her hair was dripping and clotted with slimy gore, and the skin of her cheeks was charred black. Her lips and nose had been burned from her face so that the open screaming mouth was a vast black hole of horror exposing broken teeth and festering sores that were custard yellow with puss.

A blackened tongue slithered demented from the unhinged jaw and she tottered over the rampart of bodies and flailed her clawed and broken fingers at Bannon.

The air swished before his face and Bannon flinched away as the undead woman's hand passed just an inch from his forehead. There was a yelp of fear in his throat and his eyes went wide and white with cringing horror. Bannon stumbled backwards as the woman swayed closer, her arms gnarled and twisted.

The undead ghoul took a blundering step forward. In life she had been an old woman, hunched and cronelike. In death her eyes blazed yellow and predatory with the virulent infection. She snapped her head forward and the hoarse rasping sound of her voice was a loathsome serpentine hiss.

Bannon felt his feet go from under him. His arms cartwheeled for a flailing handhold that wasn't there. He cried out in blind panic... and then he fell to the ground on his back.

Blam!

Ringo fired a single shot, the roar of it deafeningly loud in Bannon's ears, and the ghoul's head was wrenched sideways as the bullet went up through the zombie's jaw, and tore a ragged path out through the back of its skull. The woman buckled at the knees and then fell face-first into the long grass.

Bannon lay prone for one terrified moment, staring at the sightless infected face of the woman. His ears were ringing and there was a churning nausea in the pit of his guts. He was panting like a running dog – the white hot flush of his terror wrung out blisters of sweat across his brow. He sat up in the dirt, slow and dazed and blinking.

"Fucker!" Ringo growled but without visible emotion. "Get your ass back to the chopper."

Bannon turned and staggered back towards the helicopter. He saw the rotors still turning slowly, saw the helmeted face of the pilot peering through the plexiglass bubble of the cockpit. Bannon was reeling, his heart still hammering in the cage of his chest. The crew chief hunched over the machine gun was waving his arm frantically at him, the man's mouth wide open shouting words that were being whipped away by the beating sound of the machine.

Bannon hauled himself through the open hatchway. He was trembling. He slumped down heavily on the bench seat, hunched over with his head cradled between his splayed fingers. His breathing quavered in his throat. Behind his closed eyes he saw pinwheels of bright light and flashes of color. He rubbed at his temples, and then opened his eyes again slowly...

...to a fresh unfolding horror.

Chapter 2.

The slope of the hill was swarming with another wave of undead ghouls that poured down through the long grass. They came in a pulsing surge, milling with those who had fallen prey to the guns, and pushing them forward so that Ringo and George were overwhelmed. The two special forces soldiers fired long withering bursts at the tide of undead, and a dozen fell, but more came behind them. The two soldiers leaped to their feet and went sprinting back towards the helicopter.

The crew chief at the heavy machine gun tried to cover them, but the swarming press of undead was like a tidal wave that threatened to wash them all away. Ringo turned, still twenty yards from the helicopter, and dropped to one knee. Bannon could see Paul and John sprinting back towards the chopper. The two men were running hard, weighed down by weapons and kit. Paul made a fist and was frantically circling one finger into the air. George ran past Ringo and then turned back to give covering fire.

It was too late.

The zombies flung themselves at Ringo, and in a stuttering hail of bullets, the elite soldier went down. One of the ghouls reeled away from the melee, its arm severed at the elbow joint, but others flung themselves at the soldier and his blood-curdling cry ripped the sky apart. A dozen of the ghouls clawed and gouged at his body, tearing the soldier apart and ripping open the pouch of his stomach so that his entrails bulged pink from the wound. Through milling legs and flailing arms, Bannon caught a final glimpse of Ringo. The man's face was wrenched in agony, his eyes slitted and his jaw hanging slack. He was crawling through the bloody grass towards the helicopter on his hands and knees, the weight of his bowels swinging and slipping beneath him.

Bannon heard George cry out in rage, and then saw the big man open fire, sweeping the barrel of his assault rifle in a wide arc. There was a murderous fanatical roar in his throat. He emptied the magazine in one long burst and then reloaded. Those few seconds cost him his life.

The zombies swarmed over him, driving George to the ground while Bannon watched on, white-faced with abject helpless horror. For long, gruesome seconds there was just a sound of shrilling triumph, and then the tide of zombies swept on towards the helicopter, leaving the broken body of the soldier like something dreadful that had been washed upon the rocks. George emerged from the clawing, snarling atrocity, his body dismembered, his throat torn open – a pulped bloodied corpse almost beyond recognition.

Bannon leaned out through the helicopter hatch and vomited.

The whine of the helicopter turbines began to rise into a numbing wail of deafening noise. The big rotor blades began to thwack at the air with sudden urgency. Bannon felt the helicopter somehow become buoyant. Paul and John were kneeling just a few yards in front of the open hatch, and the heavy machine gun blazed its fiery breath over their heads as the special forces team made a last defiant stand against the remorseless tide of ghouls.

The fluttering deadly beat of the heavy machine gun dulled Bannon's senses as the rotting writhing bodies twitched and jerked and bucked as the stream of bullets tore them to pieces.

"Will they ever stop?" Bannon felt the stomach sliding sickness of his dread. He shook his head and swallowed the taste of his own bitter despair.

How could there be so many?

Why hadn't Chopper Two drawn these undead away?

He dropped down into the grass and ran to where John and Paul were firing with the grim resolve of men who knew death was inevitable. Bannon tugged the spare ammunition magazines from the chest rig and set them down.

He clapped Paul on the back to let him know he was there.

"Fuck off!" Paul turned and snapped. The man's eyes were bloodshot, his face caked with gore and dirt. His eyes were hard but haunted. "Get out of here, now!" the soldier barked.

Somehow the hail of fire halted the undead for long seconds. The line flung itself against the guns and then recoiled, as if a shudder had run through the masses. They fell back, like a spent wave, then gathered and returned. The sound of the heavy machinegun was an assault on the ears – a remorseless judder of death and destruction, overlaid by the lighter, more sparing rattle of automatic rifle fire as the two surviving soldiers husbanded their ammunition, and made every bullet count.

The undead swept forward yet again, and Bannon saw the surge stumble over the litter of bodies that covered the ground. Many of the corpses lay still and unmoving – shot through the head, but many others lay writhing and growling, trailing shattered limbs and clutching at chest wounds that had torn out through their backs. They crawled and slithered towards the helicopter with the infected madness still blazing fiercely in their enraged eyes.

The range was point blank. Smoke and the gagging stench of death swirled in the air, only to be whipped away by the rotors of the helicopter. The ground beneath the bodies was turned to mud, thick with gore and guts. The grass was beaten flat by the churning surge, and still the zombies came on towards the guns.

Bannon saw Paul snap off three quick shots, the range less than ten yards. Three of the ghouls collapsed, like tenpins bowled over. Two of them were women, dressed in muddied ragged clothes that were brown with dirt and grimy with soot. The women were pressed shoulder to shoulder, and they fell backwards onto the heaped corpses around them, faces destroyed, skulls collapsed. The third was just a child, virulent thick clots of blood gushing from its mouth. It had already been shot – there was a gaping wound in the boy's side, and one of its arms hung limp and wasted. Paul's bullet struck the child in the left eye and it was flung round in a macabre dancing pirouette before falling stiff and still into the grass.

Bannon began to back away the few steps towards the open door of the helicopter. The undead tide was relentless, stealing inch after inch of ground against the guns until the writhing wall seemed to hang poised like an avalanche about to crash upon them.

Then, suddenly, Bannon's eyes caught a flash of brilliant white, wavering on the far edge of the zombie horde. His gaze snapped round and he peered through the wavering smoke, shielding his eyes from the sinking sun with his hand.

The patch of white waved like a flag, like a battle flag on an ancient field, as a rally point for those who fought. The white cloth rippled and ruffled, then swung frantically from side to side.

Sully!

Bannon knew it was Sully, even before he spotted the tall shape of the man that seemed to tower over the milling mass of undead, the shaved head and broad shoulders like a beacon. He ran back to where Paul knelt and pointed.

"Sully!" Bannon shouted. "He's over there!"

Paul got to his feet, weapon still pressed hard against his shoulder, eye sighted down the barrel at his next target. He fired a short burst, and then tried to look above the gnashing moaning heads of the horde.

"Can't see him!"

"He's over there!" Bannon pointed, stabbing with his hand like it was a blade.

"Are you sure?" Paul fired at an undead ghoul that had come running and stumbling across the battlefield of corpses. It was a man. He had been dressed in a business suit. The fabric was torn to shreds, the tie around his neck hung like a noose. His shirt was streaked with dried blood and his head lolled macabrely from the sinew and muscle that held it attached to his neck. The man's throat had been gored. He ran at Paul with his arms outstretched, fingers seized into claws. Paul waited until the man staggered over the broken disemboweled body of a woman and then he fired. The weapon hammered against his shoulder, empty casings sprayed from the chamber and the roar so close to Bannon was like a hammer beating against a steel drum. The undead man was flung back. He staggered, lost momentum for a moment and then seemed to teeter on ungainly legs. Paul squeezed the trigger again, and the hail of fire obliterated the man's head so that when he fell, he had been decapitated.

Paul squinted his eyes. He saw it then, like a ship's sail, pillowed by the gentle breeze, wavering in the distance beyond the haze of smoke and the roaring clamor of noise.

The man frowned, his face a bleak snarl. "Fuck it!" he spat. "We'll have to go and get him."

"Fucking what?" Bannon shouted back, his tone horrified. His ears were still ringing from the deafening sound of gunfire. Paul grabbed him by the webbing of his harness and shook him. He thrust his blacked face at Bannon. "I said we'll have to get him!" he growled in a voice that made it clear there was no choice.

Paul punched John in the shoulder. The soldier turned. Paul pointed, and there was sudden recognition in the other man's eyes. "We're going for him," Paul shouted.

John nodded. Said nothing.

"Can you hold 'em off for thirty seconds?"

John nodded again, fired a short burst at a writhing figure that was crawling in the grass on her hands and knees towards him. The ghoul's hair was smoldering and her upper body was blackened charred flesh that hung in stinking flaps from her bones. John pulled a sidearm from the holster strapped to his thigh. He fired a single shot from the handgun and the undead ghoul's head was flung back. She collapsed in a spreading pool of thick custard-like gore.

John thrust the pistol at Bannon. "M9 Beretta. Point and shoot," the soldier gruffed. Bannon took the gun. It felt awkward and heavy in his hand.

"This isn't a last stand," Paul barked to John. He emptied his magazine into the crowd and reloaded a new one with a slap of his palm. "If we can't get back, don't wait for us. Get on the bird and get the fuck out of here."

The helicopter crew chief traversed the heavy machinegun and ploughed a deep hole in the wall of undead with a withering burst of fire, sweeping the weapon back and forth until everything became shrouded in smoke and the ammunition ran dry. John retreated until he felt the helicopter's hull against his back, squeezing off short bursts from the hip to hold the horde at bay. There was less than thirty undead now, staggering and slowed by the atrocious damage the special forces team had torn through their ranks. They milled amongst the carnage of the field, disabled and debilitated by their shocking wounds. Few had escaped the firefight without hideous injuries. Many were unable to walk. They crawled and writhed in the dirt, flailed and thrashed, but came no closer.

Paul ran.

He ran with his gun held high and sighted, firing into the throng of snarling faces, and close behind him followed Bannon, with the Beretta held stiffly out ahead of him and oily snakes of fearful sweat running down his chest. They climbed over the shapeless barricade that was the dead, scrambling over the slick bloodied grass until suddenly there were no more faces – and there were no more zombies. They were through the remnants of the horde, and standing face-to-face with John Sully.

The big crewman threw down the makeshift flag. He was shirtless, his jeans torn and ragged. His chest was laced with shallow scratches that ran in criss-cross patterns, dribbling trickles of brown thick blood. His face was carved of stone – a set and impassive expression, and there was bitter malevolence blazing behind the peculiar yellow eyes. He glared at the elite special forces soldier, and then turned his simmering gaze to Bannon.

"You didn't turn back for me," Sully said, his outrage quivering in his voice.

Bannon threw back his head and sucked in a mouthful of rancid cloying air. "I tried," he gasped. His breath sawed across his throat. "They thought you were one of the zombies chasing me."

Paul cut Sully short, glaring at the man with grisly fascination. There was a gaping ragged wound clawed out of the stranger's throat, shreds of flesh rotting from the gouge, and his skin hung grey and deathly from his body like a shroud. "We're back now," Paul snapped.

Bannon's face was frantic. He gripped Sully's arm fiercely. "Maddie!" he rasped. "Have you seen her?"

Sully shook his head. His expression was tight and restrained. Something malicious passed like a shadow behind his terrible infected eyes. "No," he said flatly, his voice coarse and parched. A burnt voice.

Bannon seemed to shrink, deflate. The last breath of hope escaped his drawn lips in a hollow sigh.

Suddenly the world went unnaturally silent, and the relative stillness was an eerie premonition of doom that Paul sensed before he understood.

The soldier turned... and saw everything in a slow motion nightmare.

The helicopter was surrounded by the last of the undead ghouls. They were pressed tightly together.

There was no gunfire – only the rising wail of the zombies and the screaming beat of the helicopter's massive rotors. John, the last man on the team, was clambering back into the open cargo door of the Black Hawk, thrashing with his legs at the flailing, clawing hands of the undead. The heavy machine gun was silent. The crew chief had a sidearm in his hand, firing into the point-blank faces that snarled and roared with the insanity of their infection. Paul heard John scream, and then the man turned his head and spat into the face of a zombie that had lunged and bitten his leg. The ghoul was like a rabid dog, gnashing its jaws and growling as it worried the man's thigh with its teeth until a gush of bright red blood spilled down the zombie's chin.

Paul saw John smash his fist at the ghoul's head...
but it was too late.

The first of the ghouls crawled aboard the
helicopter just as the wheels of the big bird lifted off
the ground. Three more of the undead scrambled
into the cargo area. They were hideous, blood-
drenched wraiths, snarling and howling as they
tore at the crew chief. The man tumbled out
through the cargo door and fell a few screaming feet
to the ground.

He fell amongst the howling horde of undead.

The crew chief cried out once – the nerve-
shredding shriek of a piteous soul suffering the
final torture of a gruesome death and then a
solitary shot rang out like the peal of a bell.

The helicopter leaped off the ground, rising
twenty feet in an instant. It hung there, rotors
thrashing the air, and then the tail of the Black
Hawk seemed to twitch and swish from side to side.
The chopper tilted over and swung away to the east,
clipping the tops of the trees as it got clear of the
rocky coast.

Paul watched, horrified.

The Black Hawk began a slow leisurely turn,
still flying low above the crests of the ocean, quickly
shrinking in size. Sunlight winked off the cockpit
windshield and fuselage windows. Then suddenly
the machine seemed to shudder and rear up, almost
in a vertical climb. It hung there, suspended for an
instant like a great black bird shot in flight... and
then fell back, and plummeted tail-first into the
ocean.

For a few brief seconds the sea was churned into
a foaming frothing maelstrom as the rotors flogged

at the crests. Then the great blades splintered apart and tore the helicopter into pieces.

Bannon stared, appalled.

"Run!" Paul shouted suddenly. He shoved Bannon hard in the middle of his back, pushing him towards the slope where the burning shops and businesses of Grey Stone lined the crest.

Bannon ran, staggering and grunting with every step, his jaw hanging slack as he tried to suck air across his swollen tongue. Sully ran beside him.

Paul shouldered his weapon and followed. At the lip of the gentle rise, he paused suddenly. They had reached the road.

The special forces soldier dropped to his knee. Bannon and Sully went to ground beside him. Bannon was panting. He still had John's Beretta in his fist. He tucked it inside the waistband of his jeans.

Paul cuffed sweat from his eyes. His face was caked with dirt. He stared hard at the closest buildings, his instincts heightened as though he was trying to sense danger. The smoke was thicker now they had crested the rise. Many of the buildings were smoldering, but he could see nothing still ablaze. All that could be burned had already gone up in flames.

There were a couple of abandoned cars slewed across the blacktop. It was a narrow road. One of the cars had mounted the curb and crashed head-on into a tree. The car was blackened and burned out. The trunk of the tree had shattered on impact and the tree had crashed down, crumpling the roof of the vehicle and effectively barricading the road.

The other vehicle was a red SUV. It was lying on its side like a broken toy in a scatter of smashed glass. There were rubber scorch marks on the bitumen and a scar of dull paint. The body of a dead woman hung suspended from her seat belt in the passenger seat. The woman's head was turned so that Paul could see her in profile. She had mop of long blonde hair that was daubed in blood. The woman had been dead for some time. Her face was gruesomely bloated, the skin purpling to black as it rotted away.

Beyond the SUV, almost directly across from where they crouched, was a bakery. The shop front was thick plate glass, cracked but intact, as though something heavy had been hurled against the window. There was an open doorway between the windows, hung with long colored streamers that flapped gently in the breeze. The inside of the shop was strewn with overturned tables and chairs and the ransacked debris of panic or maybe conflict. From the corner of his eye Paul saw Bannon was watching him closely. He made an imperceptible shake of his head, and shifted his gaze.

The building next to the bakery was two stories, with just a narrow door on the ground floor, and a row of three windows directly above. There was some kind of lettering painted onto the door – perhaps an accountant, or a lawyer's office, he guessed. The building was brick. The door looked solid. The building was on a corner. Paul's eyes scanned the side road, but he could see nothing through the swirls of lingering smoke. He narrowed his eyes and pointed.

"That door," he muttered, then turned on his knee and glanced back down the slope, staring at the killing ground that was the sporting field.

There were still some undead, staggering aimlessly in the long blood-drenched grass, milling around the pathetic crumpled shape of the crew chief's remains that lay in shreds at their feet.

The rest of the field was strewn with corpses; broken clumps of rotting flesh that had been shot to the ground in gruesome attitudes of horrible death. Around where the chopper had landed, the grass had been trampled flat and it was there that the most bodies lay, heaped upon each other like cords of firewood.

Overhead a dark pall of crows wheeled lazily in the setting sky. Paul watched as one of the ghastly big black birds dropped with a raucous screech and flurry of flapping wings. The bird landed on the body of one of the zombies. The figure lay on its back with its arms flung wide. The crow hopped onto the chest of the corpse and dipped its beak into maggot-riddled flesh.

Paul turned back to Bannon and crushed a finger to his lips.

Silent!

The special forces soldier got stealthily to his feet.

Chapter 3.

Long shadows stretched over the ground as Bannon and Sully crept quietly across the road, following the footsteps of the special forces soldier who led the way. Bannon kept his eyes on the broad of Paul's back, not daring to glance around, not risking even a breath until they had reached the far side of the blacktop and stood huddled in the shade of the doorway.

Paul narrowed his eyes and stared at the door for a moment. It was solid wood, with a sign for a natural health therapist painted in neat white lettering just above waist height. He tried the handle. The door was locked.

That was a good sign, and bad news.

It was good, because it suggested the interior was secure. Maybe the business had been closed when the zombie infection broke out through the population. Maybe the owner had left town before the infection spread. The bad news was that entry would require the risk of noise.

Paul took his KaBar from the sheath strapped to his thigh and jimmied the point of the brutal knife into the timber adjacent to the lock. He heard the soft splinter of wood. He gave the blade a twist, and shoved against the door with his thigh at the same instant. It swung open several inches on silent hinges.

The soldier let out a strained sigh of relief.

"On me," he whispered in Bannon's ear, and then nudged the door wide open and stood stiffly for long seconds, his body tensed and poised, his weapon sighted as he waited for his eyes to adjust to the heavy gloom.

He was standing in a small foyer. There was a plastic potted plant in the corner and a photo of a beach scene in a frame on the wall to his left. Ahead of him was a narrow stairway, leading up to the next floor. The stairs were carpeted. Paul took three cautious creeping paces towards the bottom step with Bannon and Sully crowding close behind him. Sully closed the door and used the potted plant to hold it shut.

The room smelled of exotic oils and scented candles.

Paul glanced over his shoulder at Bannon and held up one hand like a cop stopping traffic. His eyes were wide and red-rimmed. Bannon nodded.

Paul went up the stairs in a crouch, taking slow measured steps, keeping his center of balance low, weapon tucked into his shoulder. He reached the top floor and then disappeared from sight for several minutes. When his head finally reappeared at the top of the landing, Bannon felt himself visibly relax. The soldier beckoned Bannon with a curt wave of his hand.

The top floor of the building was partitioned into three cubicle offices. Each of the dividers was a low wooden wall topped by a long glass panel. The first sectioned off area held a small white desk, chair and a couple of filing cabinets. Behind it, long massage tables dominated the two larger areas. The walls were lined with shelves of candles and perfumes and bottled oils. Bannon turned in a slow circle, taking everything in.

"It looks like old Sylvia Marchant was running a brothel," Sully smiled, his face gruesome, his voice low and hushed. He stood in one of the larger cubicles and tested the firmness of the massage table's padding with a prod of his hand.

"Maybe," Bannon said in a distracted whisper. He had known the woman who ran the business.

She was a legitimate massage therapist, but he didn't bother correcting the other man.

It no longer seemed to matter. Sylvia Marchant was either long gone... or undead.

Paul went quickly through the desk drawers and found nothing of use. He stepped down a narrow hallway towards a closed door. He pushed it open. It was a small bathroom – just a washbasin and toilet, tiled floor, white walls. There was a curtained window set into the far wall, the glass inserted in a series of opaque louvers. He twitched the fabric aside and stared through one of the slits to the ground below.

It was almost dark, but he could see an alleyway with an overflowing industrial trash receptacle and a stack of plastic crates. He stepped back and studied the window more closely. It would be tight, but it would do, he decided.

He went back down the hallway.

"There's a window in the bathroom," he said quietly to Bannon. "That's the escape route if needed."

Bannon looked alarmed. "We just jump out the window?"

Paul nodded. "It opens onto an alley. There's a trash bin dumpster..."

Bannon lapsed into doubtful silence for a moment. "What about the downstairs door?" he asked at last. "Should we barricade it with the filing cabinets?"

The soldier hesitated. Carrying the metal cabinets down a flight of stairs was bound to make noise.

"No," he said at last.

Bannon flinched. "You're just going to leave a potted plant to hold the undead back?"

"No choice," the soldier said grimly. "If we make noise, a couple of filing cabinets might not be enough to hold them back anyhow. Our best chance is to go very quiet and hope they don't stumble over us."

Paul set his automatic rifle down on the desk. The soldier was weary – bone weary. The adrenalin still fizzed in his blood, but now the immediate danger had subsided, he felt heavy. He closed his eyes for an instant – just long enough to draw a long deep breath – and then exploded into sudden violence.

Sully and Bannon were standing in a tight knot facing him. Paul lunged at Sully, taking the big man completely by surprise. The momentum of the soldier's attack drove Sully staggering back against a wall. Paul threw a wicked right-handed punch that caught the seaman clean under the jaw. Sully's head snapped back and a sudden growl snarled on his lips. The special forces soldier was one of the world's elite. He kicked out at Sully's knee with the heel of his boot, and the big man staggered. Paul hit him one last time, a punch that began low down at the level of his waist, and was swung with all his weight and momentum. It struck Sully flush on the temple and the big man's peculiar yellow eyes rolled up into his skull. He started to teeter, jaw hanging slack. The soldier propped Sully upright against the wall and spun him round like a cop in the midst of a take-down. He wrenched Sully's hands behind his back and snatched cable ties from a canvas pouch on his webbing belt.

"What the fuck?" Sully snarled. Paul had hit him with everything he had, but the big man had not fallen.

Paul cinched a thick cable tie around Sully's wrists and then strapped another one in place. He had his knee in the small of the man's back. He stepped back warily.

"What the fuck?" Sully turned round, and his face was swollen and gruesome with his outrage. He bunched the muscles in his shoulders and strained against the ties, to no effect. Thick cords popped out along his neck. He gritted his teeth and hissed at the soldier.

"What the fuck!"

Paul stood back, his breathing quick but controlled. His knuckles hurt. He stared at Sully with stone cold eyes.

"I don't fucking trust you," Paul said. "That's why you're tied."

Sully's expression became monstrous. "You fucking came back to rescue me!" he seethed. He shot a savage glance at Bannon, and then back to the implacable gaze of the soldier.

Paul shook his head. "We didn't come back to rescue you," he said deliberately, and there was a streak of cruel harshness in his voice. "We came back to capture you."

Sully gaped. Bannon visibly flinched. He stared appalled at the soldier for long seconds. "I wasn't told –"

Paul dismissed Bannon's protest with a sneer. "You weren't told that we never wanted your wife, either," he said.

Sully's mouth tugged into a grim snarl. "What do you want with me?"

"The labs want you," Paul said. "My orders are to bring you back. You're a freak. You survived a zombie bite – the only one so far. That makes you valuable," Paul shrugged his shoulders without emotion. "The researcher teams want to cut you up and use you to find an antidote."

Chapter 4.

Paul nudged Sully into a corner of the room with the barrel of his rifle. The big man slumped down until he was sitting uncomfortably. The office was gloomy with the quickening shadows of night. Sully hung his head, staring bleakly at the floor between his boots. Bannon paced the room uneasily.

Paul propped himself on the corner of the desk, his leg swinging like the tail of a dangerous predator. He had the automatic rifle across his lap.

Bannon reached into one of the pouches of his chest rig. "I have a flashlight... You packed it before we left the base."

Paul shook his head. "No flashlight," he said. "Too risky."

"Well, could we light a candle or something?" Bannon asked. "Otherwise we're going to end up sitting in the dark."

Paul narrowed his eyes for a thoughtful moment. The office was secure. There was only the door downstairs and the narrow window in the toilet at the end of the hallway. "Sure," he said slowly. "Set it on the floor in front of the freak."

There was a cigarette lighter on a shelf in the first therapy cubicle. Bannon tucked it into his jeans pocket, then snatched up a candle and brought it into the office area. The light from the candle was a pathetic little flicker. The wavering glow caught the hard ridges of Sully's brutal face and cast them into deep malevolent shadows.

Paul reached for a canvas-covered bottle clipped to his webbing. He unscrewed the cap and sipped.

"Drink?" he offered the canteen to Bannon. The water was cool. It trickled across Bannon's swollen tongue and washed away the dirt and vile taste that had soured in the back of his throat. He sipped sparingly, the soldier's eyes watchful and measured. Bannon handed the bottle back reluctantly and licked his lips.

"Thanks."

Paul set the bottle down on the desk.

Bannon shrugged his shoulders. "Now what do we do?"

Paul turned his eyes to Bannon, and there was grim resolve in the tightness of his expression. "We wait," he said, and glanced at his watch. "An evac chopper will be back to pick us up at zero six hundred hours. Until then we do nothing. Nothing to make any noise, and nothing to draw attention to ourselves."

The hours crept by slowly. No one spoke. Bannon stared at the guttering candlelight and once, when he looked up, he saw Sully glaring at him. The big man's expression was unfathomable. Sully's skin looked waxen, as though it had a sheen of perspiration spread over it. The grey flesh seemed to hang from his skull in softening pouches, and his eyes looked out from deeply sunk sockets.

Bannon looked away. Paul was checking his weapon. The soldier finished the inspection and laid the gun down on the desktop. He reached into a holster for his sidearm.

"What kind of a gun is that?" Bannon pointed at the rifle and asked with no real interest other than to while away a few more minutes.

Paul considered Bannon's question for a moment. "It's an HK-416, which is the gas operating rod version of the M4 carbine," he said. "It's more reliable than the standard M4, and the gas regulation means it never fouls."

... which meant nothing at all to Bannon.

He pulled the Beretta out of the waistband of his jeans. "This is the gun John gave me," he said. "Should I keep it?"

Paul nodded. His own sidearm was the same model. "Did you fire it?"

Bannon shook his head. Paul checked the weapon quickly and handed it back. "It's good to go," he said gruffly. "You've got fifteen rounds. Don't waste them."

Chapter 5.

Bannon woke with a choked cry in his throat, lurching awake on the cubicle floor with his hands clenched into white-knuckled fists. Paul was crouched over him, his eyes wide, shaking his shoulder.

Bannon sat upright, staring at the walls as though surprised and mystified by his surroundings. The faint glow of the candle cast creeping shadows around the small room.

Bannon blinked – his eyes were red, raw and stinging. He scraped his fingers through the tangle of his hair and then froze as the sudden memories and nightmares of the day came rushing down upon him in a procession of sickening waves.

"What time is it?" he croaked.

"Oh three hundred," Paul whispered. He had the M4 in one hand, and his expression was tightly strained. "You need to get up. Now."

He hauled Bannon to his feet, grabbing him roughly by the webbing of the chest rig. "There's something moving around outside," the soldier said. "I just heard sound."

Bannon came alert instantly, a tingle of fear chilling down his spine. "Outside?" He clutched for the Beretta, but Paul seized his wrist and shook his head. He leaned close to Bannon's ear and his words were barely a breath.

"Right outside the door. Stay right fucking here and watch the freak. I'm going down to investigate."

The soldier pulled back, saw Bannon nod his head, then glanced over his shoulder as if to check the office one last time. Sully was sitting brooding in the corner as though he had never moved. He was watching Bannon's expression, the big man's eyes dark and sullen. Paul went down the stairs, one creeping step at a time, disappearing into the darkness beyond the flickering reach of candle flame.

Bannon stood perfectly still, staring down the staircase. He saw vague shadow – a lighter darkness against the inky black. Then the two merged together. He held his breath, and there was a cramp of raw fear across his face.

For a long time nothing happened. Bannon found himself staring into utter silence. Finally he heard a whisper of sound – a soft creak of movement – and his heart started pounding inside his chest.

He saw a vertical wedge of grey light appear, and realized it was the downstairs door slowly opening. Bannon's eyes grew wider. He took a wary step away.

Was something coming in?

He leveled the Beretta, holding it in a two-fisted grip, and aimed at the empty space at the top of the landing, waiting for something gruesome to slowly emerge from the shadows. He held his breath, felt a trickle of sweat run down his back.

Nothing happened.

Bannon waited.

From the corner of his eye he saw Sully move slowly, stretching his legs out in front of him and rocking gently from side to side as if to alleviate tired muscles. Bannon's eyes flicked nervously back to the stairs.

"Steve," Sully said suddenly, making no effort to hush his voice. "I need to talk to you."

"Shut up!" Bannon winced. His jaw was clenched and the words came through gritted teeth.

Sully shook his head defiantly. "I'll be quiet, when you agree to talk to me."

Bannon looked appalled. His eyes went very wide. He felt a sickening surge of panic. "You'll get us killed!" Bannon croaked hoarsely. "Shut the fuck up."

Sully narrowed his eyes, cunning and calculating. "I need to talk to you – now," He said, and his voice became a rumble.

Bannon glared at him and then Sully saw the moment of capitulation. Bannon's shoulders slumped. The man nodded his head.

"What do you want?" Bannon whispered hoarsely.

"I want you to let me go."

Bannon shuffled closer, still with the Beretta held distractedly guarding the top of the stairs. "You're fucking crazy," Bannon gasped. "I can't let you go."

Sully was glaring at Bannon with cold, seething rage simmering just below the surface of his expression. Then, in an instant, his entire demeanor altered.

"Steve, look at me!" Sully suddenly implored, and there was a desperate passion in his strained voice. "Jesus, Steve! It's me – your best friend."

Bannon stared. Sully was on his knees, and in his eyes was a fervent appeal for mercy. The edges of the bite that had been torn from his neck looked blackened and rotting in the gloomy light, and Bannon could see a livid purple bruise that reached

195

up around the man's jaw and down across his shoulder. The veins in Sully's neck were swollen beneath dry stretched skin.

"You can't let them do this, Steve. You know what will happen if they get me back to a government lab. They'll cut me into tiny pieces. They'll torture me like an animal. I'll be dissected... it will be cold-blooded murder." Sully's gaze filled with raw fear and despair. "My blood will be on your hands."

Bannon felt himself faltering. His resolve began to waver. He shook his head at last. "I'm sorry, Sully. I can't let you go. Millions of lives could be saved."

Sully snarled suddenly and he licked his tongue across his blackened, cracked lips.

"Shoot me, then!" he barked. He tried frantically to break his hands free of the thick cable ties that bound him. "Put a bullet through my brain! One shot! At least fucking kill me before those bastards cut me open."

Sully's breathing was ragged, his face swollen and dark with outrage. His eyes were wide and wild, like a great predatory beast. "Do me a favor. Kill me!"

Bannon gaped, his expression stricken. He could feel cold damp sweat soaking through the back of his shirt. He clenched his jaw and screwed up his resolve, so that the next words he muttered sounded harsh and ravaged. "I can't do that."

Sully's mouth twisted into a grimace of animal hate...

... and then a sudden scuffling sound – the sinister sound of heavy steps dragging – screeched across Bannon's frayed nerves. He flinched. His eyes snapped huge and fearful. He felt the thump of his heart beating like a drum, and his palms were suddenly slick with sweat.

Sully heard the sound too. His voice broke off and his infected gaze turned ominously in his head...

... towards the top of the stairs.

Bannon saw a hand first. It seemed to manifest from out of the pitch black, reaching out like a claw towards him – a bloodied, broken hand. The fingers were gnarled, the skin streaked with dirt and gore. Bannon choked down on a sudden gasp of panic. The Beretta trembled in his grip.

And then Paul's haggard, pale face appeared like some gruesome, ghostly apparition. The soldier's features were racked tight with agony, his lips curled into a grimace. There was a thin trickle of blood at the corner of his mouth. He stood on the top step, somehow limp and unsteady – and then his knees buckled and he crumpled to the office floor with a grunt of gasped breath that sounded like it had been punched from his lungs.

Bannon dropped the weapon and grabbed at the special forces soldier. Paul slid down the wall until he was lying on his back.

"Jesus! Are you okay?" Bannon drew back and stared hard into the soldier's face. Before his eyes, blisters of sweat welled up along the width of the man's brow.

"Just a scratch," the soldier whispered. "My arm."

Swiftly Bannon tugged at sleeve of the man's uniform until he was staring at a small cut, just below his left elbow. The limb was swelling, becoming bloated and discolored. Spider webs of veins around the wound began to purple and thicken like cords of rope beneath the tight skin.

There was very little blood. The soft fleshy lips of the cut pouted sullenly, but when Bannon tried to squeeze the flaps of skin back together, the gash began to weep a trickle of yellow puss that reeked of stinking corruption. Bannon felt a creep of black despair wrap its talons around his heart and squeeze the breath from him. He looked across the dark room to where Sully sat unmoving, his face impassive, his eyes seeming to glow in the flickering light of the candle.

Bannon shook his head sorrowfully, and then screwed his eyes shut...

... so that he didn't see Sully smile, sly and gloating.

"What happened?" Bannon knelt close to the soldier. The man's M4 was gone, and so was his KaBar. The Beretta was still in its holster.

"Undead, just outside the door," the special forces man rasped. "I tried to use the knife," and then the words were wrenched from his throat in a clotted rasp as Paul's face seized suddenly into a terrifying spasm of ghastly pain. He panted, gasping for air, his mouth open wide and his tongue swollen between his teeth.

"Tried to lead them away..."

Bannon gnawed on his lip. He touched his fingertips to the soldier's forehead and the skin there was blazing hot. He fumbled the flashlight from a pocket of his chest rig and played the narrow white beam across the wound.

The flesh along the soldier's arm was turning grey, as though the skin there was covered in a thick layer of dust. As Bannon watched, horrified, the infection spread to the clenched fingers of the soldier's fist, and crept up, beneath the thick camouflaged fabric of his uniform.

The soldier's eyes became clear and focused for an instant. He gazed up into Bannon's face. "Finish the job," he gasped in a whisper.

Bannon got to his feet. The soldier's head lolled to one side and he lay quite still. Bannon picked up the Beretta and thumbed the safety off. He took a deep breath, and then started to tremble. Panic and fear beat black wings against his thoughts.

He aimed the Beretta at a space between the soldier's eyes.

Chapter 6.

"Wait!" Sully snapped suddenly. He got to his feet, but stayed in the corner of the cubicle.

Bannon was standing over the dying soldier with his arm extended, the pistol just inches from the man's forehead.

"The moment you pull that trigger, whatever was outside – whatever attacked him – is going to come charging through that door downstairs. Every undead ghoul for a mile is going to be drawn to this place."

Bannon nodded and swallowed hard. Paul's breathing was shallow, sawing across his throat as though each gasp was a painful effort. The soldier's hand fluttered by his side, twitching with nerves as his life began to fade. His eyes were screwed tightly shut, his mouth agape. He licked spittle across his parched lips and one of his legs trembled.

"I know," Bannon said heavily.

"Well before you kill him, let me go. Cut me loose, because I'm your only chance of getting out of here alive."

Bannon shook his head. "Sully, I can't do that," he muttered. "There's a rescue helicopter coming. It will be here in a few hours. I need you to be on that chopper."

Sully's expression became grim and the look on his face was filled with veiled menace and foreboding.

"That's not going to happen," he said slowly.

The two men locked eyes, and for long moments there was no sound but the soldier's dying gasps for breath.

"What makes you so sure?" Bannon responded to Sully's warning with his own challenge.

"I'm not going back," Sully said flatly. "I'm not going to be cut into little pieces. I'd rather be dead... and without my help, there's no way you're going to survive until that helicopter comes. No way in the world."

Bannon shrugged. "You make it sound like I care," Bannon grinned, but it was an unconvincing effort that fixed on his face. He bared his teeth and narrowed his eyes to slits. "I don't," he said flatly. "I don't care whether I make it back or not. I only came here to find Maddie. Now...," his voice trailed away into silence.

Sully took a step closer. *"Maddie is alive,"* he said.

Bannon's eyes snapped with shock. "What?"

"Maddie is alive," Sully said again.

"I don't believe you."

"It's true," Sully said fervently. "I've seen her."

Bannon's gaze narrowed suspiciously. "Where?"

Sully gritted his teeth. "She's on my boat at the end of the marina," he sighed. "She's been there since before the outbreak."

"What?" Despite himself Bannon felt a sudden surge of hopeful relief. He stepped closer to Sully and stared into the big man's virulent eyes.

"She's been there all along," Sully confessed. The tension seemed to go out of his body. He glanced away for a moment, like he was searching for words, and then stared hard at Bannon. "I have a concealed compartment below the cabin deck. She was hiding there."

Bannon shook his head. This made no sense. He raised the pistol until it was pointing at Sully's chest.

"You're lying."

Sully grinned coldly. "We were having an affair," he said. There was a split second of stunned silence, and then it all poured out in a torrent of tortured words.

"Maddie and I have been sleeping together for over a year," Sully breathed. "Every time you put to sea, she would come and stay on the boat with me. When I sailed with you, she would stay aboard the boat. That's where she is. That's why I knew you were never going to find her in the fucking apartment complex. We're in love."

Bannon flinched and shrank away, feeling the monstrous enormity of his shock as a series of tremors that turned his legs to jelly. The gun dropped to his side. He glared at Sully, slowly shaking his head in denial, and yet somehow sensing deep within himself the sudden truth.

He felt himself reeling. The world seemed to tilt off its axis. He clutched for the desk to steady himself and as he did, the anger came surging through him – a sudden red mist of rage that clouded his mind and eyes.

"You were sleeping with Maddie?" he croaked.

Turmoil swirled within him, bubbling and hissing like the brew of a witch's cauldron – a fusion of poisons and toxic emotions that left him gasping.

Sully nodded, and his expression slowly became smug and triumphant. "Every day you were at sea," he taunted softly. He licked his lips lasciviously, as though the taste of Bannon's wife was a delicious flavor he could still savor.

"She was hot for it," Sully goaded. "She couldn't get enough of my cock. Your wife begged me to fuck her, y'know?" He stopped talking suddenly, and his expression became a thoughtful mockery. "No..." he said at last. "... I guess you don't know."

Bannon's face twisted into an ugly snarl. "You're full of shit!" he said defiantly. "You just want me to fucking kill you. You're trying to get me to blow your good-for-nothing brains out the back of your hideous fucking head!"

"Maybe..." Sully's voice was unnaturally calm, coarsened by the infection that swirled in his veins so that each word was a gravelly rasp. "And maybe I'm just telling you the truth."

"No!" Bannon hissed. "You're fucking lying!" The gun came up again, steady as a rock, and aimed between the big man's wide open eyes. "If Maddie was on your boat, you would have brought her with you to the sports field," he hissed, his words laced with venom.

Sully looked bored. "I couldn't," he said. "The entire waterfront is crawling with undead. The only way to get Maddie to the pick up point would have been for her to swim across the marina. And as you know..."

"... Maddie doesn't swim," grunted Bannon heavily, the realization like a sickening punch to his guts.

It was true!

Bannon felt himself imploding, shriveling. He felt his eyes mist over. Suddenly he felt a hundred years old – worn down by the strain and tension, the fear and the sudden devastation. He had sensed all along that once the mission was over, he would need time to mourn the death of his wife. Now – suddenly – he was confronted with the gut-wrenching shock of her monstrous betrayal.

And her survival.

He lifted his head and stared into the implacable eyes of John Sully. "You betrayed me," he said softly.

Sully nodded. "Yes, I did. So did Madeline."

Behind Bannon, the special forces soldier gave a sudden gasp of ragged breath, and then his back arched horribly as though his entire body was racked by seizure. The man's heels juddered, tapping out a macabre tattoo on the ground. Bannon watched in ghastly fascination. The soldier turned his head and his eyes came open for an instant. He saw Bannon, tried to form words but his mouth was twisted with pain. He sighed, and then went limp with the slow softening relaxation of death.

Bannon went to the body and thrust the barrel of the Beretta between the dead man's eyes. His face was screwed up into a grim, remorseless expression, suddenly devoid of compassion and hesitation... and fear. He shot the soldier, and then turned his baleful eyes back to Sully.

"Take me to my wife."

Chapter 7.

Bannon snatched the pocket knife from out of the chest rig and cut the cable ties around Sully's wrists. The echo of the gunshot had faded into the night, but the reverberation of the deafening sound had drawn the undead. They swarmed towards the downstairs foyer. Bannon heard the door crash back against its hinges, and then there was a rising shrill of demented voices, filling the air in the darkness below where he stood.

He looked around him wildly. The desk was the closest. He dragged it across the top of the stairs. Sully had his arms wrapped around one of the filing cabinets like an embrace. The muscles in his shoulders flexed and he dead-lifted the heavy metal. The drawers flew open, spilling files and papers across the floor. Bannon set fire to the litter while Sully heaved the second filing cabinet across to the makeshift barricade.

"The massage tables!" Bannon snapped.

Sully went into the closest cubicle. The table was on castors, each wheel locked to prevent it rolling. He kicked the brakes off and pushed the table ahead of him. Together they upended the heavy piece and sent it clattering and crashing down the narrow staircase.

"Want the other one?" Sully asked

Bannon shook his head. "No time," he said.

The flames had caught quickly. The thick sheaths of paper blackened and curled, then burst alight. Smoke began to fill the office. Bannon tugged the Beretta from the dead soldier's holster.

He had a pistol in each hand. The fire crept up the wooden door frame and cast leaping demented shadows across the walls. Bannon fired six shots down the stairs, aiming blindly into the smoke as the snarling growl of inhuman voices became feverish.

"We've got to get out of here – now! The bathroom window!" Bannon spat. "Go!" There was enough light from the fire to show the darkened passageway and the closed door. Sully went lumbering along the hallway. Bannon stood at the top of the stairs for a moment longer. He drew the flashlight and sucked in a deep quivering breath. The beam sliced down through the blackness of the stairwell.

The top of the stairs formed a rectangular frame for the ghastly image that burned across his eyes. Writhing bodies, struggling over each other, reached out for him, thrusting through the fire. Yellow blazing eyes, demented faces snarled. One of the ghouls lunged at the barricade and went tumbling backwards down the narrow steps, shrieking as fire swept over his flailing body. The rags he wore caught ablaze and he staggered like a human torch while other insane ghouls knocked the creature to the ground and clambered over it.

Bannon fired three shots into the head of the closest zombie. It was a woman, her wiry hair fizzing and smoldering to her skull as she hurled herself through the blaze. She gnashed her teeth, leaping at Bannon. He felt the kick of the gun's recoil pulse up through the muscles of his arm, and the woman's face disappeared, snapped back into the darkness by the brutal impact of the point-blank rounds. The shrieking sound of her voice was cut off abruptly.

Bannon turned and fled down the hallway just as bright flickering flames danced across the office floor and began to lick at the flesh of the dead special forces soldier.

The bathroom door was swinging open. Bannon crashed into the room, bouncing off a wall. Sully put his fist through the glass louvers of the narrow window and they exploded outward in a shower of glittering shards. Bannon thrust his head through the opening. Cold night air overwhelmed his senses. He could smell the salt of the ocean, and hear the faint distant rumble of surf on rocks.

And he could smell smoke.

The end of the alleyway backed onto a side street that was bright with the light of new fires. Dark silhouettes drifted before the leaping flames as the undead wandered the streets. They moved in restless packs, staggering and lunging in aimless chaos as they scoured the remains of Grey Stone for living flesh.

"Good God." Bannon tried to guess their numbers but it was impossible. The undead moved in and out of buildings, prowled on the edges of the light, and ghosted in the shadows. A house suddenly erupted in flames at the far end of the street and two ghouls came reeling from within, both of them on fire so that the pungent stench of burning flesh carried on the breeze and overwhelmed him. Bannon tasted the wretched nausea of it in the back of his throat and gagged.

"We have to jump into the trash bin," Bannon choked out the words. He spat the taste of death out of his mouth and then jammed the two pistols inside the chest rig. Flames had taken hold along the walls of the office. Billows of writhing smoke swirled into the tiny bathroom. Bannon could hear the undead clawing at the makeshift barricade. He went out through the window, clinging to the narrow wooden frame...

... and then let go.

He fell awkwardly into a muffled explosion of cardboard boxes, and the slimy refuse of rotting vegetables. The commercial waste bin was filled to overflowing. He landed on his back, felt the wind punched out of him by the shock of the impact, but got to his feet with a stunned grunt. He looked up. Sully was wriggling himself out through the window, the big man's legs dangling in mid air as he held himself steady. Bannon clambered out of the big steel bin and crouched in the shadows. His eyes swept the alleyway. He filled his fist with one of the Beretta's and waited.

Sully dropped like a stone, plummeting feet first into the overflowing pile of rotting trash. He landed heavily and the sound seemed to jar the night air. Bannon cringed, and tried to melt against the cold brick wall. Sully climbed out of the trash bin and pressed his face close.

"Get rid of the vest," Sully whispered.

"Why?"

"Because the only way you're going to reach Maddie is to swim across the marina," Sully's tone became harsh, "and you ain't gonna do that with a heavy harness weighing you down."

A twisted, tottering shadow suddenly appeared at the end of the alleyway, the undead ghoul's features shrouded in darkness, but its outline backlit by the burning flames along the distant street. Bannon cringed and held his breath. The zombie stood, perfectly still for several seconds, and then its body took on the posture of a stalking animal, suddenly alert and aware. It took three paces down the alley towards were Bannon and Sully crouched, and then it stopped again. Bannon saw the ghoul slowly turn its head and he stared, appalled and fascinated. His heart skipped a beat. He trickled air from his nostrils, not daring to move. The ghoul came a step closer, so that he was poised just a few feet away from where Bannon hid, the zombie craning forward as though trying to see shape within the dark shadows.

In one of its bloodied gnarled hands, the zombie carried the limb of a small child. It was a leg, severed at the knee, the foot still covered by a shiny black shoe. The flesh had been gnawed away, back to the bone. The zombie dipped its head and gnawed at the gristle of cartilage and stringy muscle that still hung in shreds.

Bannon gaped in fascinated skin-crawling horror.

Suddenly Sully got to his feet. Bannon's mind went white with pure fear. Sully stepped out of the darkness, moving in ungainly shuffling strides. He brushed against the ghoul. The undead growled. Sully nudged the zombie again, and the creature turned and lumbered from the alley. Bannon's mouth was dry. He stifled an uneasy qualm of fear. He watched Sully teeter to the end of the alley and stand there, his head turning both ways before he turned back to where Bannon was hiding. Sully waved his hand and Bannon rose cautiously to his feet.

He could hear glass breaking in the upstairs office and the trampling sound of stomping feet. He shrugged off the chest rig and then rummaged around in the trash bin. He wrapped the small emergency beacon in several plastic bags and stuffed it down inside his shirt.

He still had both Beretta's. He thrust one into the waistband of his jeans, and came creeping along the dark shadowed wall of the alley with the other pistol held out in front of him.

Sully was waiting impatiently. He saw that Bannon had cast off the vest but he said nothing. He pointed.

"We double around," he said. "We follow the rear of these buildings along the street to the next intersection. Then we cross the road and make our way back to the waterfront, following the headland. We've got a better chance once we get into the trees around the lookout."

"Then what?"

"Then – if you're still alive – I'll take you down the ridge to the marina."

Chapter 8.

They hugged the fence line and the walls of the buildings, keeping to the shadows with their eyes moving restlessly, breathing sharp and shallow, Bannon's nerves screwed up tight as they worked their way in starts and pauses towards the corner of the block.

The air was cold, the night inky black. There was no moon, and clouds of swirling smoke obscured the pinpricks of starlight. They ducked into a narrow alcove of deep shadow and Bannon saw his breath softly misting before his face.

Across the street, the fire was leaping from one building to the next. Most of the structures were houses. Their roofs smoldered and then burst into bright little tongues of flame. Bannon heard glass shattering. He leaned forward, beyond the veil of shadow and stared along the sidewalk.

"Another fifty feet," he said. "Maybe a bit more before we reach the corner."

Sully nodded, said nothing. The big man was staring directly across the street where one of the undead had suddenly appeared in the doorway of a house. The ghoul stood swaying on the porch, its head tilted in an attitude of concentration. It seemed to be feeling the air, its body twitching. Sully clasped Bannon's shoulder and pointed.

Bannon's gaze fell on the ghoul. He watched with fascination. The zombie came down a short set of steps and it suddenly dropped to its knees. It was hunting something.

Or someone.

For long moments, Bannon lost sight of the ghoul in the dark shadows that enveloped the house. He peered hard, eyes wide and stood perfectly still.

"Do we go on?" he breathed the words from the corner of his mouth, his lips barely moving.

Sully shook his head. "We go quiet," the man hissed.

The ghoul appeared again suddenly, coming to its feet by the front fence of the property as if it had crawled across the lawn on its hands and knees. Bannon felt his heart skip a beat. The zombie had once been a middle aged man. Its skin was white and bloated, the stomach a huge hairy obese bulge that hung heavily down over his hips. The ghoul was completely naked, and it moved in slow stalking bursts, almost birdlike, as it edged closer.

There was an open front gate and a driveway beside the home, bordered by high trees. The ghoul reached the gate and then turned away suddenly, sprinting along the driveway towards the rear of the home. Bannon felt himself sigh a slow breath of relief.

"Now," Sully muttered.

They came from the alcove and crept forward. The sidewalk was broken concrete pavement. Their steps were soundless. They covered another twenty feet before a deep hole of shadow at the back of a building beckoned them.

There was trash strewn across the ground. They were standing under some kind of awning over a door. It was probably the rear entrance to one of the main street shops, Bannon guessed. He pressed the palm of his hand against the timber. It was solid wood, and locked.

To his left and right he could see jumbled shapes of junk and rubbish. The stench of rotting food was strong, overpowering everything else. Sully stood like a statue. Only his eyes moved slowly in his head.

Bannon could sense the big man's sudden tension.

"You hear something?"

Sully nodded.

Bannon tried to focus his hearing, straining to separate individual sounds amongst the bedlam and chaos that surrounded them. Then something dark scurried across his boot. He snatched his foot away and felt himself cringe with a shudder of skin-crawling revulsion.

"Rats."

Sully nodded. The darkness beside where they stood seemed to be moving – writhing. Bannon stared hard until slowly several shapes emerged.

The rats were feeding on something – probably a pile of garbage, or maybe a corpse. Bannon didn't want to know. He couldn't smell the stench of bloated death... but perhaps his senses had been overwhelmed, or diluted by the strong odor of smoke. He shuffled a pace away, but another rat came crawling up his leg. He lashed out with his fist. The rat made a child-like screech of pain and fell away.

"Fuck this!" Bannon hissed. "Let's get going." He moved. He took three steps in the darkness towards the edge of a fence, and then stopped, as if frozen. He felt something give way beneath his foot.

He looked back over his shoulder. Sully was right behind him.

"Sully!" he whispered urgently. He had one foot suspended in mid air and he felt himself begin to teeter off balance. He had trodden on a body, lying on the concrete in the black shadow of the fence. Bannon could see a sheen of firelight reflect from a wedge of torso flesh. He held his breath.

The figure hissed. Bannon's eyes went huge with his horror.

He stumbled backwards. The figure he had stepped on came up onto its hands and knees. It was a woman. She was wearing the tattered shreds of denim jeans. Her upper body was naked. The woman hunched her back and snarled. Then she pounced to her feet.

Now she was upright, Bannon could see the undead woman more clearly. She had died young – maybe still a teenager. She had short blonde hair, dirty with filth and gore. Her face was desiccated, the eyes sunk deep into her skull, a flap of rotting flesh torn from one of her cheeks. She had been bitten on the shoulder. One of the arms seemed to hang like a broken wing, as if maybe bones had been shattered.

"Fuck!" Bannon gasped.

He threw up the pistol instinctively. The zombie drew back her lips, exposing snarling teeth that were chipped and broken and blackened. At the same instant she lunged her head at Bannon like a spitting cobra. He flinched away, felt the fetid rotting breath of the ghoul wash over his face. The gun in his hand was wrenched off target and he had to drag it back, costing him a precious split-second.

It was all the time the ghoul needed.

The undead woman flung herself at Bannon, fingers clawing at his shirt so he felt the tug and then the tear of fabric. He reeled away, hopelessly off balance, and there was a cry of utter horror in his throat as he fell hard to the ground. The Beretta was flung from his nerveless fingers and went skittering away into the black night.

The undead woman lunged, but Sully was suddenly there, swinging a mighty fist that connected with the ghoul's jaw. The sound of bones breaking was sickening. The woman's head was wrenched round, hair swishing in the air like ragged tails. She crashed against the fence and hung like a rag doll, stunned for an instant.

Sully stood protectively over Bannon's body. The ghoul hissed at him, making greedy gulping motions, her evil slanted eyes blazing with poisonous hatred and her tongue stabbing obscenely from between her lips. She came warily from the fence, circling around to the opposite side of the narrow path. Another rat scurried somewhere in the darkness, and as Bannon heaved himself shakily up onto his knees, one of the vermin scrabbled onto his shoulder. Bannon thrashed wildly, revolted by the touch. His flesh crawled as clawed filthy feet brushed over his cheek.

His flailing panic incensed the rage of the zombie woman. She attacked again, hurling herself mindlessly forward. Sully snatched the woman up by the neck and squeezed. The ghoul made wretched clotted sounds of fury, kicking its legs in empty air. Sully threw the woman down to the ground beside where Bannon sat dazed, and pinned her to the concrete.

215

"Find a weapon!" Sully hissed.

"A weapon?" Bannon was numb, senses reeling. The woman writhed and began to screech.

"A fucking stick. A knife. Anything!" the big man's voice was a raw rash of violence.

Bannon got to his feet and staggered. There was a ragged old broom leaning against the fence. He snatched it up and passed it to Sully.

"Break it!"

Bannon put the handle across his knee. The sound of the wood shattering made him wince. He thrust the shortest piece of broken wood to Sully's outstretched fingers.

With his hand clamped like a steel brace around the undead ghoul's throat, Sully raised the splintered end of the handle high overhead and then stabbed down. The jagged edge went through the zombie's eyeball. The ghoul screeched. The woman was clinging to the stick with both hands, kicking frenetically out with its legs. Sully twisted the handle to grind it deeper through the skull, and finally felt it grate against bone. He twisted, wrenched the handle with all his might until the shaft plunged deep into the thrashing woman's infected brain. Watery ooze dribbled from the burst eyeball and then the zombie went limp, finally dead.

Bannon tore open his shirt and stared down at his chest. His lungs were heaving. Sweat ran in rivulets over the lean muscles of his abdomen. He turned to Sully, his expression bleak and wrought with ominous dread.

"Do you see anything? Am I scratched?"

Sully peered close. Bannon made a half-turn so that he was caught in the flickering glow of the burning buildings on the opposite side of the narrow street.

Sully's face was rigid, his expression fixed. He shook his head slowly. "You're okay," the big man said.

Bannon sighed, and went soft with relief for a moment. His hands were trembling. One of the plastic bags that he had waterproofed the emergency beacon with was tattered. The little black box had saved his life.

Sully's eyes narrowed. "What's that?"

Bannon started to answer, and then some instinct warned him. He choked his reply off and buttoned up his shirt hurriedly. "I'll tell you later," he grunted.

Sully became suspicious. He opened his mouth to say something more, but suddenly Bannon remembered the Beretta.

"The gun!" he blurted. "I lost it in the darkness."

"Forget it," Sully snapped. "We don't have time to look. Use the other one." Behind Bannon's back he had seen a flicker of distant movement. "Right now we have more important things to worry about... and run from."

Sully stabbed his finger into the wavering shadows.

Chapter 9.

The screeching snarls of the woman they had killed and the sounds of the life-and-death struggle had drawn more zombies. They gathered in a cluster in the middle of the street, backlit by leaping flames as the houses behind them burned. They were gnarled, twisted shapes cast as black silhouettes. Bannon drew the Beretta from the waistband of his jeans.

"How many do you think?" he asked in a whisper.

Sully shrugged. "Maybe eight. Too many."

"What do we do?"

"If we run, you're dead. They'll catch you."

"We could stand here and fight," Bannon said grimly. Behind the ghouls, one of the houses suddenly collapsed. The roof caved in and the sky filled with a towering ball of flame and embers.

Sully turned his eyes to Bannon.

"This gun has fifteen bullets," he showed the Beretta in his fist to Sully. "More than enough."

Sully's expression became sour. "You won't hit anything."

That was a point. Bannon wasn't a soldier – he was a scared, tired, panicked fisherman. The chances of him shooting anything that moved in the head beyond a few feet of range were practically zero.

"So what do we do?" Bannon's voice became strained and urgent. The horrendous crashing sounds of the house collapsing had masked the whispers of their words, but it had also pushed the undead away from the flames. They had come to the gutter, and milled close together on the concrete sidewalk. They were less than twenty feet from where the two men stood in the dark shadows of the doorway. "Can you stall them?" Bannon felt his panic begin to flutter in the pit of his guts. "Go out there and lead them away?"

"No."

"Why not?"

Sully turned on Bannon, and there was real malevolence and fury in his face. He snarled, and his words grated. "Because I don't know what will happen if I get bitten again, or even scratched," he spat. "Maybe it will be enough for me to turn completely. Maybe any more exposure to the infection will turn me into one of those fuckers. Did you think of that?"

Bannon hadn't. He hadn't considered the possibility that Sully was still in danger.

"Get the door open," Sully muttered. His simmering outburst dissolved in an instant. "We'll have to take our chances inside."

Bannon looked appalled. Being on the open street had given him some small sense of security. The glowing flare from the fires had provided enough light for him to see danger coming. The interior of the building behind them would be pitch black.

Bannon opened his mouth to protest, but Sully intercepted him. "Think of it as a shortcut," the big man said grimly. "The building has to open onto the main street. It must be one of the shop fronts. If we're lucky, we'll save some time getting to the woods along the headland."

"And if we're unlucky?"

Sully's expression didn't change. "If we're unlucky," he paused for an instant, "the building we're about to break into is going to be filled with more zombies."

Chapter 10.

"The door is locked!"

"Bust it open," Sully growled. "Fuckin' hurry!"

The undead had heard them. It was inevitable. As the house on the far side of the street crashed to rubble and the smoke and dust swirled high into the sky, the sound of the men's voices – even hushed and strained – carried to the infected. They came snarling and lunging... and hunting.

Bannon took a step back and then launched himself, kicking out hard and striking the door an inch below the lock with the heel of his boot. The door exploded inwards and Bannon's momentum carried him across the threshold. Sully came crowding after him, stepping into a world without light.

The darkness was absolute – a claustrophobic nightmare where every sense was subdued and made useless. Sully slammed the door shut and braced his back against it. Seconds later the hammering fists and outraged snarls of the undead came vibrating through the wood. The door bucked and lurched against Sully's broad back.

"Hurry! Find something to barricade the door!" the big man hissed.

Bannon groped hopelessly in the blackness. His hands reached out blindly. He felt something like soft silk brush over his face and he cringed away. He shuddered. He could hear the wailing of the zombies undulating: rising and falling like waves crashing on a beach. The sound of their pounding fists became louder. He flailed his hands in hopeless desperation.

And then froze.

Bannon's outstretched fingers brushed something that felt... familiar. His breath hitched in the back of his throat and jammed there. Slowly, fearfully, he crawled his fingers over something that felt like a face.

"Fuck!" he cried out. He stumbled away, tripped over something heavy in the dark, and staggered to regain his balance. "They're in here!" Bannon screamed, his voice filled with blind terror. "The place must be full of them!" He had the Beretta in his fist and he fired twice from just a few feet of distance. The roar of the shots was a detonation of deafening sound in the confined space. For a split second the black night lit up, and then the darkness came down again like a crushing anvil.

"Fuck!" Bannon gasped again. "I think I got it." He was panting. His heart was racing faster than he thought humanly possible and there was a terrified feverish tremble in his hands. He blinked. The dark was swirling before his eyes. Pinwheels of light sparked across his vision.

Suddenly he remembered the cigarette lighter he had taken from the therapy office. He fumbled it from his pocket and took a slow fearful breath.

The lighter sparked, then flamed.

The pool of light was small, a soft wavering glow of weak yellow that spilled like a puddle around his feet. The light caught the edge of a row of shelves against the far wall, and turned the shapes around him into threatening shadows.

His hand was shaking. Bannon held the lighter close to him...

... and stared down at the ground.

The shop mannequin lay on its back on the floor, a ragged hole punched into the forehead of the figure, and another hole smashed through the shoulder.

Bannon's expression became incredulous. He flicked a glance at Sully, and then held the cigarette lighter high above his head. They were standing in a dress shop.

"Good shooting, Annie fucking Oakley," Sully sneered with derisive contempt. "You killed a store dummy."

There was an open doorway near where Bannon stood. He held the lighter out ahead of him. It was a small office at the rear of the shop. He could see a foam coffee cup and a litter of invoices spread across a sturdy desk. He upended the desk and edged the heavy piece out through the opening. They braced the desk hastily against the back door of the shop and then piled heavy cardboard boxes on top of it.

"That will hold them – for now," Sully grunted. The chorus of snarling cries from outside had diminished. He pressed his ear to the door for a long suspicious moment.

"Maybe some of them have lost interest," he shrugged, his tone puzzled and unsure. There was still a ragged relentless beat of fists pounding through the door, but not so many, nor so frantic. "Or maybe they've found something else to hunt."

Bannon crept between the racks of dresses and women's fashion pieces, shielding the flickering light with his cupped hand. The floor was polished timber boards so that every step he took seemed an unnaturally loud echo. There was soot and flakes of black ash on the ground that had either been blown in through the doors, or maybe fallen down through the ceiling from the roof above as it had burned.

The front of the shop was plate glass – two big floor-to-ceiling windows on either side of a glass-fronted door. The windows were painted with 'Sale' and 'Discount' signs, and there was an arrangement of several more mannequins before each window. Some of the fiberglass figurines were standing in dresses. Others had been posed sitting on boxes and delicate chairs.

"Wanna shoot them too?" Sully gruffed dryly.

Bannon said nothing. He felt a flush of acute embarrassed heat on his cheeks.

In the middle of the shop floor was a sales counter, standing like a small island. There was a cash register on the polished counter top and several shelves underneath. Bannon crept to the counter and peered cautiously out through the shop's display windows.

Nothing moved.

Far off, through the ragged black outline of distant trees along the headland, the sky seemed to be lightening with the first hint of the coming dawn. He glanced at his wristwatch. It was 4.30am.

He had just ninety minutes to reach Maddie, talk reason into her, and then get her back to the sports field for the rendezvous with the rescue helicopter. His expression became tight and grim.

"We need to get across the street and into those trees," he said, pointing out through the darkened glass.

"No shit," Sully said. In the weird light of small flame, the big man's face looked ghastly – a gruesome mask of grey hanging flesh and the sharp lines of his skull showing as deep hollows and jagged highlights. His eyes were haunting – somehow soulless.

Bannon could smell the whiff of corruption. It wrinkled in his nostrils.

Sully got slowly to his feet and went to the front of the shop. There was a small bell fixed above the door. He unfastened it carefully, and then turned back to where Bannon hesitated. "Come on," he whispered. "There's no time left for hiding."

Bannon got to his feet. He crept to the front door and pressed his nose against the cold glass, eyes fearfully hunting the heavy darkness of the street beyond.

There were black masses beyond the windows – the hulking shapes of cars that had been parked, or abandoned. They were deep shadows without distinct form. Bannon sucked in a series of deep ragged breaths, like an anxious athlete about to run the race of his life.

It was a hundred yards of lush grass from the street to the edge of the woods, where the ground slowly rose and roughened to become the rocky headland that protected the southern arm of Grey Stone harbor. Bannon knew the area well. He could see it in his mind – see the park benches and the children's playground equipment where tourists and locals gathered on sunny summer afternoons after a morning at one of the beaches. He could visualize the bushes and shrubs that had been planted for shade and shelter against the winds that came off the ocean.

A hundred yards seemed suddenly a very long distance.

"Are you ready?" Sully asked.

Bannon nodded.

Sully reached for the lock. "When we get outside, we just fucking run, okay?"

"Okay."

"We make for the trees at the top of the headland – the ones at the end of the tourist loop."

Bannon nodded again.

Sully's expression became fierce. He thrust his face close. "If I lose you," he warned, "– if we get separated for any reason – I won't come back for you."

Bannon nodded. "I understand," he said, and then narrowed his eyes, and his voice became stinging. "That works both ways. If I get to those trees and you're not there, I'm going to get Maddie, and you can fucking rot for all I care."

Sully's smile was unexpected. "Good," he said harshly. "Just so we understand each other." He unlocked the glass door and cracked it open.

Fresh salty sea air swirled into the shop – the sweet smell of the ocean. Bannon tasted it in the back of his throat and his eyes watered. Then Sully pulled the door wide open...

... and they began to run.

Chapter 11.

Bannon exploded through the open front door of the shop like a sprinter, bursting out of the blocks. There were two cars parked nose-to-tail on the side of the road. He weaved between them, and then his boots were slapping on the blacktop.

He ran with the Beretta in his fist, arms pumping, keeping his eyes fixed on the distant smudged darkness of the wooded crest. He heard sound behind him, but didn't look back. Sully was not beside him.

Bannon kept running.

The grass on the far side of the road was long and unkempt. He leaped the gutter and his legs buckled, but he stayed upright. He ran with fear and desperation.

But he didn't run fast enough.

There were undead in the park, wandering aimlessly. They emerged from the night, seeming to peel away from the shadows of a high shrub near the park's playground equipment. Bannon saw them coming towards him and knew that he was trapped.

He stopped running, slowed to a walk.

He stood still.

His breath sawed across his throat and there was a fierce cramp of pain in his chest. He stole a glance over his shoulder. Backlit by the faint glow of distant fires, he saw Sully's big lumbering shape coming towards him with an awkward ungainly gait. The man was twenty yards back, running on grimly.

Bannon turned around and faced the undead.

There were two of them – maybe a man and a woman. Bannon couldn't be sure. It was too dark, and they were too far away to see detail. The decomposition of the bodies seemed to have ravaged their appearances beyond identification. One was taller and broader than the other, but they both moved as though it required great effort – as though it was the fury of their infection that compelled them.

Bannon raised the Beretta.

The closest undead was the broad shouldered one. He seemed to creak with effort, the body stiff and withered, but the eyes still filled with the blazing malevolence of its madness. It loomed closer and as it did, Bannon at last was able to see features.

The ghoul was a rotting, filthy corpse. Ragged, tattered clothes hung from the body and the flesh of it had blackened and bloated. The zombie's face had been ripped and clawed. Flesh hung in livid flaps, and there were hideous lacerations and weeping ulcers along the line of its jaw.

The ghoul's throat had been gnawed, so that the head seemed to hang. The flesh around the wound was black, and the stench of corruption and decay was almost a physical thing.

The zombie raised its loathsome head...

And Bannon flinched in abject shock.

"Peter?"

The crewman Bannon had sailed with – the polite young man with the steady gaze and calm confidence – was long gone. This hideous infected monster was not the youth that Bannon had set to sea with, and trusted at the helm of *'Mandrake'*.

Bannon remembered Peter Coe dying on the cobbled pavers in front of the marina, recalled the undead ghoul tearing at the young man's face and throat, and the pain of his own anguish. He took a staggered step back. The zombie came on, mindless with its madness.

Bannon raised the Beretta reluctantly.

"Peter. Don't."

The zombie stopped, just a few paces from Bannon and stood teetering. It's head lolled, and then the body began to rock. The ghoul hissed at Bannon, and its tongue slithered from the dark gaping hole of its mouth. Bannon felt the shake in his arm. The gun wavered.

"Peter…?"

The other ghoul moved around to Bannon's side, stalking him with slow predatory steps. It was a woman. Her expression was a snarling slash across the revolting face that looked like it had been gnawed by vermin. Her hair hung in ragged tufts, and one of its eyes was missing. The dark hole of the empty socket oozed thick brown slime that ran down her cheek and dripped from her chin. She flapped her hands madly in the air like the wings of beating birds and Bannon was forced to follow her with his eyes, compelled by his ghastly fascination.

Which was the instant the ghoul that had once been Peter Coe suddenly attacked.

The zombie charged at Bannon in a frenetic lunge, arms and legs tangled into a writhing fit of fury. It flailed at him, its jagged black fingernails like little knives that swished through the air before his face. The ghoul was vomiting rancid clots of slime from between his bloated snarling lips.

Bannon wrenched the pistol round and pulled the trigger instinctively. The bullet caught Peter Coe full in the chest, just below the breast bone, and hurled him to the ground. The female zombie shrieked cruelly. She twisted and growled – and then sprang forward. Bannon swung his body neatly from the waist, bringing the Beretta around and squeezing the trigger at the same instant. The first shot flew wide. He fired again, just as the woman's thrashing clawed hands reached out for him. The barrel of the handgun pressed brutally into her face as the sound of the shot ripped through the dark night.

The ghoul's head seemed to disappear in a mist of gore and clotted shards. The round punched a neat hole through her cheek, but such was the extent of her corruption and decay that when Bannon stared down at the mess that splashed his boots, there was little of the head remaining.

He reeled away. Loud, pounding steps came from behind him, heavy enough that he could feel the tiny tremor of them vibrating up through the ground. He spun round and saw Sully. The big man was hefting a long piece of wood that was slick and wet and stained.

Sully slowed but didn't stop. He saw an undead ghoul in front of Bannon, and another one lying in the grass beside the man. One of the zombies was sitting up slowly, rising upright from the waist. To Sully it might have been a man. He swung the lump of wood like a two-handed broadsword, without slowing his stride, and smashed the zombie in the head. The sound of the blow was a meaty, satisfying thud – like a dinger hit way back into the bleachers. Peter Coe's skull caved in.

"Come on, fucker!" Sully shouted over his shoulder at Bannon without turning or stopping. "Keep running."

Bannon ran.

He caught Sully quickly, and the ground beneath their feet began to rise. Bannon could feel the grass underfoot give way to small stones that squirmed and popped beneath his boots. They had reached the base of the headland.

Clumps of trees rushed out of the darkness. Bannon clawed at them to keep his balance and heave himself higher. Wind rustled through the leaves, swirling and sighing. Bannon gritted his teeth and scrambled on.

The headland that overlooked Grey Stone harbor was like the hump of a whale's broad back. The two men reached the crest. Bannon was gasping painfully. He bent at the waist and propped his hands on his knees, sucking in cold, wind-chilled air that was swept straight off the ocean. They were concealed in the woods, and it seemed like another world. The sound of the pounding surf was loud in the stillness, and the air was sweet, free from the taint of corruption and decay. Ahead of them was the rocky cliff-face and then endless vast miles of ocean. To their right, was the tourist road that meandered up the rise and then looped back onto itself. Behind them were the burning ruins of their town.

Bannon breathed deeply until the tremble in his aching legs had subsided, and the sweat of fear and panic had dried on his skin.

There was a pale line across the horizon, a scar of milky grey light. Sully was gazing at it pensively.

"That zombie you just killed – the one you hit with the lump of wood. I think that was Peter Coe," Bannon said.

Sully didn't seem to hear. Bannon grunted. He glanced over his shoulder, back through the trees and narrowed his eyes warily. It was still dark, but the distant town seemed a lighter shade with the imminent approach of dawn. He could see nothing moving. He swept his eyes carefully through the trees and concentrated his gaze on the open ground near the clump of playground equipment.

Nothing.

"I said, that zombie –" he started.

"I heard you," Sully cut him off abruptly. He was leaning on the length of lumber, like it was a walking stick. He turned to face Bannon. "But I don't care who it might have been. It was a zombie – pure and simple, and if you had just shot the fucker in the head the first time, I wouldn't have had to clean up your mess."

Bannon felt his temper boil. "Peter was a friend," he said, and his tone was like acid. "Maybe it's easier for you, Sully... because you've always been a fucking jerk. You never had friends."

"That's right!" Sully's tone became venomous so that he spat the words out. "I don't have friends – but I do have your wife, Bannon," he became malicious. "In fact, I've had her time and time again."

232

There was a moment of tense silence. Bannon had the pistol in his hand. Sully carried the heavy length of wood. With a huge effort of will, Bannon relaxed his fingers from the trigger.

He turned on his heel and crept through the trees towards the tourist loop. The road loomed out of the gloom, and he saw a couple of park benches and a picnic table. Bannon stalked to the edge of the woods and crouched. His eyes swept the open ground before him. On the far side of the road was a fringe of low shrubs beyond which, he knew, the ground dropped away suddenly – down to the southern arm of the marina's break wall. He was tempted to cross the road – aching just to stand on the lip of the promontory and gaze down into the harbor. But caution made him wary.

He heard Sully's footsteps behind him, crunching over fallen leaves and debris. For a moment, Bannon did not turn. Instead, he had a sudden flashed premonition – an image of Sully's gruesome death-like face twisted into a malicious grimace as he lifted the heavy piece of lumber above his head and then crashed it down, murdering him. Bannon turned his head slowly. Sully was standing over him, a dark brooding hulk, his expression fixed and unfathomable. The two men locked eyes, and Bannon wondered if Sully had read his thoughts.

"Wait here," Sully said thickly, his voice tight and strange for a moment, as though he too had recognized the opportunity – and lamented letting it pass. "I'm going out to check the road."

Chapter 12.

Sully stood in the middle of the blacktop, staring defiantly back down the road to where it joined the main artery into town. Nothing moved. The area around the lookout was cleared and level. During the holiday season, the grounds were filled with a throng of tourists who sat in the grassy field and perched on the wooden benches, staring out at the distant horizon and the misted panoramic view along the rugged coastline.

Sully gave a curt wave of his hand. Bannon came cautiously from the fringe of the woods.

Dawn was rushing across the horizon, watery pale light creeping up the sky and pulling the world out of darkness and back into gradual detail.

Sully threw the piece of lumber down onto the ground. "How this ends is going to be up to you," he said suddenly.

Bannon kept his expression blank. "Meaning?"

"Meaning you've got decisions to make."

"Such as...?"

Sully sneered. He folded his arms across his chest. "Maddie and I are in love – that's a fact. You're going to have to decide how you deal with it."

Bannon raised a taunting, mocking eyebrow. "I will believe that when I see it – and when I hear it from Madeline's mouth."

Sully nodded. "Fine," he said. "But when you talk to her – when she tells you what I've already said, you're going to have to decide whether you let us go – leave us to try to find peace... or whether you want to play the hero."

"Hero?"

Sully nodded. Then he thrust a finger into Bannon's face. "It's not the choice I'd recommend," he warned. "I hope you can be a man about this. I hope you do the right thing by Maddie. Because if you don't – if you try to get me into that helicopter, and if you think I'll let myself be taken back to a lab somewhere... you're fucking out of your mind. I'll kill you before I let them take me."

Bannon's expression was tight. He glared at the bigger man for long seconds, neither of them blinking, as if the confrontation was a direct test of wills that neither was willing to concede.

"You could have killed me already. You could have left me to die," Bannon said at last. "You didn't."

"No, I didn't."

"Why?"

"Because I'm trusting you to put your wife's happiness above everything else – and out of consideration for Maddie. She still cares about you. She just doesn't love you anymore."

"That's very noble of you."

Sully's eyes darkened and his expression turned nasty. "So far I haven't needed to kill you for my own survival," he said bluntly. "But if I ever do – I will."

Bannon was unflinching. He stared hard into Sully's virulent eyes, measuring the man with frank appraisal. He put his hands on his hips. "Since we're having this little heart-to-heart, there's something I want to know," he said.

"Yeah? Make it quick." Sully narrowed his gaze and stared unmoving for a moment back towards the burning buildings, like a hunting dog distracted by the first hint of scent. The dawn's light was coming on quickly. He could see the shapes of individual buildings, and make out the bodies of the two undead laying in the park. Gulls were picking at the remains. Bannon waited until the alert tension had gone from the other man's posture.

"I want to know why you waited," Bannon's voice had an edge of challenge to it. "Why didn't you come back to town last night after the chopper picked me up, and make a run for it with Maddie."

"How? On the boat?"

Bannon nodded. "You could have tried clearing the harbor."

Sully nodded slowly. "Yeah, I could have," he said, "and I thought about it."

"But?"

Sully shook his head. "Too dangerous in the dark."

Bannon nodded. He accepted the risk of trying to navigate the wreckage-strewn harbor at night would be monumentally dangerous. "Then why not try in daylight. Why didn't you take your chances yesterday morning, before the helicopter came?"

Sully's lips peeled back into a humorless smile that showed his teeth. His expression was fixed and frozen.

"The marina looks like a mini Pearl Harbor after the Japanese attacked," he said darkly. "Half the boats moored along the jetties have sunk, or burned down to the waterline... and a couple of yachts were drifting. I thought they might get drawn out through the heads with the tide, but they didn't. They wrecked on the break wall." Sully glanced away, galled and frustrated. "If I had tried to get out of the harbor, I would have ripped the bottom out of the boat."

The two men were silent for several seconds. Bannon watched the pale light of the approaching day begin to spread across the rim of the world. "The army will come back for you, Sully. You know that, don't you?" he changed the subject suddenly.

Sully said nothing and Bannon went on relentlessly, filling the strained silence with his hushed voice. "This won't be the end of it. If you don't board that helicopter when it returns, the military will just send another team, and another after that. They won't give up. You're too important. You might contain the key to curing this hideous infection." He sighed. "There are just too many lives at risk for them to let you get away."

Sully looked unflustered. "They'll never find me," he said confidently, and then turned to face the ruined town that spread out below where they stood. "Take a look around," he gestured. "The whole population is undead. How would they ever find me?" He shook his head.

Bannon thought about that. Sully had a point. He could move freely, maybe even make it cross country, further down the coast to one of the other towns that had been overcome with the infection. It would be like trying to find a needle in a haystack.

Chapter 13.

The slope down to the marina was rocky. Bannon scrabbled to the water's edge and stared for long seconds. There were tufts of long grass growing between the rocks. He crouched behind cover and Sully dropped onto his haunches beside him.

The complex of buildings that fringed the harbor was completely destroyed. The shops and restaurants had all burned to the ground, a mess of black charred rubble. Smoke still rose in lazy tendrils, and some of the debris had been hurled into the water. To his right, he saw the long rocky arm of the break wall, reaching out into the ocean. The line of huge quarry boulders that formed the wall was distorted by the wreckage of two sail boats. The first one had been driven bow-first into the rocks. The hull of the boat had been chewed open as the ebb and flow of tides had ground the vessel further onto the jagged teeth of the wall. She lay askew, across the channel, listing to one side so the high mast pointed skyward at an accusing angle. Gulls and crows perched in the tangled wreckage of rigging.

The second boat was nothing more than a lighter ethereal shade within the deep murky water. She had sunk stern-first, so that only the tip of her bow and mast still showed. There was a litter of wreckage – lifejackets, plastic buckets, sails and rope – bobbing on the surface.

Directly across the harbor, Bannon could see the three jetties, pointing like fingers into the calm water of the marina. Pleasure boaters had used the closest concrete jetty. There were several small sailboats and a couple of luxury yachts normally moored.

Now there was just black charred chaos.

Several of the smaller boats had sunk. One of the luxury yachts had burned to the waterline so that just the black ribs of her hull structure showed, like the ravaged carcass of some great animal. Bannon shifted his gaze.

The second marina jetty was the largest, and widest. It was the dock used by the commercial fishing fleet that still operated out of Grey Stone. Bannon saw *'Mandrake'* moored in deep water and apparently undamaged, and closer to the shoreline, a trawler. The trawler's superstructure had been burned so that the boat looked like a featureless hulk, and there were black charred streaks down the side of the once-white hull.

Game fishermen had used the furthest jetty. The boats there were sleek, luxury cabin cruisers with graceful flowing lines and high flying bridges. Many of the boats were gone from their moorings, but Bannon barely noticed. Suddenly all his attention was on the twenty-foot half-cabin cruiser at the deep end of the dock.

Sully's boat.

She nudged placidly at her moorings, the boat's bow bobbing listlessly with the ripples of the incoming tide. Bannon gave the boat his full attention.

She was white, with generous lines along her hull. There were two Perspex windows facing him, like close-set eyes, and fitted above the windshield was a blue canvas tarp. Bannon stared hard for long seconds, then turned to Sully.

"What's your plan?"

Sully shrugged. "You swim across the marina to the last jetty," he said. "I'll be there waiting for you."

"What if the zombies see me?"

"You'll be safe in the water," Sully said. "They don't like it."

Bannon looked thoughtful. It was about a hundred yard swim to the jetty where Sully's boat was tied. That was no problem for him. He had been in and around the ocean all his life. He knew he could comfortably cover the distance. "What about you?"

"I'll meet you at the end of the dock."

"You're not swimming across?"

Sully shook his head, and seemed uncomfortable at the suggestion. "No," he said bluntly, and then sniffed. "I'll go back around along the waterfront."

Bannon became wary. "I thought you were scared about getting another bite – further infection."

"I am," admitted Sully. "But as long as I just mingle and don't provoke them, or get in the way of something the zombies are hunting, they pay me no attention. It's like I don't exist."

Bannon smiled cynically. "You mean it's like you're one of them, right?"

Sully said nothing, but his eyes glowed with a sudden flare of anger. His lip curled into a snarl. He got wordlessly to his feet and glanced into the dawn sky. "Don't take too long," he made the words sound like some kind of an ominous threat. "You don't want to miss your helicopter ride back out of here." He turned and walked away, wandering towards the burned out buildings of the marina complex, leaving Bannon all alone...

... and suddenly feeling exposed and vulnerable.

Chapter 14.

Bannon stared down into the water of the marina, and shuddered. The surface was slick, rainbowed with stains of spilled fuel, and littered with floating wreckage. He could see burned timbers and the debris from sunken boats bobbing on the tide.

And bodies.

Corpses – their flesh pecked from their bodies – drifted with the current. They were bloated, sun-blackened, hideous lumps. Some of the bodies were clothed, others floated naked and were made obscene by their gruesome wounds.

Bannon kicked off his boots, and then peeled off his shirt. He put the Beretta inside one boot and then wrapped everything into a tight bundle. There was a rock a few feet to his left – one of the quarry boulders from the break wall. It was a peculiar light grey color. He stuffed the wad of possessions behind the rock and went bare-chested to the water's edge. He wedged the tightly-wrapped emergency beacon down the front of his jeans and checked his wristwatch. He was running out of time. He eased himself into the murky water like he was lowering himself into a scalding hot bath and sank slowly down to his chin without making a splash.

Below the surface, the rocky break wall was thick with moss and slime. Bannon pushed himself off with his feet and began to swim in a kind of breast-stroke... careful to keep his arms, hands and feet below the surface... and even more careful to keep his chin and mouth above the surface.

242

The murky water smelled like rancid effluent, thick and greasy so that Bannon felt the wretched odor of it like a coating of slime on his skin and on the back of his tongue. He kept his mouth closed, breathing slowly through his nose, and began to draw his way out into the deeper water, casting a wake of low ripples behind him.

On the distant shoreline, he could see figures moving. They drifted into and out of sight with no apparent purpose – the undead meandering through the carnage of the destroyed buildings, pausing like vultures to pick at the ruins in search of anyone who might have survived.

None of them seemed to notice him.

Near the first jetty Bannon suddenly felt something beneath the surface of the water brush against his left leg. His heart stopped beating. His eyes went wide. He felt a surge of pulsing dread.

He suddenly wondered if the drifting bodies that bobbed like lumps of wood had attracted sharks. An unbidden image of sleek grey predators hunting through the murky depths came to him, his imagination so real that he felt himself cringe and tuck his legs up tight against his torso. There hadn't been a shark sighting in local waters for decades... but then there hadn't been a harbor full of decomposing dead bodies to lure them before now either.

Just as he felt himself begin to panic, Bannon's other leg brushed against the same obstruction. It wasn't a shark. It was hard... and it wasn't moving. He prodded at it carefully, mindful of the dangers of getting tangled in debris. He thought he felt something like maybe a yacht's mast, or perhaps a spar. Carefully he trod water, and edged himself away from the obstruction. When he felt he was clear, he stretched out again, and stroked towards the barnacle-encrusted piers that underpinned the closest jetty. He was breathing hard. He could feel the burn of tired muscles in his chest and across his shoulders. He slinked into the shadowy gloom underneath the pier and reached out for a dangling jetty rope to support himself.

The severed head of a woman bobbed up in the water, floating like a cork close beside where he rested. The face was bloodless, the waxen skin pale and bleached as marble. The eyeballs were missing so that Bannon stared into two gaping dark holes. The lips had been nibbled from the face, and part of the nose was missing. There was a bullet hole in the side of the head. A school of small fish darted in the water around the decapitated head, worrying the soft flesh. The head turned over slowly and then drifted past him, out into the soft light. Bannon shuddered and pushed himself away from the pier.

Bannon guessed it was only about thirty yards to the main marina pier where the 'Mandrake' sat gently tugging at her mooring lines. He fixed his gaze on the squat shape of the big fishing boat and tried to work through the water with purposeful rhythm. A couple of gulls were perched on the bow of the boat, and a dozen more of the scavenger birds were squawking and bickering in the air above the main deck. As Bannon swam closer, he suddenly realized why.

The stench of rotting fish was withering – a reek so fierce that Bannon's eyes watered. The air seemed thick and cloying. He reached the broad stern of the long-liner and clung to one of the fender tires that had been hung from the side of the pier to protect the hull of the docking boats.

Mandrake's' hold was filled with thousands of tons of rotting fish. Bannon had ordered the hatches opened before they had sailed into Grey Stone, ready for a quick unload into the fishery's refrigeration rooms. Now that cargo had spent a full day spoiling in the warm sun. The air was filled with a cloud of swarming, crawling metallic green flies.

He hung in the shadows of the fishing boat's hull, floating in diesel fuel and filthy water for a full minute. He could hear movement along the pier, but it was indistinct – a fusion of muted sounds that could have been the swarming flies, or perhaps the struggled awkward gait of a zombie. He hesitated. If one of the undead was on the jetty, they would surely hear his soft splashes in the water as he swam away. He counted slowly to ten, knowing that every second was precious. The noise seemed to rise and fall, sometimes sounding right overhead, and other times fading so as to be almost indiscernible.

"Fuck it," he thought to himself at last. His lips were quivering. He had been in the frigid water for several minutes. His fingers and toes felt numb. He couldn't waste a single second more.

He hung in the water and began to pump his lungs with air like a bellows, cleansing them of carbon dioxide. When he felt himself on the verge of hyperventilation he took one last long breath and then duck dived below the surface, striking out with great kicks of his feet, and clawing through the water with his hands.

His vision was distorted, and his eyes began to burn. Dark jagged shapes loomed menacingly out of the distance. The water around him swirled and billowed with clouds of sediment.

He swam trickling air from his nose like a miser, until his chest felt like it was on fire and his lungs began to pump convulsively. He felt a sense of disorientation begin to creep over him, a dizzy vertigo that turned his arms and legs to slow lethargic lead.

When Bannon finally knew he could swim no further, he dashed desperately for the surface like a submarine that had blown its main ballast tank.

His head and shoulders crashed through the water, and he gulped and gasped for air. His lungs heaved, his breath gagged in the back of his throat, and his mouth filled with putrid water. He retched pitifully.

The undead heard him.

There were two ghouls standing on the jetty where *'Mandrake'* had been moored. One of them looked up. Bannon glanced over his shoulder. Sully's boat was just twenty yards away.

The ghoul stared at Bannon with some kind of fascination for long seconds, tilting its head from side to side curiously. It came to the edge of the jetty and peered down into the water, then shuffled away warily. The zombie turned its gaze back to Bannon – and it snarled.

Chapter 15.

Bannon hung in the water for thirty precious seconds, re-filling his aching lungs with putrid air, and then he dived one last time, back beneath the filthy surface of the harbor.

He swam towards the last jetty, fighting against the gentle relentless push of the tide, and when he saw the white bloated shapes of boat bottoms suddenly loom out of the murky haze, he paused for an instant to get his bearings. His vision was horribly distorted and his eyes stung. He saw the dark pier posts of the jetty, standing like ghostly silent sentinels, and he kicked off again, following the murky stilts until there were no more.

He was running out of air. He felt his lungs pump but he fought against the urge to rise immediately. He could see the bobbing keel of Sully's boat, almost directly above him, and he could see pale light refracting off the water's surface, glinting and glittering into a thousand tiny shards with the first touches of sunlight.

Bannon let the last of his air spill from the corner of his mouth as he rose slowly. Detail became clearer. The light became brighter. He could see the end of the jetty, the wavering shape of bowlines, and the steps of an iron ladder attached to one of the piers that sunk down into the depths. He swam towards it and grasped at the rusted rungs, pulling himself upwards until his head eased above the bobbing surface and at last he could breathe again.

He gasped.

He was clinging to the rungs of a ladder at the end of the game fishing jetty. Looking back towards the foreshore he could see three or four big sleek cruisers, desolate and left abandoned. He went up the ladder slowly.

As his head rose to the level of the jetty, Bannon paused and swung his eyes warily across the concrete wharf. The entire length of the dock seemed to be littered with abandoned debris. He could see tangled lengths of rope, suitcases and clothes, boxes and bodies.

And he could see Sully.

The man was standing ten feet away, waiting cautiously beside the boat tied at the end of the dock.

His boat.

The boat where Maddie was hiding.

Bannon came up the ladder and heaved himself onto the concrete. He was shaking, his breathing ragged. He felt the chill of the frigid water deep within his bones. He blinked water from his eyes.

There was a wall of wooden boxes and plastic crates of rubbish behind Sully so that part of his cruiser was obscured. Bannon frowned. It was as if a large dumpster had been upended at the end of the dock. Sully pressed an urgent finger to the blackened rotting flesh of his lips, imploring Bannon to silence. He gestured back towards the shoreline.

"Trouble," he whispered hoarsely. "I can sense them."

"Where?" Bannon muttered.

Sully shrugged, like the instinct was like some vague nagging premonition that persisted. He studied Bannon.

"You made it," Sully said, sounding just a little disappointed.

Bannon said nothing. He was staring at the reeking mess of rotting garbage and stacks of assorted debris behind where Sully stood.

"It was the best I could do to hide Maddie," Sully grunted, sensing Bannon's question, and explaining the high barricade in a hoarse guarded voice. "I figured it would cut down the chances of the zombies seeing the boat and getting curious."

Bannon nodded. He was shivering, his lips pale and bloodless, teeth chattering, and his hands and feet numbed from the cold water. Suddenly his stomach gripped into a vicious cramp of pain, and then he folded at the waist and retched explosively into the putrid slopping water of the marina.

Chapter 16.

Sully's gaze snapped towards the waterfront and he glared for long seconds. His eyes seemed to be searching the ruins of the marina complex. He cocked his head, and then his expression became grim and vindictive.

"They heard you," he snarled. "They fucking heard you."

Bannon straightened unsteadily. He scraped the back of his hand across his mouth and then spat. He lifted his eyes to the end of the dock and saw movement – undead gathering.

A small group of blood-drenched rocking shapes stood at the far end of the jetty. Bannon looked for an escape.

"How many?" Sully barked. He was casting about him wildly, looking for a makeshift weapon.

"Four," Bannon choked. He felt his stomach heave again and he vomited over his feet, purging the last of the stinking seawater from his guts.

He felt shaky, but better. He took a deep breath.

"Untie the boat," Bannon said.

"What?"

"Untie the boat!" Bannon barked. "We need to get off this dock."

Sully understood. He crashed through the barrier he had built, scattering the refuse and debris like a battering ram. He crouched over the stern line. Bannon cast off the bow line. Bannon leaped aboard the boat and Sully bunched the muscles in his broad shoulders and gave a mighty heave. The boat began to drift away from the end of the pier. Bannon thumped the engine start button and the twin outboards gurgled throatily. Sully took a running leap and landed in the cockpit, just as the undead came rushing along the pier.

One of the ghouls hurled itself off the lip of the jetty, enraged and maddened by the insanity of its infection. It had once been a young man, but his death had not been kind. The ghoul had only one arm, the other limb just a ragged tattered stump of flesh that hung from its shoulder. It leaped across the widening gap and crashed into the stern of Sully's boat. Gnarled bloodied fingers clawed at the transom, as the zombie's thrashing body dangled in the water. Bannon gunned the big outboards. The water around the stern of the boat erupted into a white roaring froth as the big propellers tore the silence apart, sucking the shrieking ghoul into their wash. The zombie was shredded between the spinning blades, its decomposing body minced, the infected oozing entrails sprayed across the scummy water.

Bannon conned the boat out into the deep water of the marina and then let the outboards idle. Sully went forward and dropped the anchor. The cruiser drifted with forward momentum for a moment then pulled up tight against the heavy chain, swinging her stern around as the hull responded to the tug of the tide like a weather vane in gentle breeze.

Bannon stared back towards the game fishing pier. More of the undead had gathered, standing precipitously on the edge of the jetty as if it were a cliff face. They snarled and hissed in futile madness.

"We're safe... for now," Bannon said grimly.

Sully said nothing. He came down off the bow and dropped easily into the wide, open cockpit area.

Sully looked dour. "Yeah, for now," he grunted like he was pronouncing a delayed death sentence. "But not for long. We can't just anchor here in the harbor, and we can't get out through the channel. I already told you that. There's too much wreckage. I'll rip the guts out of her. And sooner or later, the last of the food and water is going to run out. Then what, hero?"

Bannon smiled thinly. An idea was forming in the back of his mind. "You're going to need a bigger boat," he said.

Chapter 17.

Bannon stole a fretful glance at his wristwatch and then at the sky. The first rays of morning light were stretching across the ocean. He was running out of time. He turned on Sully, his voice pitched low but thick with menace.

"Where's my wife?"

Sully ducked down below the canvas cockpit tarp. There was a narrow wooden cabin door set beside the boat's wheel and controls. The door was double latched and double locked. Sully took a set of keys from a compartment and unlocked the door.

Sully paused, then glanced back over his shoulder, eyes smoldering in a glare that seemed a compound of triumph and trepidation. Steve Bannon was holding his breath.

The cabin door swung open slowly...

Chapter 18.

Sully shuffled back and a woman's face became framed in the narrow doorway. Her hair was a blonde tangle, her face drawn as though she were racked with appalling tension. Her eyes were blue and haunted – and the traces of her ordeal were a dark smudge the color of bruises below her eyes.

She saw Sully and her expression became one of overwhelming relief. The woman threw herself into the man's arms, hugging him fiercely. She buried her face in Sully's shoulder, and began to sob. Her body shook, her hands trembled. She clawed at him with her fingers as though to convince herself he was real.

"I was so worried," Madeline Bannon sniffed against his chest. She pulled away suddenly, and studied the man closely, her face torn with sudden confusion. "I thought you weren't coming back."

"I got held up," Sully said in an understatement. "I spent the night running from the undead... with your husband."

Maddie Bannon flinched, and then, at last, realized that there was someone else on the boat – someone standing in the open cockpit. She untangled herself from Sully, suddenly self-conscious and flustered. Bannon stood, staring at her, his facial features carefully composed, but with deep hurt stinging in his eyes. Maddie pressed at her hair and made a fluttering gesture with her hands to straighten the clothes she was wearing.

"What are you doing here?" her voice was dead and flat.

"He came for you," Sully intercepted the question. "The rescue team – the whole broadcast – was a sham, Maddie. They weren't coming to rescue us. They came here to snatch me. They wanted to take me to some fucking lab and cut me open. They think I have some cure for the virus running through my blood. Your husband came with them to identify me to the goon squad."

There was a long silence. Maddie's expression slowly altered as she assembled and understood Sully's words. Finally she stared hard at her husband in a gesture of defiance.

"Is that true?" her face became pinched.

Bannon shook his head.

"I came for you, Maddie," Bannon snapped. "I came back here to find you. I didn't know it was a set-up until we were hovering over Grey Stone. I agreed to identify Sully to the soldiers in exchange for them including you in the rescue."

Suddenly Maddie lashed out at Bannon, lunging forward to strike him flat-handed across the cheek. His lower lip ground against his teeth and the warm coppery taste of his own blood filled his mouth. Bannon glared at Maddie for a long silent moment of shock, and then his eyes turned stone cold. He smeared away the blood with the back of his hand.

"Leave us alone, Steve," Maddie's voice was low with her resentment. "I don't love you – and I haven't for a very long time. I'm with John now… and I've been happy." There was a barb of spite in her voice, and a twist of cruelty in his wife's expression that Bannon had never seen before.

He glared at her. "Maddie, I risked my life to rescue you."

"Well you shouldn't have." There were tiny crows feet lines at the corners of her mouth and eyes. She thrust a finger at him suddenly. "It's been over between us for a long time, Steve. You knew it and I knew it, so don't pretend to be that caring husband now. It's too late. You had your chance... all those years I waited around for you while you were out catching fucking fish!" Maddie closed her eyes and shook her head like she was reliving a bitter dream. Her cutting words trailed off.

Bannon nodded his head. "Fine," he said stiffly. He straightened his back. "If you want the marriage over, that's fine with me – the marriage is over. But the fact remains that you're still in danger, Madeline. Lying cheating heartless bitch or not – you're still a human being," his lip curled up in distaste, "and staying here puts you at great risk."

She raised a mocking eyebrow. "Staying here...? Do you mean staying with John?"

Bannon said nothing. He didn't need to. Maddie read the meaning in his cold silence.

She propped a hand on her waist and shifted her weight, her stance aggressive. "I might be at risk staying with John, but I don't care!" her voice became suddenly strident with her passion. "For the first time in a long time I feel alive. John makes me feel that way – something I hadn't felt in your bed for a very long time. So, yeah – my life might be in danger... but at least I'll feel alive right up until the moment I die." Maddie was breathing hard, her panted breath making her shoulders shift beneath the fabric of her blouse. She looked away for a moment to stare back at the edge of the jetty where the undead ghouls cried out and howled in maddened frustration, then turned her eyes slowly back to Bannon. All her anger seemed spent. Her voice was suddenly soft, almost weary.

"This is the way I want it," she said with finality. "I want to stay with John. What we had – you and me – that's over, Steve. And it's been over for so long that I don't care about you anymore."

Chapter 19.

Bannon glanced again at his wristwatch. Daylight was just about to break across the horizon. He glared at Maddie and then swung his eyes onto Sully. The big man's face was gloating so that his features seemed somehow coarsened into stark sharpness. Bannon's mouth tightened.

Sully's infected blazing gaze seemed alight with his triumph. "Satisfied?" the man goaded.

Bannon nodded curtly, but there was turmoil behind his eyes. He took a deep breath, felt his hands bunch into bony fists and then slowly relax again.

"I know how you can get out of Grey Stone," he said to Sully. "I know how you can escape the pursuit of the army."

Sully narrowed his eyes suspiciously. "How... and why?" he interrupted.

Bannon shot him a withering glare. "You can use *'Mandrake',*" he said. "She's big enough and solid enough to bustle her way through the boats wrecked along the channel wall. And she's still got fuel. Not enough to get you to the far side of the world, but enough to get you the hell away from here."

Sully shook his head. "I can't – not on my own."

"I'll help you," Bannon said. "Once the boat is clear of the dock and running out through the heads, I'll jump overboard and swim for the break wall. Hopefully I'll make it to the landing zone in time. And hopefully the helicopter will be there waiting to pick me up."

"And the wreckage?" Sully went on with selfish concern. "It's not just those yachts in the channel – the whole marina is littered with sunken and burned out boats."

"I just swam it," Bannon said frostily. "Remember? I just swam all the way across the marina. Apart from the boats close to the waterfront that went down at their moorings, there's nothing big enough to damage *Mandrake*. She'll get you out into open water." He paused, choosing his next words deliberately. "You'll be free," he said. "The army will never find you."

Bannon saw Sully's eyes come sparkling alight.

"Why?" Sully edged closer. Bannon saw Maddie's eyes harden with her own interest.

"Yes. Why?" she repeated. She folded her arms across her chest and her expression was severe with mistrust.

"Because I want something in exchange."

"What?" Sully asked.

"I want five minutes alone with Maddie," Bannon said. "That's the deal. I'll help you get *Mandrake* free from her moorings and running out through the channel. But I want to talk to Maddie first – alone."

"Why?" Maddie frowned.

"Because I want one last chance to convince you to come with me."

Sully and Maddie exchanged glances. Some silent message passed between them. A cold little smile of defiance tugged at the harsh lines of Maddie's mouth. "It will be a waste of your time."

"That's okay," Bannon said, shaking his head and smiling thinly. "It's my time to waste. You've got nowhere else you can go. I have a helicopter waiting for me. It's your choice. If you want my help escaping Grey Stone, you have to hear me out. Decide now."

Chapter 20.

They ducked into the narrow cabin at the bow of the boat and Bannon pulled the little door closed behind him. There was a crawl space in the floor between two V-shaped bunks. Bannon stared down into it.

"That's where you've been hiding?" Bannon looked down into the dark horrid little hole. "It's like a coffin."

Maddie ignored the question. She said nothing for a long moment. It was like she was keeping her composure on a tight leash. She smiled at Bannon, baring her teeth, her expression brittle.

"What do you want?" Maddie curled up like a cat, her eyes slanted and feline. She was impatient. There was hardness in her voice and tension in the way she was poised.

Bannon took a deep breath and clamped his hands together. He looked down at his bare feet for a moment, and then into his wife's cold eyes.

"Did you ever love me?"

There was a perspex hatch in the cabin roof. Maddie cracked it open and rummaged through the tangled bedding for a cigarette. The packet was crumpled. She shook the box. There were only a few cigarettes left. She lit one and a tendril of blue smoke crawled up her face. She winced, blinked her eyes, then blew a long feather of smoke at the low cabin ceiling.

Maddie thought hard. For a moment her features became severe, and then softened, just a little. "Once," she said. "A very long time ago."

Bannon stared at his wife. "Until...?"

"Until I realized that you loved fishing more than you loved me."

Bannon looked incredulous. "Sully is a fisherman too!"

Maddie shook her head. "It's not the same," she sparked. "You lived to work. John worked to live. For you, fishing was everything. John is different. Fishing is just his job."

"I worked for our future," Bannon's jaw became set and his lips pressed into a thin bloodless line. "I worked to give you all the things you wanted – the unit, the furniture, the jewelry..."

She laughed then, a cruel, spiteful chortle. "And look where it got us!" she threw her hands in the air. "All that working and saving for a rainy day... well it's pouring right now, Steve. It's fucking pouring with rain, and all that work for our future has been wasted – because suddenly there *isn't* a future. Not for us – not for anyone. Life is measured in moments, not promises. That's why I had an affair with John," she snapped brutally, "and that's why I'm staying with him now. For the moments – the ones we still have remaining until the inevitable."

Bannon shook his head. "We can still have a future – even if it's not together. This virus hasn't spread any further than a few towns along the coast," he explained. "You can come with me. There is a helicopter flying back to pick me up at 6am. Come with me now. You'll be safe. You can start again on your own. The world is going on, Maddie. Beyond this town, life still goes on."

She shook her head. "I don't want the life I had – not the life with you. I don't want to survive anymore. I want to feel alive. I know I should be racked with terrible guilt for cheating on you with John... but I'm not," she said maliciously, as though the matter was trivial to her. "I just don't feel guilty. I stopped caring for you, Steve... and then I stopped caring *about* you."

Maddie paused to draw deeply on the cigarette and then exhaled in a long harsh breath." Every night you were home from sea I would lie in bed and count the hours until you were gone again. And then I would pray that you didn't pick Sully for that trip's crew, so I could be with him. I got to the stage where I hated you – where everything you did and everything about you repulsed me. It's how I feel now."

"Your mind is made up?" he tried one last time, merely to clear his conscience.

"My mind is made up," Maddie repeated. "I never want to see you again. Just leave John and me together. Go back to civilization and forget me. I'm already well on my way to forgetting you."

Bannon stood up. He was hurt, but not shocked – not completely. He had known there had been difficulties in the marriage, but he hadn't known the problems had been so irreconcilable that Maddie had turned to adultery and betrayal. He looked at his wife now, and saw a totally different woman – one he didn't recognize. A cruel, selfish woman he didn't like.

You reap what you sow.

It made his next decision easier.

Chapter 21.

"Here, take this," Bannon said as he came from the boat's cabin. He had the emergency military rescue beacon in his hands, unwrapping it from the protective layers of plastic. He passed the small black box to Sully, carefully controlling the pantomime of his expression.

"What is it?" Sully asked warily. He recalled Bannon's evasiveness when he had asked about the box the night before.

Bannon sighed. He took one final glance at Maddie. She had her arm around Sully's waist, and the final lingering tendrils of Bannon's doubts faded from his conscience.

"The army thinks it's a cure," Bannon lied smoothly. "They think the electronic waves that this box generates can fight the spread of the zombie virus."

Sully gaped. Maddie's face was frozen in shock.

"Serious?" Maddie asked.

Bannon nodded. "I brought it with me for you," he said. "I thought you might have been bitten, or if you got bitten I could set this device to fight the spread of the infection before it overtook you."

Sully narrowed his eyes and stared down at the innocuous little box. "Why didn't you use it on the soldier – the one who died last night?"

Bannon shrugged. "No time," he lied smoothly. "It has to be set up – activated. It wasn't. Paul was infected before I had time to program it. Remember when he came back up the stairs, he had already been infected."

"Program it? Sully's mind picked up on a critical word and he focused on it as though the death of the special forces soldier had been forgotten in the blink of an eye. "How?" Sully saw the keypad. "With this?"

Bannon nodded. "It has a three digit password. That starts the regenerative frequency. If it's running, and the victim keeps it with them – I mean close to them – the process begins to fight the virus almost immediately."

Maddie looked at the box like it was wondrous. She took it from Sully's hand and turned it over, inspecting it closely. Sully stared Bannon in the eye.

"Why?"

"Why what?"

"Why give it to me?"

Bannon shrugged. He was no actor. The temptation to reach across and tear Sully's throat out was like a blazing itch of vindictive temptation. He forced his face into something like weary submission.

"I still care for Maddie," the untruth almost scalded his tongue. "But she doesn't want to be with me. She wants to be with you. She just told me that." Bannon's eyes hardened. He squared his shoulders. "I think you're a piece of fucking shit – a lying, devious back-stabbing prick... but I'm putting Maddie's welfare above how I feel for you. If she is going to survive, she can't stay here in Grey Stone. Like you said last night, you can hide here and the army will never find you amongst the swarms of undead... but Maddie will end up getting bitten. You won't be able to prevent it."

"So?"

"So she needs to get out of here, and she won't come with me. She'd rather die with you than fly back in the helicopter and give you up." Bannon shrugged. "What choice do I have? You need to be around to keep her safe – and you need to get out of Grey Stone if she is going to survive the virus."

Sully and Maddie looked at each other with beaming smiles of hope. Sully had one more question – one more suspicion.

"Ever since you arrived in that helicopter you have wanted to take me back so the army could cut me open. You said you couldn't let me go – there were millions of lives at risk. Now, suddenly, none of that matters?"

Bannon conceded the point, acting like his decision weighed heavily on his conscience. "It matters," he said. "But I realized last night that if the army gave me this box as a cure for Maddie, then they obviously have more of them. I thought you were the only chance to save countless lives. Clearly," he pointed down at the box, "I was wrong. They have other cures they're working on."

"What's the code?" Maddie asked impulsively. "How long will it be before John starts to feel better?"

"I'll tell you the code when we're aboard *'Mandrake'*," Bannon said firmly. "The army told me the effects would start to show within thirty minutes."

"Thank you," Maddie said sincerely.

"Don't thank me," Bannon said. "You're a human being. But, Maddie, ... as a *person*, you're a lying filthy whore who would rather spread her legs than work through her marriage problems, and Sully here, is a fucking snake that should be killed for his betrayal. You two pieces of shit deserve each other."

Chapter 22.

Bannon stood in the boat's cockpit and stared across the harbor to where *Mandrake'* lay moored along the main pier of the marina. Sully was beside him, the big man's attention fixed on the distant waterfront.

"We have no weapons," Bannon said.

Sully shook his head somberly.

"I don't even have the soldier's handgun," Bannon lamented. "I left it under one of the break wall rocks."

The two men lapsed into brooding silence. *Mandrake'* was at the end of the main wharf – maybe forty or fifty feet away from where they were anchored. There was a small cluster of undead at the end of the game fishing pier, still howling at them, the zombie's snarling voices carrying clearly across the water. Bannon frowned and tried to make calculations.

"How long do you think each wharf is?" he asked Sully.

The big man grunted, then shrugged his shoulders. "Maybe a hundred feet from the waterfront out into the harbor."

Bannon nodded. His guess had been similar. "And how far between each pier?"

"Maybe another forty feet."

Bannon rubbed his chin. "So those zombies will need to cover a hundred feet back to the waterfront, then forty feet to the main pier... and then another forty or fifty feet to reach the bow of *Mandrake'.*

Sully nodded. "That's not far. It doesn't give us any time."

Bannon made a wry face and then shook his head. "It gives us time…" he countered. "It just doesn't give us time for any mistakes."

"You got a plan?"

Bannon turned and stared into Sully's grey sunken face. "No," he said. "We just have to race in and get aboard as quickly as possible. I'll get the diesels running – you'll have to cast off the bow and stern lines. Once we're away from the jetty, we'll be safe. As soon as you clear the lines, I'll con *Mandrake'* out into deeper water."

Sully frowned. "The lines – they're going to take some time."

"Cut them," Bannon shrugged. "The panga is still in my cabin."

Maddie had been listening intently. She had her lip trapped between her teeth and her expression was fraught. "What's a panga?" she interrupted.

Bannon glanced over his shoulder at her. She was sitting in the swivel seat near the boat's steering wheel. She had one long brown leg slung over the armrest, lolling indolently.

"It's like a machete," Bannon said. "A crude blade, about eighteen inches long. We use it on fish sometimes."

Maddie frowned. "I thought you were supposed to be out catching fish, not hacking them into little pieces."

Bannon could barely be bothered with the woman. Suddenly she was like an obnoxious stranger to him. "Some fish we don't want," he said vaguely, then turned his back on her.

Bannon suspected one or two of the undead wailing at them from the end of the game fishing jetty had drifted away. He glanced at his wristwatch again and his expression became grim.

"It's now or never," he sighed.

Sully hauled up the boat's anchor and then leaped down into the cockpit and gunned the twin outboards. The little boat lunged forward. He swung her bow in a shallow arc and then lined up for the stern of *Mandrake*. Over the throaty roar of the engines Bannon could hear the undead become agitated. It was as if the sound of the motors was a gnawing torment to them. He clung on to a stainless steel handrail and the speedboat skipped across the calm oily surface, bearing down on the broad black hull of the long-line fishing boat at incredible speed.

At the last possible moment, Sully cut the engines. The boat's bow dropped down in the water, the speed and grace gone from her. She wallowed, still drifting towards *Mandrake*, carried on by her forward momentum. Sully spun the wheel hard and the boat crunched into the side of *Mandrake*.

Bannon was standing ready in the cockpit. The two vessels came together with a terrible rending grind of wood and aluminum – the impact jarring him off balance. He steadied himself and leaped for the side of the big fishing boat, using the stern scuppers as a foothold. He went over *Mandrake's* gunwale and landed heavily on the boat's stern deck. Sully was a few seconds behind him. Bannon didn't wait. He ran at a crouch past the big open hatches, and the tangle of lines and winch equipment. The fiberglass deck was slippery and streaked with slime. A swarm of flies took to irritated flight, buzzing around the reeking rotting catch still in the hold. Bannon swatted at the air until he crashed through the open doorway into the dark gloomy spaces of the *'Mandrake's'* superstructure.

The big diesel engines kicked to life. Bannon threw back his head with a sigh of relief. He heard Sully scrabbling around in the captain's cabin.

"Hurry up!" Bannon shouted. He peered hard through the boat's windshield. The pier was littered with debris, and much of his view of the waterfront was obscured by the smoldering ruins of the trawler, moored to the jetty in front of him. He thought he heard an undulation of sound – a moaning rise and fall of clamoring voices.

"For fuck's sake, hurry up!" he cried again.

He fiddled with the controls – settled the engines until they were throbbing. He saw a flash of movement, and then saw legs pass in front of his view. It was Sully. The big man was scampering over the forward deck, holding the brutal blade of the panga low by his side.

The mooring ropes were as thick as a woman's wrist. Sully chopped hard at the bow line and it severed neatly. Bannon felt the nose of the big fishing boat begin to inch away from the jetty. Sully turned and ran towards the stern.

Bannon waited impatiently, counting down from ten in his mind. It would take Sully that long to reach the stern of the boat and sever the line. When he reached zero, Bannon threw the lever control into reverse, and *'Mandrake's'* big engines began to claw her backwards.

The fishing boat's hull shook and shuddered in protest. The whole vessel seemed to come alive under Bannon's feet, trembling and tremoring so that he thought she might break apart. He saw the stern of the burned out trawler inch away from him – and then the pylons of the main peer began to slide past.

Bannon waited as long as he could. He could hear cries of rage now, carrying down the length of the jetty and he knew the undead must be rushing along the concrete pier. He left the controls and burst out onto the stern deck. At the side of the boat he could see Sully, heaving Maddie aboard in his big muscled arms. Bannon ignored them. He clambered up the narrow flying bridge and lunged for the fishing boat's dual controls.

The undead were shambling along the pier. There were at least a dozen of them. They were drenched in blood and gore, hurling themselves forward on broken limbs and oozing stumps of rotted flesh. Bannon wrenched a last look over his shoulder – the fishing boat's blunted stern was just creeping out beyond the end of the pier. He toggled the controls and swung the boat around in a tight reverse turn.

'Mandrake' swished her stern, and the boat hung broadside to the end of the pier. They were barely clear of the wharf. Bannon pushed the throttle control forward, and the boat's propellers churned the water into white frothing wake. Her backward momentum halted – she hung motionless for a second in the lapping calm water... and then slowly began to nose her way forward, towards the distant rocks of the break wall and the harbor's deep-water channel.

Chapter 23.

Bannon swarmed down from the flying bridge and shouldered his way along the narrow passage, back to the fishing boat's wheelhouse controls. Maddie and Sully were standing in the small kitchen area waiting. Maddie was peering fretfully out through the starboard windows as the marina's main wharf slid slowly away behind them. Only then did she allow a sigh of relief.

Bannon took the wheel. He had conned the big fishing boat out through the heads of Grey Stone more times than he could remember. He eased the boat's speed up to four knots, and his touch at the controls was light and instinctive.

"Where's the regenerator device?" Bannon didn't actually know what to call the little black box. He couldn't call it what it really was.

Maddie had it. She thrust it into his hands.

Bannon took his eyes off the view through the fishing boat's broad windshield and programmed the three-digit code the special forces soldier had given him before the Black Hawk had lifted off.

Six, zero, two...

For an instant nothing happened. Bannon frowned. Then a pinprick of red LED light began to flash from one corner of the keypad panel. It was unimpressive.

"That's it?" Sully looked doubtful.

Bannon shrugged, nodded. "It's been programmed, and I've set the code," he said. Bannon didn't know how the emergency rescue beacon really worked. He had expected some kind of rhythmic pulse of sound...

He only hoped that every military radio along the coast and the army's defensive perimeter was picking up the distress message and taking action to respond.

"Keep it with you," Bannon urged Sully, his eyes steady and the conviction in his voice compelling. "It will only work if it's within a few feet of you."

Sully nodded. He set the emergency beacon on the saloon table and watched it.

"Thirty minutes," Bannon went on. "That's what the army doctor told me. "You should start to feel an improvement within half an hour."

Sully nodded. Maddie reached for the big man's hand and interlaced her fingers with his, gripping him tightly. She smiled up into his eyes. "We're going to make it, John," she said softly. "I just know it."

Bannon turned back to the wheel to cover the sudden withering blaze of contempt that crept into his eyes. The *Mandrake'* was on a straight line for the narrow channel, bordered by the two long arms of the break wall. Ahead, he could see the stern of the wrecked yacht skewed across the path. He nudged the big boat up to five knots, and then six.

He pointed out through the windshield glass.

"We're going to hit that first yacht near its stern," he spoke to Sully. "We'll take her on our port side. As we get close, I want you to call out the distances to me. Okay?"

Sully nodded.

"We can't do anything to avoid the other yacht – the submerged one. We're just going to ride right over her."

'Mandrake' was a big vessel with a high, blunted bow. As she drew nearer to the dark blue water of the channel, the stranded yacht was going to disappear from Bannon's view. Sully went out through a sliding wheelhouse door. There was a slight breeze coming off the ocean. He slitted his eyes and braced himself. Maddie wedged herself into one of the narrow saloon benches and clung to the edge of the table.

Bannon finessed the spoked wheel, shifting *'Mandrake'* in the water as he approached the channel marker and the beginning of the break wall. He saw the light grey rock where he had hidden his shirt, boots and the gun roll past the starboard windows, then turned all his attention to the hull of the stranded yacht that loomed directly ahead.

It disappeared under the bows of the fishing boat.

"Forty feet!" Sully called.

Bannon thrust out his jaw and gritted his teeth. He kept the bow of the boat lined up with a marker he had picked out near the far end of the break wall. Overhead gulls began to circle and wheel in the air above fishing the boat, their raucous cries filling the tense silence.

"Thirty feet!"

Sully's voice rose, becoming strained. Bannon saw Maddie fidget in her seat. Her face was drawn. She was gazing sightlessly at the little black box as though mesmerized by the tiny flash of red light.

"Fifteen feet!" Sully called. "You're going to hit her amidships."

Bannon touched the wheel. The bow of the boat swung a foot to port. He braced himself, spreading his legs and tightening his grip on the wheel.

"Ten feet!" Sully called. The big man grabbed for a handhold. Bannon touched the throttle control and the *Mandrake's* big engines roared out in response.

The big fishing boat crashed into the hull of the deserted yacht, hitting her near the sleek stern and shattering her timbers to splinters. The fragile structure collapsed before the weight and momentum of *Mandrake*, and was crushed down beneath the keel, smashed into floating debris that gurgled and churned in the big boat's frothing wake. Bannon heard the rending grind echo up through the *Mandrake's* keel, a mournful groan that was sickening. The sound dragged out for long agonized seconds – and then she was free.

Bannon allowed himself an instant of sighed relief.

"Coming up on the next one!" Sully barked. He had run forward to the bow of the fishing boat. He peered over the side, then turned back to stare at Bannon through the thick glass. He signaled 'left' with his hand.

Bannon touched the wheel.

Sully held up his hand again. 'Hold'.

Bannon steadied the wheel and took a deep breath. The channel was opening up to the rolling swells of the ocean. He could feel the boat beneath his feet, suddenly restless, as if she was eager to be free of the harbor and once again out in the deep ocean. Bannon eased the throttle down until *Mandrake's* speed was steady and sedate.

The sudden scrape and ragged vibration came as a surprise. Bannon had underestimated the distance to the sunken yacht. He felt the wheel suddenly kick in his hands, and then a sound like a juddering vibration hammered up through the water. He glanced up in alarm. Sully was bent over at the waist. The big man straightened and came lumbering back through the wheelhouse door.

"We're clear of the sunken yacht!" Sully said in an excited gasp of relief. "We made it!"

Bannon nodded. He felt his fingers unclench from their grip at the wheel, and the tight strain seep from his back and shoulders. He took a step away from the wheel, and only then realized that he was sweating. The cold breeze through the open doorway felt chilled as ice.

"She's all yours," Bannon made a sweeping gesture with his hands. The end of the break wall loomed just ahead. *'Mandrake's'* motion became suddenly lively as the ocean swells reaching the long rocky arms of the harbor entrance crashed into milling confusion. "Just hold her steady until you get well offshore."

Sully nodded. He stepped to the wheel and frowned with concentration. He had rarely been at the helm before. Bannon had never trusted him. He peered hard through the windshield, craning his neck forward with total attention.

Bannon watched the big man for a moment, and then suddenly a shaft of sunlight came streaming through the glass – a golden ray of blinding morning light – as the huge round orb of the sun finally rose across the rim of the world.

It was morning.

Steve Bannon had just run out of time.

Chapter 24.

Bannon went out to the starboard rail. He could see the end of the break wall, white surging foam boiling around the rocks. He glanced over the side. The water here was dark green, deepening to shades of blue.

Maddie appeared suddenly behind him. She stood silently, her arms folded across her chest, her expression unfathomable. Her mouth was tight with some kind of restraint.

Bannon stared at his wife for an instant, and realized he couldn't muster any kind of emotion. He was done with her, and the finality of the feeling was like a release.

"You reap what you sow," he warned.

Then he leaped over the side of *'Mandrake'* and splashed into the foaming wake of the big boat's wash.

The water was ice-cold, carried into the mouth of the channel from the deep ocean currents that swept and swirled in endless cycles along the coastline. Bannon came to the surface gasping, feeling the frigid water like a clamp around his chest. He struck out quickly for the southern break wall.

It was just a dozen strokes. His hands and feet clawed at the slime-covered rocks. He went up the face of the wall like a mountain climber, and when he reached the lip of the wall, he stood for a moment, with one last life-or-death decision to make.

Before him was the rocky face of the headland promontory, rising maybe thirty feet. He could climb the ledge, or run back along the break wall to where he had hidden the gun and his clothes. It would mean wasting precious minutes, but the climb over the rise to the tourist lookout would be easier.

He hesitated.

He stole a glance at his wristwatch.

5.53am.

But the watch had stopped.

How long ago? He panicked.

Cold despairing dread washed over him.

What time was it really?

Bannon started to run along the break wall, back towards where he had concealed the gun.

Shards of jagged rock cut and slashed his feet, but he barely noticed. Bannon ran with the desperation of the hunted, leaving a trail of spattered blood behind him. He ran with his arms pumping, staggering across the broken ground until his panic seemed like an impossible burden that turned the world around him into a slow-motion nightmare of fear and dread.

He found the rock, fumbled for the gun. He stared down at his feet. They were slick with dripping blood. Tattered shreds of flesh hung from his toes. His heels had been slashed open. He dropped to the ground. There was a thumping beat in his ears – a relentless pounding of blood hammering in his head, made so loud that it numbed his senses. He tried to control his breathing. His heart was racing. His hands were trembling. He turned and shot a glance over his shoulder, scanning the waterfront with his eyes. He could see no movement – see nothing hunting him. He screwed his eyes shut and gritted his teeth. He forced one of his bleeding feet into a boot... and then realized that the pounding in his ears was getting louder.

And clattering.

He wrenched his eyes skyward. There – in the distance – he could see the dark dragonfly shape of a helicopter, suspended on the blurred disc of its rotors, swooping in low over the trees. It was flying in from the north. The air began to fill with the thumping vibration of its approach.

Bannon threw the boot away and started to run.

He went up the gentle rise, scrambling hand over hand at stringy clumps of grass until he crested the hill and reached the side of the road that looped back into town. He paused for a moment. The helicopter was back over his shoulder, but coming on quickly. He could see dark shapes in the open cargo doors. The helicopter began to descend.

Bannon started running again.

He went across the road and into the woods. Through the filter of the trees he could see the helicopter dropping down out of the sky. It swooped over the sports field and seemed to hang there for an instant, maybe fifty feet off the ground. Bannon ran with his eyes fixed on the big bird, stumbling and tripping until the woods began to thin and he was running downhill – down the rocky slope that sheltered the sports field from the ocean breeze.

The bodies of the undead that had attacked the special forces team lay spread across the long grass, many of the corpses bloating with gases so that their hideous shapes were almost impossible to recognize as human. Bannon ran down until the ground began to level out. He was waving his arms frantically.

The wash from the helicopter slapped against his face and threw debris into the air. Bannon staggered, exhausted into the open field and looked up.

The swollen drab green belly of the helicopter was almost directly above him. He shouted, but the words were whipped away as they reached his lips. He thrust the pistol into the air, aiming away at the distant buildings of the town.

And he fired.

The helicopter jinked – yawed sideways, and then came rocking back. Bannon could see the blurred darkened shapes of men, leaning out through the cargo door. There were four soldiers perched on the lip of the opening, weapons across their laps, their faces obscured by camouflage paint and heavy Kevlar helmets. The helicopter crawled across the sky and then turned tightly.

It began to descend.

All of Bannon's attention was on the helicopter, watching it drop from above. His head was craned back, his arms thrown up to his eyes to shield it from the swirling debris.

He didn't see the undead come from the buildings.

He didn't see them swarm at the top of the hill, gathering on the edge of the road.

He didn't see them congeal together into a hideous writhing mass, and begin lurching down through the long grass.

The helicopter dropped the last thirty feet, heavy as a stone. At the instant before landing, it leveled, and then sank down onto the heavy suspension of its struts. Bannon felt the air become a howling blast – like a physical fist that punched at him so that he staggered back a pace. The helicopter had landed thirty feet away, amidst the carnage of zombie bodies that were strewn across the field. The four men sitting in the open cargo door leaped out from the body of the beast and ran...

... away from him!

The men went at a run, hunched and weighed down. They fanned out in an arc around the perimeter of the helicopter, dropping into the grass and taking up firing positions.

Bannon suddenly saw why.

The hillside was swarming with undead. There seemed no end to their number. Hundreds of ghouls, incensed and maddened by the thunderous roar of the helicopter, swayed on the skyline as the sun crested the edge of the ocean and painted the world in glorious golden hues. It was a dreamlike scene. A moment of nature's true beauty made gruesome by the stench of death and the frenzied howls of the zombies. They spilled down the slope in a relentless rushing tide of virulent madness.

Bannon ran for the helicopter. A soldier in grey camouflage fatigues leaped to the ground to help him aboard. The man was wearing a flight helmet. He stared at Bannon for just long enough to be sure he was human.

"Who the fuck are you?" the man roared at Bannon. The soldier had a face full of crags, and steady dark eyes that looked like they had seen just about all life had to offer.

"Bannon! Steve Bannon."

The man pressed his face closer. "Where is the team that came with you?"

"Dead."

"All of them?"

"Yes."

The soldier flinched, and then narrowed his eyes. "I'm crew chief, Staff Sergeant Walters," he shouted into Bannon's face above the thudding roar of the big rotors and the whine of the engines. "I'll be your hostess for today's flight. Now get on the fucking chopper!" Then he seized Bannon by the arm and unceremoniously hurled him like a heavy sack in through the cargo door. Bannon crashed against a steel support of a seat and heaved himself upright. He was panting. His legs and arms felt weak. He buckled over and vomited across the floor of the cargo area.

The howling clatter of the helicopter's big rotors had not slowed. The chopper was prancing in little buoyant leaps across the grass, eager to take flight, while the two pilots in the cockpit held the beast tethered by careful control.

Bannon heard a sound like canvas being ripped, and realized the men spread out in the field had begun shooting.

The zombies hurled themselves against the defensive line of soldiers like a seething wall of water that crashed against rocks. The roar of automatic fire was deafening. The crew chief clambered aboard behind Bannon and flung himself into a small seat forward of the cargo area. He hunched down behind the sights of a machine gun and opened fire. A hail of shiny spent shells sprayed across the cabin floor, and the sound was like a chain saw, ripping through the morning sky.

The undead line wavered, fell back, and then came again. Bannon crawled to the open cabin door. He could see the soldiers working manfully over their weapons, not bothering for accuracy, but merely firing at the mass of undead to stem the surge. Then the two outermost soldiers suddenly got to their feet and sprinted back to the helicopter. They flung themselves aboard and opened fire once more.

Under the cover of the helicopter's heavy machine gun, the last two men retreated. The storm of fire covering them was like a solid wall of lead. Ghouls were ripped apart, spread splattered and broken into the grass. Others simply disappeared into ghastly mounds of shredded flesh. It was a slaughter-house – a horrendous carnage of gore and awesome firepower.

Two of the zombies reached the helicopter. They came on at an insane rush. They were spitting blood, their bodies torn apart by countless ghastly hits. They were both men. Their eyes were a deep glittering yellow, their snarling mouths wide open ravaged holes. A soldier thrust the barrel of his weapon into one of the thrashing faces and held the trigger down until the ghoul's head erupted in a spray of misted gore.

So many rounds had hit the other zombie, that its flesh had been flayed back to the bone. It collapsed, just a few clawing feet away from the helicopter, shrieking its hideous horror. A soldier emptied a full magazine into the body.

The last two soldiers reached the cargo door and Bannon helped haul them aboard. Instantly the helicopter seemed to spring from the ground, rising up in a gut-swooping lurch. In seconds they were forty feet in the air, the soldiers still firing down at the undead, until, at last, the big bird's nose dipped down and it swooped away, heading north.

Towards safety.

Chapter 25.

Steve Bannon slumped against the rear bulkhead of the Black Hawk's cabin and stared numbly out through the window. The sun was glittering off the ocean, and in the mid distance he could see the black squat shape of the *'Mandrake'* nudging her way out into the rolling swells.

Bannon smiled.

Further away, at the very limit of his vision, he could see other dark specs massing together close to the horizon. They were coming on with purpose, and in the sky – below the scudding clouds of sunrise – there were more dark silhouettes racing through the cool morning air. Bannon couldn't hear those helicopters, but he could see them, converging on the signal from the emergency rescue beacon he had activated aboard the fishing boat.

Bannon sighed.

He had fulfilled his promise to the dying special forces soldier.

He had finished the job.

Sully would be captured. Now that he was isolated on the fishing boat, there was no chance he could escape, no chance he could hide and blend in with the thousands of undead that ravaged and raged across the countryside.

Bannon only prayed that the scientists and teams of USAMRID doctors would make the big man's remaining days in a laboratory cage painful and torturous. The fucker deserved it.

His thoughts turned then to Maddie. Bannon made a pensive face, and then shook his head. He felt no guilt for deceiving her.

You reap what you sow.

Maddie and Sully had betrayed him. He had his revenge on both of them. Maddie would be saved from infection, to live a life alone and in fear, without hope for a future.

Just like him.

Just like everyone who survived the apocalypse.

The End.

Also available: by Nicholas Ryan:

'Ground Zero: A Zombie Apocalypse' - "A bloody zombie smash!" DJ Molles, author of 'The Remaining' series.

'Die Trying: A Zombie Apocalypse' - "A heart stopping zombie thriller!" DA Wearmouth, author of 'First Activation'.

You can follow Nicholas Ryan on Facebook and Twitter.

9201115R00161

Printed in Great Britain
by Amazon.co.uk, Ltd.,
Marston Gate.